FINDING

Martin Flatman

To my sons, Sam and Joe, and all the people I have worked and worshipped alongside in Reading, Newbury, Oxford, and Eynsham, especially my partner Frances.

About the Author

Martin Flatman is a retired Catholic priest who remains active in spreading good thoughts and ideas on the internet. He is a married priest, as well as a grandfather and great-grandfather. Martin enjoys gardening, trains, and history. He resides near Oxford, where he worked for many years.

Contents

Chapter 1: Surveying the Ground

Walter could not quite believe what he was doing. Here he was acting like an amateur detective, the sort you see on the TV, sitting in his car watching for a man to come out of his house so he could follow him. He wasn't the sort of person to do this kind of thing. He was a respectable recently retired Geography teacher from Oxford, and yet here he was far from home, acting suspiciously. The man in the house must not see him, must have no idea that someone was watching him, or his whole reason for doing it would fail, so he worried that he might be seen by someone, even by the man, and questioned or even accused of being a stalker.

He hadn't even told Penny what he was doing this early in the morning out in the car. He had never really lied to his wife before, so what he'd said was almost the truth, that he was going out for a drive and a walk and to expect him back by lunch time. He knew that she would be cross with him if she found out what he was really up to, so a white lie was for the best. Indeed, she had been surprised that he had so easily agreed to come up to Marston Green from Oxford to stay with her cousin again, and so had no idea what his unusual enthusiasm was all about. "I suppose she thought I was just being kind to Angela," he said to himself. Angela's husband had recently died, and she was all alone and sad. Penny had said to Walter, "Couldn't we go up and stay with her for a bit to cheer her up?" She had been expecting to meet reluctance, because he had never shown much enthusiasm before, but this time he said "Yes, why not? Great idea, and whilst you chat to her, I can go for long walks or look at the planes or the trains."

That was the nice thing about where Angela lived. Penny remembered many happy holidays there as a child, staying with her Aunt and Uncle and having great times with Angela. They used to love wandering down Newlands Lane and sitting on the field gate at the bottom where they had a good view of Birmingham Airport. Not that much happened in those days. The bottom end of Newlands Lane was now part of the Airport, and a huge grass-covered earth bank prevented any view of the planes. Penny had told him how way back then they had rarely seen a plane. They could wait for what seemed like hours and finally give up waiting and go back home, but it didn't matter because it was a great place to sit and chat and watch the flocks of peewits on the grass in front of them. Now things were very different, and sometimes Angela wondered why she had persuaded her husband that they should move back into the family home, a rather nondescript bungalow, except that it was just that, her family home, the place where she had grown up, and she didn't really want to see it in someone else's hands.

Walter loved planes almost as much as he loved trains, and that was the one advantage of Marston Green, as you could go and stand on the Footbridge at the Station and more or less watch both at the same time, and so escape Angela's chatter. It had been even worse in the old days, as he had absolutely nothing in common with Tom, Angela's husband. But Tom wasn't there anymore; and so provided he could escape from the house regularly, he could happily go along with Penny's plans. Penny was even more surprised when he said "I think we should stay for a few weeks, don't you, so we can give her lots of support. And I'll take my gardening clothes." "You're being really nice about this" she said. "Thanks for being so understanding." Little did she know why he really wanted to be there!

His plan had come about quite unexpectedly. On their last visit, just before Tom had died, Angela had pointed out to them the house where Colin lived. He was surprised she knew this, but assumed it must be because of her contacts with the police. Colin's house was literally just at the top of the Lane and across the road – one of those earlier properties built for those who wanted to travel into Birmingham every day. At first he had thought nothing of it, but gradually the idea had begun to creep up on him, to follow Colin and see if he could get to know him and find out why he had behaved the way he had, and so when Penny suggested the visit he was really quite keen, indeed he had to be careful not to appear too keen, or she might smell a rat!

Anyway, they had driven up from Oxford on Wednesday and here he was on Friday morning having failed on Thursday, sitting in the car almost opposite Colin's house. Almost, because he wanted to be far enough away so as not to be noticed. Just one more parked car.

It was lucky it was quite pleasant weather because he sat there for almost an hour before a slim, dark-haired man in his late 30's emerged from the house. He was in a light grey well-fitting suit with an open-necked shirt and he began to walk briskly up the road towards the station. Walter assumed that this was the man he was seeking, that this was Colin. He had worried that he might go to work by car, but it was clear that he was lucky, for he was either heading for a train or a bus.

Quickly but cautiously, Walter got out of the car and began to follow him. It was easy really, because why should anyone suspect another person walking down the road at that time in the morning, but Walter was still a bit nervous. The pavement was only on one side of the road as the other side was all grass and trees intersected by the driveways up to the houses over there. He knew that he mustn't skulk along slipping from tree to tree as people might do in some rather bad movie. All he needed to do was simply walk steadily along the path as if he did this every day; but he still worried that somehow he might be found out. He then began to worry that Colin might be going by train. He thought he might be delayed and lose touch with his prey as he bought a ticket, but then remembered that you just got on the train without a ticket here; but he needn't have worried, because Colin went over the line by the footbridge and headed for the Bus Stop. There were quite a few people waiting, so Walter simply joined the queue, but then he froze in panic because how would he know where Colin was getting off? So when the 72 came, he asked for a ticket to Solihull, the bus's destination, thus covering every eventuality.

He was slightly annoyed at having wasted the money, because Colin got off in Sheldon, so he did too, and then wondered what he should do. How could finding out where he worked make much difference? It wasn't long before he found out. Colin went into an entrance that clearly led to some rather dull-looking offices above some shops, and that was that. He took a note of the names of the firms who advertised themselves at the entrance, but didn't go any further into the building, as that might have given the game away. All he could do now was walk around and explore Sheldon for a bit, and then get the bus back to Marston Green. Sheldon wasn't exactly the sort of place where someone like Walter could find much to interest him. Lines of shops on either side of a broad busy road was not exactly the kind of place where you lingered for long, so soon after 10.00 am he was back at Angela's and wondering what to do with the rest of the day.

The ladies announced that they were going into Birmingham shopping and asked if would he like to come along, but he said as they expected "No thanks. Shopping is not my favourite pursuit. I'll stay at home and spend some time on the computer, and then maybe have a look at what needs doing in the garden," And that's what he did. "Help yourself to lunch, won't you Walter?" Angela said. "There's cheese and some ham in the fridge and you'll find some cake in a tin." "Ok, thanks", he said, and then waved them goodbye as they headed for the station.

He had taken a note of the various companies whose names were displayed at the entrance to those offices, and so he looked each of them up online in case he could find which was the one where Colin worked. Scrolling through each Company's Website took him some time, but none of them named the people they employed, except a Solicitors, and Colin wasn't one of the partners they named, and so after a while he gave up. The next thing to do was to try to forget all about Colin for the rest of the day. Indeed, he told himself that there was nothing more he could do until the next morning, so he spent some time on Facebook seeing what the family were posting.

They had three children scattered in various parts of England, and there were pictures of the grandchildren appearing regularly, showing the latest things they were up to. He had loved being a Dad, and was a bit sad that being a hands-on Grandad wasn't possible. As with many families nowadays, they all lived some distance from Oxford, so seeing them on Facebook with the occasional visit was the next best thing.

After lunch he went out in the garden to see how it was looking and soon realised that there was quite a lot to be done. The roses were struggling through the weeds, and needed a deal of help if they were to bloom well this summer, so he went back into the house to change into the gardening clothes he had brought up with him. He was soon out again and began to weed the bed nearest the house. Clearly not much had been attempted in the weeks leading up to Tom's death, and more or less nothing since then. He remembered how they had come up for the Funeral a few weeks ago, but he hadn't really looked then at how the garden was doing, so he was glad he had guessed that it might have been neglected and that he could be useful. Anyway it had been raining then, making a sad day even sadder. It had been the kind of funeral where a clergyman who had never known Tom, desperately tried to say something meaningful, but didn't really succeed. Tom and Angela had never gone to Church, and so that kind of Funeral was inevitable. He wished Angela had been brave, and given up the religious bit. It would somehow have felt more genuine, except that Angela had said later that she couldn't have coped if they hadn't sung "The Lord's my Shepherd", as it took her back to her childhood. Such hypocrisy irritated him, and he remembered telling himself off for being so uncharitable. Digging up the weeds, he now remembered all this, and realised how differently he and Penny viewed death. He thought of the great funerals at their local church in Oxford, full of prayer for a church member they all knew. Sad yes, but full of the bright promise of immortality.

But thoughts about Colin soon came back into his mind. How could he get to know him and gain his confidence in just a few weeks? He tossed all sorts of schemes around in his mind, but didn't really come up with anything very clever. Then, before he knew it, there was a call from the house. "Would you like a cup of tea?" Penny and Angela were back. "Yes please," he replied. "I'll come in." Angela was full of thanks for his work in the garden. "I keep meaning to get round to it, but somehow never find the time." Walter knew the real reason. Tom had spent many hours in his garden, and going out there reminded Angela all too vividly that Tom was dead. The two women spent some time looking at the things they had bought, and occasionally trying to get him interested, but Penny laughed. "It's no good Angela. Getting Walter interested in clothes is a waste of time." He laughed too, "That's not quite fair," he said, "I often admire your new clothes once you've got them on." "Yes" she said to Angela, "He is quite good at that…. when he notices." "Oh Tom never notices," Angela replied, and then burst into tears. "Sorry, sorry," she said, and Walter and Penny hugged her and said they understood. They were glad to be there for her.

Chapter 2: Making Contact

Walter now had a weekend of anxiety as he prepared himself for an attempt to make contact on Monday morning. He had always been an early riser, needing to be at his school to get things ready before the kids started arriving, and he hadn't got out of the habit after he'd retired. He left the house at precisely 7.50 am knowing that he would then pass Colin's house just before he came out, provided he was a regular timekeeper too. He was. And so just after he passed the house and slowed down, he heard the front door open and close, and soon knew, without looking round, that this time Colin was following him. He had decided on a very simple plan. He got out his phone and allowed it to slip out of his hand onto the ground. "Bother," he said, turning round to pick it up, only to find Colin catching him up and picking it up for him. The plan had worked. "Oh thanks so much," he said. "Getting clumsy in my old age." "Go on," said Colin. "You're not really old. You were walking along ahead of me at quite a pace." "Ah yes," said Walter deviously "I don't want to miss the Bus." "Well I'm heading for the Bus too" said Colin. "So let's get going," and they walked on together.

Neither of them spoke much after that, until they reached the station. They were crossing the Footbridge when they heard the recorded announcement telling people to stand back behind the yellow line, so they knew that an express was coming. Colin paused, so Walter stopped too. "Don't wait for me" said Colin. "I just love feeling the train woosh past so powerful and so close, not as good as the roar of a steam engine of course, but I still love the feeling of power." Walter stopped and laughed "Well we've certainly got one thing in common," and they stood there together as the fast electric train roared through at speed. It gave Walter an easy way to link up with this man. "It reminds me of standing on my trainspotting bridge near Wimbledon station. There were lots of electric trains, but once in a while an express would go by hauled by a steam train, and we all loved it. I still remember it now, it was called The Atlantic Coast Express, but I never knew till I was much older exactly where it was going." "Ah yes" said Colin "The great competitor with the Great Western. It would have gone to Exeter wouldn't it, and then on to Okehampton? Where did it go then?

Well, I think it split there and part went on to Bude, and thus to the Atlantic Coast hence the name." Walter actually knew this and more but disguising his knowledge a little he said "You are clearly an expert. I love trains but I would not know details of someone else's region." They walked on to the Bus Stop talking trains, or rather Colin talked trains, and Walter only had to pop in the occasional comment to keep him going, fascinated at how much information poured out of him. It continued when they got on the Bus, with only a few questions from Walter to prompt Colin's continued enthusiastic flow.

They both got off in Sheldon. This time Walter knew which stop to ask for and so, without Colin realising it, he was on the way to achieving his aim. As Colin had talked, Walter had realised how lucky he was that this was happening so quickly. Getting to talk to another man could be a hard business. Normally you might say "Good Morning" after seeing the same person every day for a week or two, and then maybe begin to strike up a conversation after that, but the train event had opened up the floodgates, and since he was keen on trains too, he didn't have to pretend. The conversation just flowed. As they parted, they exchanged names and mobile numbers. Yes he was definitely Colin. Walter was delighted at how fast he had got to know the man he was searching for.

He felt rather silly getting on the bus and going back to Marston Green only a short while after he had set off but, provided Colin didn't see him, there was no point hanging around, and that garden needed a lot of work. On the bus, he sat and wondered if what he was doing was really as good as he intended it to be, especially when it required him to be so deceptive. The problem was made worse by the fact that he and Colin had already begun to set up quite a good friendship, and Walter had found himself liking the very man that he had wanted to hate. Well, perhaps hate was too strong a word, as hating was not something he would ever have thought good about doing, but he knew what he meant. It reminded him of some of the kids he'd had to deal with at school. He was often infuriated by their disruptive behaviour, and yet often they were quite likeable once you got to know them individually. And once you got to know them, then often dreadful stories of neglect or abuse emerged to partly explain their erratic behaviour.

He began thinking about Simon who had been such a nuisance to start with, until he had managed to get them sat down together, and Simon had been able to pour out his anger and bitterness against his stepfather. "My Mum doesn't seem to notice how awful he is, and I just don't know what to do," said Simon, almost in tears, except that big 14-year-old boys weren't supposed to cry. "I wish I could go and live with my real Dad over in Norwich, but I doubt he would want me." Walter remembered the moment when he realised that Simon visited his Dad regularly, and so could ask the simple question that made all the difference. "Why not ask him?" It was like giving someone a permission that they had never had before, for light suddenly dawned in Simon's eyes. "I could, couldn't I?" Then a pause and then, "Yup, I will." Soon after this it was a transformed Simon who came to tell Walter the good news. "Thanks so much Sir for your help. I asked my Dad, and I'm moving over there almost straight away." Walter remembered too how he had met Simon some years later, and that then they had linked with each other through Facebook. Simon was now happily settled down with a lovely wife and family, and a good job, yet out of the blue he messaged Walter to explain to him why he had hated his stepfather so much. It was the first time Walter had actually had anyone he knew admit to being sexually abused, and he was amazed. He felt slightly guilty that he hadn't enabled Simon to tell him all this way back when he was 15. "In his case," he thought, "It has turned out for the best. But I must be more aware in future." And he was.

Getting to know Colin had to be a bit like getting to know Simon. There was no point feeling angry about what Colin had done, the thing that Walter's investigation was all about. He just had to aim to be his friend, despite this bit of deception, and see then whether the real truth might eventually come out. He was so wrapped up in his thoughts that he almost missed his Bus stop. He walked home, wondering whether anything at all would come of all this. He paused, as he came to Colin's house, and noted for the first time the immaculate front garden. There was a paved driveway where a car was standing, and then a curved flowerbed on one side where some blue campanula tumbled down the low wall at the front, whilst neatly trimmed shrubs of different shade of green, and one of purple, filled the rest of the flowerbed. He guessed that Colin's house was as neat as his garden, so after having a look round to see if anyone was watching, he went into the garden and up to the front window. Peering in, he could see that it was just as he suspected. The house was as neat and tidy as the garden. There was a big black sofa on the left, a glass coffee table with a few books and magazines neatly piled together, plus the usual remotes. There was an armchair as well and a large TV and everything looked very clean. Here was a man who appeared to be in control of everything.

Walter looked round again, noting as he left that the car was equally immaculate, and walked quickly out of the garden and back to Angela's, hoping no-one had seen him and phoned the police to report a suspected burglar "Casing the joint." Seeing Colin's garden, had reminded him of the work that he wanted to do in Angela's, to get it back to the way Tom had once kept it. This time Angela came out with him. "This is so kind of you Walter, but I just don't see how I can keep it the way Tom had it. So much work, and I wouldn't know where to start." "Well," said Walter "Perhaps we should adapt it to make it less labour intensive. We'd need to dig up some of the herbaceous plants and the old worn out Roses, and buy some shrubs to replace them. Then they would only need a bit of pruning, and I could always come and do that every now and then." "Oh that would be marvellous. Let's get on with it. But I also need that paving repaired or replaced." Tom loved to let plants grow in the cracks, but I really need something more practical. Can you manage that as well?" Walter's face fell, but he tried not to show it. "I'm fine with plants, but no good at hard landscaping. Do you know someone, or a firm that might do it?" But she didn't, and he had to promise to see what he could do.

The next morning he was back out to waylay Colin, and once again, as regular as clockwork, he appeared and joined him in the walk up to the Bus. "You're a strict timekeeper," he said, and Colin looked amused but slightly grim. "Yes, and that's one of the things that destroyed my marriage. I'm a control freak and eventually she couldn't cope with me."

"I'm not surprised," thought Walter. *"Looking at your Sitting Room had already told me that."* Meanwhile Colin was already pouring out the story of how his marriage had got worse and worse until his wife told him he was a control freak, and needed to learn to live in a house which was less than perfect. "She more or less threw me out," he said "And I haven't been in touch since."

Walter listened and sympathised. He knew how easily marriages can go wrong. There was a time when he wondered if Penny was going to leave him. He was a workaholic with a strict timetable that he didn't like disrupted. Up at 5 every morning, for his cup of tea, and then time to sit quietly and drink it and do his thinking. Bill had told him that he was actually praying when he did this, but he wasn't sure about that. His mind would wander all over the place, and still did, and God hardly came into it at all. But Bill had told him the story of the old French peasant who sat in church every day. One day the priest plucked up the courage to ask the old man what sort of prayers he said to keep him concentrated for such a long time. There was a long pause, and then the old man said, "Well, I just look at him, and he looks back at me." Bill had said, "Just remember every now and then, when you sit there, that God is there looking at you." The idea had actually made him feel even more comfortable, because it required so little effort. So different from the way he had been taught to pray as a child before he had rejected all that.

Wisely, he didn't push Colin further on the subject of his failed marriage. It was clearly a wound he found hard to cope with, but he felt brave enough to ask him a bit about his children, and since Colin was so proud of them, he learnt a lot more about Colin. Eventually on the bus, Colin began to question him about his children. "We don't see them often." He said. "They live so far away. Chris is the youngest. He and Julia have three children but live in York. Teresa has two in Milton Keynes, and then there's John our oldest who lives in London. But we keep in touch, and see the photos on Facebook, mainly the grandchildren." Walter had let Colin do most of the talking on trains the day before, but it was good now that he wanted to hear him talk about his family, and so he told him quite a lot, telling him funny stories of family life when the kids were growing up in Oxford, and what they were doing now. "That's what I miss," said Colin.

As they parted at the Bus Stop in Sheldon, Colin said "Will I see you tomorrow?" "Yes, sure," said Walter, aware that for Colin this growing friendship meant quite a lot. Back in Angela's garden, he realised how lonely Colin was, and remembered his time of loneliness in his first year at University. He had seen people at lectures and got to know a few others in various ways, but the fact that there you were alone in a crowd had been very unsettling. In his second year, he had found Penny, or maybe she had found him, and everything had changed, and now they had been together for more years than he cared to remember. Poor Colin, he thought, had also expected a happy marriage, but now he was alone again. No wonder he was happy to have someone like Walter to talk to.

The problem was that these conversations were all very public. Walter knew that the only way to get Colin to open up on the more private side of his life, was to find some way of meeting and talking to him in private, but how to do that without appearing to be intruding?

Once again he found himself mulling over this the following morning and getting nowhere. Perhaps he should just give up the idea? It was a bit of a drag to get the bus to Sheldon and back every morning when he could have been doing a lot more interesting things. It was just a fluke that he had found out that Colin lived just round the corner from Angela, and if he hadn't discovered that, then his life would have been so much more simple. He had some sadness that getting to know Colin wouldn't make any difference. It wouldn't get Bill out of prison, but he just had to see if he could find out why this man had made his false accusation. He knew that most of the time things happen in life that we have little chance of controlling or changing, but it was still worth making the attempt. He was pretty pessimistic about all this, but somewhere there was the nagging thought, "Go on. Go on. You never know what might happen." And so, once again, he set off at his usual time, met Colin as before, and continued his ridiculous scheme of sitting with him on the bus, and then coming straight home again.

This time however he was glad he had prepared his ground, for Colin suddenly said "I thought you were retired Walter, so why are you getting this bus every day?" Walter hoped Colin wasn't looking closely as he produced his prepared lie. He could feel his heart beating faster. "Just helping out with a bit of supply teaching to keep my hand in," he said. "Most schools are desperate for experienced teachers when someone is off sick." "Oh I see" said Colin. "So how long will it last?" "It all depends on how long the teacher is off sick, and also how long I am up here in Birmingham," And then he added, to divert Colin's attention from the lie, "Didn't I explain to you that I actually live in Oxford?" He was relieved that Colin accepted the lie so easily. He had assumed that Colin, like most people, would know little about the staffing of schools. He remembered once going back to his old school down in South London and finding it incredibly difficult to go into the Staff Room, even though he was now a teacher, because his memories had still been so strong. No boys, and it was all boys in those days, ever passed through that door, although sometimes they might be made to stand outside as a kind of punishment. He was right in assuming that Colin wasn't that interested in how schoolteachers were employed, and just took it for granted from his own good experiences that teachers were to be trusted; and so he accepted the lie without question. Walter justified himself with the thought that it could have been true. He could have contacted the school and got some supply work if he had wanted to, and so somehow didn't feel so bad about it.

Actually Colin was distracted by something that really did concern him. He had just made a friend, and since he didn't really have any friends, he was now worried that he might soon lose him. Walter might be old enough to be his father, but he didn't behave like a father, and certainly nothing like his father. Colin shuddered. That man had helped to ruin his life, but Walter was nothing like him. His mind seemed much younger and more active. He was the kind of father he had always wished for, and now it appeared that he had to face the fact that he might go away and leave him alone again. "So how long are you staying up here then?" he said, trying to conceal his anxiety. "Probably a few more weeks yet," said Walter. "We are staying with my wife's cousin just a little way down Newlands Lane. Her husband Tom has just died and we are keeping her company and trying to help her get used to her new life."

"Oh I see. How sad for her. Will you come up again?"

"Oh yes. Penny, my wife, and her cousin Angela, are almost like sisters. She used to come up here for holidays when she was little, and they get on really well. And I make myself useful in the garden."

Walter was relieved that the conversation had gone so well. He had been able to hide that lie in a lot of things that were true, and which had helped Colin to know him better. But still, it was hard to see how that private talk that he so wanted would ever come about. They chatted about this and that on the bus and parted as usual, saying "See you tomorrow then." The Sheldon shops were as boring as usual, and Walter was soon back on the bus just as he had been for the last few days.

Chapter 3: Colin Takes the Lead

Colin had a lot to think about that day. He realised how much he liked Walter. He wanted this friendship to work, but how could he do that without appearing too eager? He actually became quite agitated by the idea of losing contact with him. He knew how lonely he was. A woman friend never seemed to work for him. The Counselling he had gone through after the break-up of his marriage had made him see how wounded he had been by his childhood experiences, and how this had pushed him into being a loner. He knew now that his marriage had gone wrong because when tensions arose, as they do in all marriages, he had retreated back into his shell, and then even sex with his wife which had always been great, had just stopped happening. He was so mixed up about it all. He had tried Internet Dating, but the one woman with whom he thought it might work had soon given up on him when she discovered what he was really like. His counsellor had wisely told him that it probably wasn't a good idea to think that one day he would be sorted out sexually. Facing up to what had happened to him in the past had helped to some extent, but it didn't really solve present day relationships.

So he was very lonely, and he knew it. The people at work were Ok, but he had always felt the need to keep a professional distance from people who were his employees, and anyway most of them seemed to have partners which made him feel awkward in their company especially as he was their boss. Being more than a bit of a nerd didn't help. They always appreciated his support when they had particularly difficult problems to solve, but he felt that they slightly resented the way he tried to explain to them his remedy. It was so much easier to take over from them and put things right quickly, and though he knew he ought not to do this, he often did it, as he felt himself getting more and more impatient with their slowness to grasp what he was trying to teach them. And then there was his fanaticism about trains. They all thought he was a little touched in the head whenever he mentioned some fascinating fact, and when he went on his trips to various preserved railways. None of them were the slightest bit interested. Then, almost out of the blue, he had discovered Walter. A good friendship with an older man like Walter was really very important for him, especially when he discovered their mutual love of trains, and each day this last week he had looked forward with more and more eagerness to that chat on the way to work.

Funnily enough, as he thought about Walter, he remembered how it was some of the teachers at his school who had supported him best through his troubled teenage years. He never really told them why he was so troubled, but their support and encouragement, as he had discovered his fascination for computers, had been a life-saver. Knowing that Walter was a teacher had somehow given him a confidence in this friendship that he probably would have found difficult to achieve in other circumstances. But now he had discovered with some sadness that Walter actually lived in Oxford and was just visiting Marston Green, and his heart sank as he realised how easily his new friend could slip away and leave him alone again. He had a restless night. He knew that it was worrying about this that was keeping him awake, especially since he had no idea how to solve this kind of problem. Computers were easy in comparison.

He was relieved the following morning to find Walter once again just outside his house at the right time. It was almost as if he were waiting for him, although he knew that was nonsense. "Hi there," he said. "Great to see you. How are you doing?" Walter said he was fine and then there was a bit of silence as they walked towards the bus stop. Colin knew he had to make an effort. "So did you teach in Oxford all your life?" he asked, and Walter began to tell him a bit about his teaching career and his final job at a school just north of Oxford in Kidlington. Colin discovered that although he was principally a Geography teacher, he had taught a bit of History as well; and had turned his hand to other things when there was a need. Walter told him about his responsibility for discipline which meant working out how to deal with pupils that were disruptive. He smiled as he told Colin that his greatest success was getting them to all wear their ties tidily. "It was simple. We gave up on ordinary ties and they all wore clip-on ones. Problem solved."

They had reached that bridge over the Railway, and once again they were lucky, so they both paused as an express sped under them. "Not quite so much fun as a steam train," said Walter. "But still magnificent." It was then that Colin had a brainwave. "I go regularly to visit one or other of the Steam lines that are fairly near here. Would you be interested in coming with me?" Walter's enthusiastic response delighted him. "Oh yes. I'd love that but which one?" "Well, the one I know best, is the Severn Valley Railway. But I suppose this weekend's too short notice? Will you still be here the weekend after?" Again, he was surprised to hear Walter say "Yes, what a great idea, and why not this weekend?" And he replied, without telling Walter why, "I always go on Saturday rather than Sundays, would that be OK?" And so it was arranged.

Colin often visited the Severn Valley Railway. His Dad had taken him there as a boy, and despite the fact that he and his Dad were no longer speaking to one another, his enthusiasm for the Severn Valley was still as intense. But he knew his Dad always went there on Sundays whilst his Mum went to Church, and that was why he had suggested Saturday to Walter. He explained to Walter that it was only about a 40 minute drive to Kidderminster on a Saturday or Sunday when the Motorways were not so congested, and after they had got on the bus, he began to tell Walter a bit about the Line he knew so well. Walter had been on the Watercress Line and visited Didcot but, as he said to Colin, "It is not so much fun visiting alone. We used to take the kids, but once they were grown up, my wife wasn't interested in coming with me, and so I haven't gone much since." Nothing could have pleased Colin more. His ex-wife had been equally dismissive of his railway mania, but here was someone who genuinely wanted to go with him. He found it difficult to contain his excitement, and had to control himself from going on and on about the technicalities of his favourite line. What he did tell Walter seemed to be accepted so easily that he laughed and said, “Now I am teaching a teacher,” and Walter laughed too. They were getting on really well.

Sheldon came all too soon. “See you tomorrow” said Colin.

“Sure thing. And then Saturday for the trip.” Both went their separate ways pleased for different reasons at the way their friendship was developing. That night, Colin slept well, happy to look forward to his day with Walter. Walter was also pleased at how easily he appeared to be getting nearer to his goal.

Chapter 4: Penny Wonders

It was at lunchtime that Walter announced that he was going to visit the Severn Valley Railway on Saturday. "I've realised how near it is from here." he said, "Only 40 minutes, and it's one I've never visited." Angela knew of Walter's steam train hobby from Penny and thought it rather a nice idea. She knew that he felt a little out of it when she and Penny started on their innumerable chats, often talking about the old days when they were girls, so she was glad he was finding things to do to amuse himself. But being a sociable person she wondered if he might be a bit lonely going by himself, and said so. Walter had hoped this question wouldn't be asked, but he was ready for it. "No," he said "I'm going with a friend I met watching trains on the bridge at the station. We started chatting and he asked me if I'd like to go with him, so I said yes." Angela thought that was lovely and said so, but Penny was immediately suspicious. It just wasn't like Walter to make friends with someone quite so rapidly. She knew him as a cautious sort of person who took time to get to know people. She didn't say anything in front of Angela, but Walter knew from the look she gave him that he would expect an interrogation when they were alone.

He was out in the garden again that afternoon. There was a lot to do, and he liked to see the difference a bit of weeding made as the dark earth was revealed. The roses already looked so much happier and he began to regret his suggestion that they be dug up. Deep in contemplation, he suddenly found Penny standing beside him with a mug of tea. "Oh thanks," he said, and then was not surprised that she said "Walter, who is this friend you are going with on Saturday? How have you got to know someone so quickly? Can you trust him?" He told her all then. He explained how he had made a point of meeting Colin once Angela had pointed out the house to them, and how the friendship had developed. "He's a really nice bloke," he said. But before he could say more she butted in "And so you think you might get him to admit he made a false accusation? I think you're wasting your time. If he admitted it, he'd get sent to prison for perjury. He's not likely to do that in a thousand years, is he? And anyway Father Bill pleaded guilty." He had to admit she was probably right, but explained that although he had pushed forward the friendship for that purpose, he had soon found how much he actually liked Colin, and was now looking forward to the trip for its own sake, and not as a way of dragging the truth out of him.

"Well, be very careful Walter. I don't want accusations made against you."

Walter felt her fears were a bit over the top. Colin was a grown man. It was so different from dealing with his pupils where false accusations could so easily ruin a career. But trying to point out to her that she was overreacting would not have gone down well, so he let it pass. "Ok," he said. "You know how careful I am."

Penny knew she had overreacted, but she knew how easily her dear Walter could be taken for a ride. He was such a softie, forever giving his money or his time to people in trouble, just as he had spent too much time at school dealing with troubled pupils and neglecting his own family in the process. Well, not neglecting them exactly, but certainly pushing himself too hard and finding less time than she would have liked him to spend with them at home. She had always loved him for it, but was always ready to warn him when his attempts at being kind went too far. She walked back to the house, sighing to herself, and wondering what she could do to stop him from going too far in befriending this clearly troubled young man.

She remembered when she had first met him at University. Her current boyfriend had got too drunk to walk her home, so Walter had shyly offered to take his place. He had clearly never had a girlfriend, but she found herself immediately attracted to this kind gentle boy, and found it easy enough to encourage him. Walter had been very reluctant at first, worried that he was stealing her from his friend. She remembered how he had told her that he had sat down with George and told him what was happening. She was a bit annoyed when he then told her that George had said he wasn't that bothered, just glad his friend had found a girl at last. She liked him for that, but always reminded George when they saw him, that she had been his girlfriend before Walter had whisked her away. This always embarrassed Walter of course, because as she knew only too well, the last thing he would have done would have been to steal a girl from a friend, but it was just Penny's way of seeing things.

She went back in the house to report the delivery of the tea, and had to cope with Angela being rather too enthusiastic about how wonderful Walter was. "I remember when you first introduced me to him. Such a quiet shy boy, but very sweet. How on earth he ever controlled a class of schoolchildren, I shall never understand."

Penny laughed. She had soon discovered that although Walter might appear soft on the surface, he was not really like that deep down. He had been a very successful teacher, eventually becoming an Assistant Head in charge of discipline at the school where he had spent the last 20 years of his working life. Many people had tried to persuade him to apply for jobs as a Deputy or a Head, but he had always resisted that kind of thing. He hated the administration. What he cared about were the students, and especially helping those who were causing the most trouble. She knew how often they had met young people in Oxford when shopping, young men usually, who bounded up to him to tell him how well they were doing. Afterwards he would share a little with her of what their troubles had been, and how the school had helped them. She was proud of him at moments like this, because although he said 'The School', she knew that the person at the school who had really helped them was her own lovely husband.

So Penny knew that Walter was no fool, and that if he felt he could deal with this young man he had befriended, then he could. She knew too that if anyone could help a man like this with some of his traumas, then her husband could. But she was less certain of his motives in this case, for as she had said to him, getting someone to admit that they had made a false accusation was a pretty tall order. Like Walter, she had been troubled that someone they knew and trusted could have been falsely accused like this and then imprisoned, but she had resigned herself to the fact that with people like this you could never tell. It was clear that what people were like on the surface, and what they actually did in secret, were two very different things. It had made her far more suspicious of all sorts of people, especially men! She hated being like this, but was stuck with it. Walter, on the other hand, stubbornly, refused to accept that their friend was guilty, and now she had discovered that he was out to prove it. Once again, he would go to any lengths to help someone that he thought had been unjustly treated. She sighed once more, realising that he would never change.

Meanwhile, she and Angela were remembering further back before she had met Walter. Talking about him as a teacher, had reminded Angela of the games they had played as little girls. They used to line up their soft toys in front of a blackboard and give them lessons in spelling and multiplication tables. "You were always so much better at learning than me," Angela said. "You could do some of the more difficult tables. whilst I was still struggling with seven twos are fourteen." Penny wondered how Angela remembered all this. She had a vague recollection of these teaching games, but the details eluded her, and she wondered why. Her memories were more of playing outside games in what had been an enormous garden, until Angela's parents sold off the far side of it for another house, and lost that great lawn and the enormous Copper Beech Tree that had once stood there. She assumed that nowadays you wouldn't be allowed to chop down such a beautiful tree. She still missed it. She and Angela had so many common memories that Walter could never share, so she was happy that he was busy, as ever, doing his own thing. Then suddenly it came to her why Walter had been so open to visiting

Angela. He had already planned to find a way to befriend this young man if they were up with Angela, and now in less than a week he had done it. Yes, she worried about him, but she was also impressed once again that when he was determined to do something, her soft-spoken gentleman was not to be underestimated.

"Still," she thought "He cannot be allowed to do this alone." So as soon as she could get a word in, she suggested to Angela that they might ask this young man to dinner with them when he and Walter came back from their Train Trip.

"Oh what a lovely idea. We can cook a splendid meal for them and find out who this man is." Penny didn't tell her that she already knew who he was. She assumed Angela would find out soon enough, and hoped she would not blurt out something inappropriate. After all, how had she discovered in the first place where he lived? Surely such people were protected by anonymity in Court? She supposed it was simply because he was so local, and as she knew only too well, Angela seemed to know all her neighbours.

Walter looked slightly surprised when he was told that Colin was to be invited to dinner. He suspected his Penny had organised this, and was slightly irritated that she was muscling in on his project. But actually, when he thought about it a bit more, he realised that it might help the softening up process, and soon became quite enthusiastic. "You better let him know straightaway Walter," Angela said. "Just in case he has other plans." Walter said he would, knowing that he could just give Colin the invitation when he met him tomorrow morning. He was glad there was something good on the TV to take his mind off all this subterfuge, except that these detective stories where you tried to work out who committed the murder before they told you, made him think that his own little story was a bit like a detective story too. He said as much to Penny as they went to bed. "These detectives almost always find the truth in the end but I bet it's not the same in real life."

"You mean you, don't you? I think you are quite right not to hope too much will come of this. But still it will be interesting to meet him."

"He really is a nice bloke. I think you'll like him. And that's half the problem."

Chapter 5: The Train Trip

Colin was surprised when Walter said that the "Girls" (as he called them) wanted him to come to dinner after their Train trip. He had already organised the day in his mind The 10.25 from Kidderminster arriving Bridgnorth at 11.33. An hour at Bridgnorth to go up and down the Cliff Railway, and then on the 12.35 back as far as Highley. Then lunch by the River Severn, and lots of time to visit the Engine Shed and get the 15.45 back to Kidderminster and home by 17.30 at the latest. He had anticipated a quiet evening at his own home after that, but he had to admit that the idea of having dinner and meeting Walter's wife and her cousin really appealed to him. "That's very kind of you," he said. "If they are going to cook for us, we can just buy a sandwich at lunchtime. Or bring our own? There's a pub by the River at Highley where we can get a drink." He gave Walter a copy he had made of the proposed Itinerary. "Does that look OK to you?" he said, and was happy that Walter agreed. Once he had made a plan, he liked to stick to it.

Walter was pleased that Colin had responded so positively, because he didn't want him to think he was getting too pushy, and begin to suspect him of something rather different from friendship. He knew he was getting a bit neurotic about this, and he knew why. He didn't like deceiving people, and yet he had to live with the agonising fact that deception lay deep within this growing friendship. So he was glad once again to let Colin do the leading, and he was certainly doing that. Information about the day was now pouring out of him. He made Walter promise to be at his house promptly by 9.00 am.

"That gives us plenty of time in case there are any hitches or hold-ups, and if we get there early, there is plenty to see at the Station."

It was clear to Walter that if he was a minute late, Colin would be outside the gate anxiously looking for him, so he assured him that being a teacher all his life had made him an excellent timekeeper. "I don't anticipate any problem, but if there was, don't worry. I'll text you straight away. And I'm only staying down the lane."

That got Colin into asking a bit more about the house where he would be having dinner at the end of the day. Walter explained that the house was called Merrymead, and was the third house on the right down Newlands Lane. "I've never been down there," said Colin. "Where does it lead to?"

"To nowhere. Except for an emergency gate to the airport which is overgrown, so clearly never used. My wife remembers the time when the Lane went further and you could see the whole Airport, but in those days there were only about six planes a day."

Then he had to explain that Angela had been brought up there, and although she had lived elsewhere after she got married, she and her Tom had moved back into the house after her parents died, because she couldn't face the idea of her beloved family home being sold to anyone else. He didn't share much more. He could see that family history was not Colin's favourite topic, and steered him back onto trains. The bus journey was a mutual sharing of the various lines they had visited. Colin knew most of the more northern ones and Walter those in the south, so there was no let up in the conversation, even though at times Colin's knowledge of the technicalities took Walter a bit out of his depth.

It was a rainy day, so once he arrived back at Merrymead, he decided to do some research on the Computer. He could never attempt to keep up with Colin's technical knowledge, but he realised he knew much more about railway history than Colin did, and so he reminded himself of that bit of history that related to this particular railway line. Wikipedia had a very substantial article for him to read, but as a Geography teacher he was frustrated that his books of railway maps were back home in Oxford, and that he didn't have an OS Map of the

Kidderminster – Bridgnorth area and no chance of getting one in the less than the 24 hours available to him. He knew there was no point asking Angela, for she and Tom, to his despair, had always relied simply on a large-scale Road Atlas, and then latterly on SatNav. He sighed, and used Google Maps in order to get some idea of where they were going.

Saturday was a much better day. Bright sunshine lit up the Lane as he walked up to Colin's house. He arrived 5 minutes before the agreed time, and was not surprised that when he rang the doorbell Colin opened the door almost instantly. Colin had actually been ready for at least 20 minutes and now, almost before Walter realised it, they were in the car and on their way. Walter knew that a car journey was always a good place for a more personal conversation, not least because although you were very close to one another in a private place, you could not look into each other's eyes, which somehow made personal revelations much easier. He always thought of that when he had a haircut! So, knowing this, he asked Colin how old he was when he'd started visiting the Severn Valley Railways with his Dad.

"Mm. I reckon I was about 5 or 6. I'd always wanted to go with him, but he said that until I started school, I wasn't old enough. So I remember longing to start school so I could go and see the steam trains with my Dad."

He paused a moment, his thoughts saddening. "I began to take my Peter when he was about 5, just as Dad used to take me, but although he liked it at first, he soon got fed up and didn't want to come with me. He preferred to stay at home and play with Maria."

"Older or younger?" said Walter

"She's about two years older, but they always got on well. Still do, I think. Anyway after that I went alone." "Alone?" said Walter. "So you never went as a family?"

"Well my wife came once when we were first married, but she just complained about the grit getting into her contact lenses, and never came again."

Walter had to control his anger. He was fairly used to doing this with annoying teenagers at school, so it wasn't too difficult. But no wonder this man's marriage had broken up. There his wife was with two little children, and he sailed off for days at a time to visit a railway line! He wanted to ask why Colin had never thought of taking his daughter. She might have enjoyed the trains more than the son. But clearly Colin came from a world where only boys liked trains. How stupid, he thought. Perhaps Colin had sensed his thoughts, because next he said, "It wasn't long after, that my marriage started going wrong. Rita spent all her time complaining about me. She really went for me. There was I working like mad to bring in enough money to buy that lovely house, and all she could do was complain that I was never there." "Ah yes," said Walter, aware that he needed to show some sympathy. "My wife used to complain that I was more often at the school than at home. But somehow our marriage survived." "Women!" said Colin, and Walter was lost for words. He could imagine how furious his wife, and even more his daughter, would have been if she had heard a man speaking like this. He imagined Colin wilting under their sarcastic fury. Walter was proud of his Teresa, now in a very high-powered job in her 30's and also raising two great children with her husband Sharad, but he had sometimes been the subject of her ticking off when he had inadvertently said something even slightly sexist. "We couldn't do without them," he said rather feebly, but Colin was now too wound up thinking of his ex-wife to take much notice, and began to tell the whole story of how angry he was at the way everything had gone wrong. "I still love her," He said. "But I can't live with her."

It had been an awful time for him, and he still wasn't over it even 5 years later, and so he was glad to be able to tell all to Walter. Walter listened patiently, adding an occasional sympathetic noise to keep Colin going. This, after all, was what he had come for; to see if as this man opened up he might reveal the lies he had told about Bill. There had clearly been faults on both sides of the marriage. Colin's wife had made the typical mistake of someone in love. She had seen all the good things about him, and ignored the things that she found more difficult. She'd lived with that common but rather silly idea that once they were married she would be able to change him. Colin was brutally honest about this. He knew he was a control freak, that he liked everything carefully ordered and organised. It was why he was good at his job, why his computer consultancy firm was so successful. He had also made the mistake of thinking he could change Rita just as she thought she could change him. He made careful plans about what they should do with their time, only to find that she would decide to do something different at the last minute. "I used to plead with her to make the changes sooner. I could have coped with that. I'm pretty flexible. Plans can be changed."

Walter suspected that this wasn't true, but Colin went on. "But she seemed to deliberately wait until it was too late, and then announce that she wanted to do something else, something that wasn't in the plan. And then we would end up shouting at one another."

"I suppose it was after one of those shouting matches that you left?" asked Walter. Colin was pleased that he was so understanding and went on.

"I actually planned it all in advance. I had my luggage already in the car and was driving off almost before she realised what I was doing. And after that, I was all alone." His memory of that moment was all too vivid, and tears came into his eyes, but he covered it by swearing at someone he thought was driving badly ahead of him. It was always other people's fault. He remembered how things had gone wrong at work too. One of his employees had actually walked out on him, and he'd found it hard to be tolerant of some of the others. Finally, he had been persuaded to go to the GP. He had been prescribed anti-depressants, but they made him feel so woozy that he had soon asked if there was some alternative, some other kind of help. "That was when she sent me to a Counsellor, and with help from her, I began to work out why I was so depressed and what I could do about it."

They had reached Kidderminster by now, and so this more personal conversation came to an end as they entered the Station Car Park. Walter was really impressed by the lovely replica station that was the southern terminus of the line, and then their talk turned to the trains. They went to the far end of the platform and watched the Engine slowly and gently backing onto the Carriages. Colin was soon explaining which engine it was, and some of its technical details, but although Walter showed some interest, part of him just enjoyed marvelling, as he always did, at the atmosphere a steam engine created, at the power that vibrated out from those great wheels and pistons shining in the sunshine even as it gently came to a halt. Then they got on the train and set out on the way to Bridgnorth. Walter was pleased to be able to show Colin he had done his homework, as they looked together on the left for where the original line from Bewdley had run, and then they enjoyed later the great bridge that took them to the western side of the River.

After their trip to Bridgnorth, and their shared enthusiasm at their ride up and down the Cliff Railway, they got back to Highley precisely as Colin had planned it, and were soon sitting together drinking a Beer and eating their sandwiches beside the River Severn. The River's dark water flowed past them slowly and steadily amidst the fresh May greenery. The day was the best kind of May Day, not too hot and yet very pleasant, with fair weather clouds sailing across a blue sky. This, and their common enthusiasm for trains, gave them a relaxed feeling as if neither had any troubles at all. But Walter knew only too well, that this was far from the case, and so deciding now was a good time, he went more personal again and asked Colin about his children. "Do you see your children very often?"

There was a long silence as Colin's face fell. "No. I've never seen them since the day I left. The money goes to them every month by Standing Order, so I do my duty by them." He paused, "I know what you're thinking. I should be in touch with them. Perhaps I should do something about it and try to see them every other weekend like some men do, but now I hear nothing, and I suppose I never will."

"That's really sad. Do they live far away?"

Colin sighed. "Only in Coleshill. Less than 10 minutes in the car." There was silence, and then he clearly made an effort to think of Walter, "I suppose you see your children and grandchildren regularly?"

Walter felt this was a good time to share a bit more about himself, although he hoped he wouldn't make Colin jealous in the process. "They've all got very busy lives so we don't see them that often. John isn't married but seems always to be working on one Court Case or another. He's a Barrister. Chris and his wife in York met at the University there, just like Penny and I did. They have three lovely children, but it's a long drag down to Oxford for them, so we try to get up and see them a couple of times a year. That's always lovely. You would think we would see Teresa most often as Milton Keynes isn't that far, but I think Sharad her husband comes to see us very reluctantly. You see Gary, their oldest, is 10 and is into weekend football, and so Sharad spends all his spare time encouraging him. They're both fanatics and so when they do come over, I can sense them both sighing as I show my ignorance of everything sporty."

"Oh I'm the same. If Peter was into football, I would find it really difficult to talk to him, but if he was into computer games, and wanted to go further into computing, then we might have something in common. But now of course I have no idea what he's like."

Colin didn't want to bore Walter with his sad life, but as they sat in silence, he felt the anger about his situation welling up in him. The children had been 9 and 11 when the separation took place. When they were younger, they had been really keen on time with their Daddy, but in the end they had begun to defy him when he tried to control the things he didn't like them doing. Rita had always let them get away with murder, and she had said that she wasn't prepared to make them do things they didn't want to do, and this had been yet another reason for the rows, until eventually she had just started walking out on him whilst he shouted at her to come back, as he hadn't finished. Had he been right to leave her? He didn't know. Perhaps he should get back in touch? After all it was his money that supported them. But sometimes he felt angry when he saw that money leaving his Account. He sighed again, "Come on. Let me show you the Engine Shed."

Chapter 6: Dinner at Angela's

When Walter arrived back at Merrymead, Angela had expected Colin to be with him. "Isn't he coming?" she said, disappointed at the thought that she had prepared too much food. She was relieved to be told that he had just popped home to freshen himself up and would be with them in about half an hour. Walter did the same, and was not surprised when precisely half an hour later, Colin was at the door. "Oh," said Angela as they were introduced. "Aren't you… I mean … er aren't you younger than I expected ." Colin knew straightaway that she knew who he was. He had sort of got used to local people recognising this, but still found it difficult. He deflected this by launching into profuse thanks for inviting him round to dinner. Angela brightened, glad that the moment of embarrassment had passed, and happy to see a young man, quite similar in age to her son, at her dinner table. She took them all out in the garden for drinks and nibbles and began to tell Colin how she wanted to improve the garden. "Tom, my late husband, just kept it like this with the formal rose beds and the crazy paving because this was what it was like when I was a little girl, but I was only saying to Walter the other day that I would really like to change it, to have it properly paved, and with less to weed… and you can see the problem every time this table wobbles."

Colin surveyed the garden. Angela was right. It was very old-fashioned. Four rectangular rose beds, with a small circular one in the middle, sat amongst very wobbly old paving stones. The rose beds now looked immaculate, as Walter had been working hard at weeding them, but the whole area clearly needed a makeover. "Perhaps you should have one much larger circular raised bed in the middle with lots of different shrubs in it that are easy to maintain and then have paving up to and around it. It's always important not to be able to see the whole garden in one glance." "That sounds lovely" said Angela. "Have you any ideas of local people who might do it?" "You ought to see Colin's front garden," Walter said, "Beautiful paving with one curved bed full of plants." Angela resisted the temptation to tell Walter that she knew exactly what Colin's front garden was like. It was she, after all, who had pointed out the house to Walter in the first place when she told them who lived there, and she had often admired that particular front garden. Walter too suddenly realised this, and was grateful that Colin was too full of new plans forming in his head to notice this second embarrassment. "Well," he said proudly "I am afraid I don't know of anyone, because I did it all myself." He paused and then "Would you like me to do it for you? You pay for the materials and I'll do the labouring?"

Angela was slightly startled by this offer. "Oh no. I couldn't ask a busy man like you to do that." But Colin was firm "My counsellor always tells me to take time off, but living alone I never know what to do when I'm not working, so this will be a wonderful way to relax. Things quieten down in my business in late July, so how about us booking a date for then?" His phone was out and open in his diary, and he wouldn't take no for an answer, so Angela gave way, astonished and yet pleased at this turn of events, not least because the victim, whom no one was supposed to know about, would now be working in her garden. Her Marston Green friends would be fascinated, since many knew where he lived, but no one seemed actually to know him. Walter had served up a surprise for them all.

She hurried off to do the last-minute preparations for the meal, refusing Penny's help. "No. You have done tons to help me earlier. Sit back and chat to Colin." And so that's what Penny did. "I'm afraid my Walter has told me nothing about you except that you love trains," She said. "But you just said you live alone. Don't you have any family?" So Colin told her about his ex-wife and the children and she was full of sympathy. "So sad for you. But what about your parents, or your brothers or sisters?" Colin was not keen on talking about the difficult relationship he had with his parents, but Penny's sympathy and Walter's friendship after their day together made it easier for him to open up to them. And so he did.

Walter pricked up his ears when Colin began to talk about his father and how difficult he had found him as he became a teenager, it reminded him of Simon, the lad at school. Could it be that Colin had actually been abused by his father? After all most children were abused by men they knew, family or family friends, rather than teachers or priests. Colin was talking about how his father had tried to control everything he did, and since his mother wouldn't stand up to him, he no longer saw either of his parents. "My Dad was great when I was little," he said. "He helped me join a swimming club and took me on regular trips to the Railway, but later things went wrong. Then after my divorce, both my parents took my wife's side, and I haven't seen them since." He then explained that his sister lived in Australia, so there was little chance of seeing her, except for her very occasional visits back to England.

Actually, his relationship with his father was even more problematic than he shared. As a boy he had got on really well with his Dad, but after an enormous row when he was about 16, he had hardly spoken to him since. He had then longed for the day when he could get away to University. After that, he found coming home an ordeal, and soon began to make excuses about how much work he had to do and how he had found a vacation job there in Loughborough. It was during that time that on one of his rare visits his Mum had got him alone and asked him why he appeared to hate his Dad so much. He had found it very difficult to explain to her his very mixed emotions. He didn't really fully understand it himself, even now, though his counsellor had worked with him to try and unravel the reason. Once again his Mum had tried to defend her husband and that had just made him angry, and he had stormed out of the house, leaving her in tears.

Penny's question had brought all this back, so he was relieved that at this point Angela called them in to eat. Penny, realising how difficult he'd found talking about his family, steered the conversation in a different direction, and they shared stories of their time at University, and she told Colin the story of how she'd met Walter, and they all laughed. Colin found himself telling them about his studies at Loughborough, and how he had then got a job with a large computer firm where he had done his Placement as part of his Degree Course, but always he had hoped he could work for himself. "I'm not very good at working for other people," he said. "I always thought, and sometimes said, that I could do the job better than them, so when the chance came, that's what I did." He tried to explain what his firm specialised in, but like most people they clearly didn't understand, so he soon asked them about their jobs, and was intrigued to find that Angela had worked all her life for the police. He looked slightly alarmed, until she explained that she had worked behind the scenes in various support roles rather than donning a uniform. She could however tell many funny stories about life there, and was soon sharing them with Colin, although she wisely didn't tell him that it was actually through her police contacts that she had found out about him and where he lived. Of course, Walter and Penny had heard most of her police stories before, but they were happy to see their friend enjoying herself with her new audience. She was still mourning the loss of her Tom, and a happy time of laughter was just what she needed.

She was also happy, as most bereaved people are, to talk about Tom with a new person. It was always easier with someone who had never known him, and she chatted away sharing memories, until Walter thought he would die of exhaustion. Finally, guessing that Colin too had probably had enough of Angela's chatter, he brought up the subject of the garden again, asking the two of them whether they had any ideas about what plants they might like in the new beds. Angela said she had no idea, and hoped that Walter and Colin might advise her, which led to a long discussion by the two men on the various plants that might suit.

Colin actually found Angela quite delightful, just like the Mum he had lost through sad misunderstandings, and was happy to join in and help take out dirty plates to stack in the dishwasher, and generally be useful. Angela's two children lived a long way away, but they were of a similar age to Colin, and she easily saw him as another son, so the bond between them grew quickly. Indeed, she soon discovered that her son Paul, and Colin, were almost exactly the same age. "Oh you're both February babies?" she said. "How lovely. Perhaps you knew him?" But she soon discovered that they were brought up in different parts of Birmingham and went to different schools, so clearly had never met. Then he noticed her dripping tap and offered to come and mend it for her tomorrow morning. She was really chuffed. Coincidentally back at the table, Penny was saying to Walter how wonderful Colin was for Angela. "I really like the idea that he will be just round the corner for her when we go back home. I know she's got lots of other friends, but they're all getting older, whilst a practical young man like him, will be someone to turn to, especially as he does her garden." Walter nodded. He had been impressed by how much Penny had got out of him, and as they came back in, he was thinking to himself that even if he couldn't achieve his aim, Penny and Angela might.

Hearing that Colin was coming back tomorrow to fix a tap in the kitchen couldn't have been better news. He wondered about asking Angela for help with his project with Colin, but swiftly realised how wrong it would be. Colin already had one person, himself, befriending him for ulterior motives, another would be wrong. Angela would hate it anyway. She was such a natural easy-going person. No. If she were to get out of him what Walter wanted to know, it would have to come from a natural friendship not by deceit. But this didn't come without its problems. What if Colin mentioned to Angela his lie that he was doing supply work at a school? He felt a pang of fear as he wondered what would happen if it was discovered that his meetings with Colin were part of a deliberate plan? But it was too late now, he would have to hope for the best. Colin did indeed say to him as he was leaving "See you Monday?" but either Angela didn't hear, or she just assumed that it was only because of Walter's very regular early morning walk. Perhaps he should tell Colin the truth? Perhaps he should admit the lie on the grounds that he felt foolish to admit this rather too regular habit? But then how and why could he explain the bus ride to Sheldon? No. It really wouldn't wash. He had better say nothing.

Chapter 7: Angela's Story

When Colin arrived round at Angela's at 11 the following morning, just as they had arranged, he was surprised that there was no sign of Walter or Penny. He was soon at work on the tap which didn't take long, and sat down with Angela for the Coffee she offered him. Then he asked where they were. "Oh, they'll be back soon" she said. "They've gone to Church." Colin was startled. "I would never have thought that Walter was religious," he said. "He's so normal. Does he just go to keep Penny company?" Angela explained that it was indeed Penny who had first got Walter going to church with her, but that many years ago Walter had made the decision to become a Catholic, and was now very involved back home in Oxford.

"But they are very nice and never get at me about it. All I know is that we can't do anything on Sunday mornings because they will be doing their religious thing. And it's no good asking them to come up at Easter because there's too much going on in their church that they want to be part of." "I was brought up as a Catholic," said Colin. "My Mum is at Mass every Sunday just like Walter and Penny. I quite enjoyed it as a kid, even when I was a teenager. I was an Altar Server, but once I went to Uni I never went again, apart from weddings and funerals of course."

Angela nodded with tears coming into her eyes "The Vicar was very kind and helpful to me when Tom died. I thought he might not want to do the Funeral as we never went to Church, but he came round here and helped me plan everything, and then took it beautifully." She got out a hanky to wipe away her tears, apologising for them at the same time. Colin did quite the right thing. "You miss him a lot, don't you?" Then she really wept as she shared her grief, apologising all the time. She told how Tom had been able to retire at 60 and it was then that they had lots done to improve the bungalow. She explained how it had been her parents' home where she was brought up, and that then some 10 years ago when her mother died, they had moved back in. "We had such a happy time together. But then they found he had cancer, and although he fought it very bravely, in the end he just got weaker and weaker, and then died here at home. The Macmillan Nurses were wonderful, but it was still a very hard time. In a way, when he passed away it was a relief because at least, he was out of pain."

Colin had had little contact with bereaved people, so he just listened, nodded and found himself holding her hand as she wept over him. Finally, having told her story, and shed some tears, Angela found herself telling him about her parents. Her father had also died in this house many years ago, and she had popped over often to help her mother look after him, but when her mother was taken ill, she had been admitted to the hospital and died there. Sharing this made her think of Colin's situation. "Are your parents still alive Colin? she said, forgetting how difficult this question might be for him. So he told her a bit more about his split with his parents, but that he knew they were still alive. He found it easy to share confidences with Angela. She was after all about the same age as his Mum, and he found a warmth in her that was just what he needed. She was really sympathetic when she heard that he wasn't even in touch with them at Christmas. "They send me a Card. Although I know it is actually my Mum who sends it. But I never send one back. I just don't want anything to do with him." He stressed the word "him" and was very firm about it, but Angela was not the sort for a quiet life when people disagreed with her, and this issue was close to her heart. So she told Colin her story.

She told him of her son Paul, who'd had a big argument with his father some years ago. The argument was about his lifestyle, for Paul was self-employed, if you can call it that, and had no regular income. Tom had expressed to him some worries about this, as a concerned parent might, but Paul took it as a personal criticism and shouted at his father, stormed out of their house in Edgbaston, and had never been back since. In fact, he had never visited them at all in their Marston Green home, although he knew it from visits to his grandparents when he was younger. He had turned up for their Funerals, but hadn't stayed to talk to anyone, even though Angela had managed to get him on one side and plead with him to make peace. It was a classic father/son split and, as Angela told Colin, both were too like one another to work a way out of their conflict. Paul's sister Becky was still in touch with him, and saw him occasionally, but she had also had no luck in healing the wound, but at least she acted as a go-between, letting them know how Paul was doing.

Then Tom had died, and when she told Paul, his reaction was anger and confusion. He came to the Funeral with a face like thunder, having already had a go over the phone on separate occasions at his Mum and then his sister for not telling him earlier that his Dad was ill. Their explanation that they hadn't known he was ill, that it was all so sudden, just seemed to make him more irrationally angry. In Church he had found himself crying, something he never did normally, with Julie his partner trying to comfort him. This time he did come to the house after the service, but had been unusually quiet as people tried to speak words of comfort to him, and had then slipped away with Julie when nobody was watching. Since then, Angela had gone to visit him, because Julie had been in touch to say he wasn't working and seemed very depressed. He had just sat there while Angela tried to talk to him, and eventually she had gone away utterly confused about what she could do to help him. She and Julie had kept in touch however, and at Angela's suggestion had been persuaded to go to the Doctor. Now he was on anti-depressants, but still not working.

Angela wanted Colin to know all this because she didn't want Colin to make the same mistake. "You may not want to see your parents now, but one day they will die, and then you may end up like my Paul, and I wouldn't like to see that happen to anyone." Colin was genuinely moved by her story. He knew what it was like to face depression, but he reckoned that his break-up with his control freak of a father was a far more serious matter than just a row over a lifestyle.

"I'm sorry Angela, but I just can't stand the idea of seeing him face to face."

"Ok. Maybe not face to face, but perhaps keep in touch for Christmas and Birthdays? And anyway what about your Mum? Couldn't you arrange to see her?"

"How would I do that? They're always together."

"Surely not always? Doesn't she ever go into Birmingham sometimes to do a bit of shopping? Why not arrange to meet her for a coffee or for lunch? She'd probably jump at the chance."

"You know, I've never thought of that, but I doubt she'd be prepared to go against my Dad." "Well try it and see" said Angela. "Is there a way of contacting her without your Dad knowing?"

It was soon clear that Colin did know a way of doing that, and with Angela's nudging he soon had it planned for a time when he knew his father would be out of the house on his allotment. It was then that Walter and Penny appeared, and they spoke of other things, but the seed had been sown, and Colin became determined to take Angela's advice. He didn't want to face the anger and despair of another bout of depression. He knew all too well how awful that was, and he remembered his Counsellor gently asking him if he could face getting back in touch with them. Angela's story was the final nudge. Now he was determined to attempt to remake the connection.

As he left, she made a point of saying to him. "Pop round any time you'd like a chat. Don't wait to be asked." And as he walked home, he still felt the warmth of that conversation. It was so different from the way he had shared things with his Counsellor. That had helped, but it had always been a bit impersonal. The planned hour-long sessions set on a regular timetable couldn't ever have the genuine spontaneity he had just experienced. His counsellor never shared anything of herself, whilst Angela had wept with him, and so he knew that although he had gained much from those Counselling sessions, and benefited from getting many things off his chest and out into the open, he felt he could share things with Angela in a very different way, and she was just round the corner. As he thought about it, he warmed to this idea, because he knew he would be supporting her as much as she was him, and there would be no need to make the effort of phoning and making an appointment. With Angela, yes he might well phone just to check she was in, but then he would be able to walk round and see her almost straightaway. He felt really good about the whole thing. "Thank God, I met Walter, and so found Angela," he thought.

His next action was to follow Angela's advice and phone his Mum when he knew his Father would be out. Unfortunately, it didn't work. It was his father who answered the phone. Colin cancelled the Call as quickly as he could, his heart beating as his anxiety welled up. It almost made him feel sick. At least their home phone didn't show who was calling. Then he thought how stupid he was to panic, for now as he thought about it more clearly he remembered that they didn't know his mobile phone number. He was stuck however. Clearly his father's timings had changed, so how could he know when to phone when he wasn't in? Perhaps it wasn't worth trying again? The idea of making endless calls and finding his father answering each time was more than he could face. Later, when he told Angela, she told him to try to think of another time when his father might be out and to be brave and try again. So he plucked up his courage and did begin a call a number of times through the week that followed, but each time with his panic levels rising, he cancelled the call before it began to ring at the other end.

He had told Walter all about this on their daily morning journeys to Sheldon, and Walter had reported back to Angela the anguish that Colin appeared to be going through. Finally, she asked Walter to get

Colin's parents' phone number from him, saying she would make the calls for him, but Colin said it wasn't right to ask her to do this, and anyway what would she say when they answered, and so stalemate continued. Meanwhile Walter thought it best to take Colin's mind off this troubled subject and back on to areas where he knew Colin felt safe. So there was much talk about trains, and Walter's experiences as a boy when steam trains were still part of normal life and not just specials. Colin was also able to help him with his Smartphone when he got muddled with it, which was pretty often, and from that there was often talk of the new advances in artificial intelligence. Sometimes Walter got a little lost in the technicalities, but Colin was a good and very patient teacher, and Walter actually enjoyed learning from him.

In fact he told him what a good teacher he was, which made Colin laugh. "I may be patient with you. But when the people who work for me get things wrong, I am more likely to just do it for them rather than teach them what to do." Walter didn't really believe this about Colin. He felt the fact that he knew taking over was his danger was probably a sign that he mostly managed to restrain himself, and he told Colin what he thought. Colin shrugged. "Maybe you're right. My Counsellor is always encouraging me to think more positively about myself. She says I am a classic perfectionist, always feeling I'm failing when I'm actually doing pretty well!"

It was the first time he had told Walter he still went for Counselling, and that led to a long discussion about how the Counsellor had helped him. Walter wondered if talking about this might lead to the breakthrough he was seeking, but then discovered that the Counsellor he used now was not the same person as the one he had first been helped by. Colin certainly was prepared to share quite a lot of personal stuff, but the really difficult area in Colin's life seemed to be strictly off limits. It wasn't the kind of thing that Walter felt he could bring up in general conversation, so no progress was made. However, at least their continued shared confidences might bear fruit eventually.

Meanwhile Angela was busy trying to find out the details of Colin's parents for herself. She was a very determined lady, and having worked for the police she knew all sorts of ways in which you could find people you were looking for. She knew his surname and she knew that his parents lived in Sutton Coldfield, and from that she soon found two addresses that might fit the bill. Next, she primed Walter to try and find out where in that area Colin actually lived when he was a boy. Walter was hesitant, until she asked him to find out if his house was near the railway, for one of the addresses was actually next to a railway line. Walter didn't even have to ask Colin that, because Colin had already shared in their train discussions how as a boy he could watch the trains go by in his back garden. Walter had been somewhat envious until he heard how noisy it could be with trains rumbling past. It hadn't stopped Colin from being keen on trains, but he had certainly made sure that he never lived too near a railway line.

Angela now decided that it would be best to do something about it herself, so roping in Penny they set off to find the house, and see if they could work out when Colin's father might be out so they could catch his Mum when she was by herself. It wasn't a long car ride, and Walter was told he could busy himself doing something else whilst they did their detective work. Walter was relieved. He had already found stalking Colin difficult enough. To stalk Colin's parents as well, even if it was for a good cause, was more than he could face. They found the house easily enough. It was in a relatively modern group of houses in a culdesac. The sort of unimaginative ones built in the 1970's with open-plan front gardens and one of the upstairs rooms over the garage. They sat in the car and wondered what to do next. They listened to Woman's Hour and a couple of programmes that followed it to stop them from getting bored, whilst watching carefully for any action from the house, but absolutely nothing happened. There was no sign of any movement at all. They waited another hour and then gave up and went off to have a spot of lunch in Macdonalds, determined to try again the following day. Walter was amused that they, unlike him, were clearly enjoying being amateur detectives, despite the fact that once again they had no luck. They tried again the following day in the afternoon, but again had no success. It was as if nobody lived there. “Third time lucky,” said Angela, as they set off again the following morning before Walter came back from his “walk”. Angela had decided that if nothing happened this time they would have to take more direct action, but then soon after they arrived a man came out of the front door and went off down the road. Angela didn’t hesitate, she leaped out of the car telling Penny to wait, and went to knock on the door he had emerged from.

Chapter 8: Colin's Mum

Monica always got anxious if someone came to the door when John was out. He had always insisted on answering the phone and going to the door whenever he was in, so she looked through the peephole first. Seeing a woman about her age dressed very respectably with fair hair and glasses, she plucked up her courage and opened the door. The woman smiled and said "I'm so sorry to bother you, but are you the mother of Colin Bransted who lives in Marston Green." Monica felt panic rising at this sudden question "Is he all right? Has something happened to him?" "No.. no. don't worry," said Angela. "He just wants to make contact with you without his father knowing. He tried phoning, but you never seem to pick up the phone. He'd almost given up trying, but I'm just a friendly and rather nosey neighbour, and so I thought I would help by calling while your husband's out." "Oh!" said Monica, panicking again, "He'll be back very soon." "No worries," said Angela. "Here's Colin's Mobile number and here are my details. Just phone him the next time your husband's out." And handing over a piece of paper with all the details clearly written on it, Angela turned away quickly and headed back to the car.

Monica stuffed the paper quickly into her apron pocket, closed the door, and feeling slightly faint, went and sat down in the kitchen, hoping John wouldn't notice her agitation when he got back. Memories of her lovely son came flooding back to her, and she wiped away a few tears, as she tried to control herself. She remembered the little boy who would never remember his real father for he had died so tragically when Colin was only a baby. John had married her when Colin was about three, and had been a great Dad for Colin and his big sister Jessica. She remembered so many happy times they'd had as a family. Toy trains of course, and then that wonderful train-set that John and Colin had played with together. Then there were the visits to that Steam Railway that Colin so enjoyed. They got on so well, and had been so close, and John had really encouraged Colin as he became more and more interested in technical things. She had been so happy that she had found a good father for him, until it all went wrong.

She still didn't know what had happened at that time. Suddenly there was Colin now a teenager shouting at his father "Keep away from me. Stop telling me what to do. I don't want anything to do with you." And there was John trying to calm him down and getting nowhere. It was so unlike Colin to get angry like that. He was normally such a quiet friendly boy, and she was bewildered by the change. Colin had ran up to his bedroom and slammed the door, and John had persuaded her to leave him to calm down, reminding her that teenagers could sometimes behave irrationally. Colin had come down later when John had gone out, and she had tried to reason with him, but he had very quietly but firmly refused to talk about it. And that had been that. Colin had cut himself off as much as possible, using the excuse that he had homework to do, and hardly speaking at all when he was downstairs with them, and after a few more attempts to get him to see reason, as he saw it, John said it wasn't worthwhile trying, better to let him stew. Saying that one day he would come round. So Colin would eat his meal fast and retreat upstairs again, and she just hoped he was working and not simply sulking. She would occasionally pop up to his room and take him a cake and a cup of tea and was pleased to find that he was usually immersed in his work, even if he was listening to his music at the same time.

She jumped as the front door opened and John appeared with his paper. "There's nothing in it as usual," he said. "I'm going out to the shed." She couldn't help smiling, because this is what he said almost every day, even though he could only have quickly scanned it walking home. Mind you, later on she knew that he would pick it up again and read it more carefully. The unusual day was when there was something in it he thought worth commenting on straight away, and then she would listen as he shared with her his thoughts on the matter. This would often lead to an interesting discussion in which he did most of the talking. He was not stupid, and so she liked days like that even though she had to be careful to ask questions rather than disagree with him, but today she was quite glad there was nothing worth commenting on. His quick disappearance to the shed gave her more time to think about Colin, and the strange woman who had just been at her door.

She knew she could think about this more easily if she was doing something, and since it was about time to clean the bathroom, she went upstairs and began the work in her usual methodical way. Put cleaner down the toilet and leave it whilst she did the rest of the cleaning. Damp the cloth, spray the surfaces, wipe them down with the cloth and then polish off with some kitchen towel, then scrub out the toilet with the toilet brush, and finally wash the floor. Little did she realise that when Colin cleaned his bathroom, keeping it as spotless as she did, he did it in exactly the same meticulous manner. She was glad in a way that this woman had befriended him, because she knew what a loner he had become, especially since he had split up with Rita. She just hoped the woman wasn't in it for what she could get out of it, that she was a real friend rather than a false one, but her visit seemed a sign that she simply wanted to help. Why else would she have taken the trouble to find her and leave the message which was now hidden in her apron pocket? Yes, Colin had become a loner. He had been a happy little child, but as a teenager, especially after that row with his father, he hadn't made many friends. Instead, he'd spent most of his time on his own in his room, apart from the early morning Swimming Club before school once a week.

Holidays with them were a nightmare. He would walk along behind them as if he didn't belong to them. Gradually he had actually managed to speak to his father if he had to, on practical matters, but the old friendship had been replaced with a coldness that she found very distressing. She'd asked his sister what she thought had gone wrong, but Jessica had no idea at all. "You know I never could talk to Colin," she said. "He was always so different from me, and the more he's got into his computer stuff the less I can understand what he's talking about. I did once ask him why he didn't get on with Dad, and he said it was none of my business, so I never asked him again." Monica had also tried once or twice to talk again to Colin about it, but all he would say was, "We just don't get on Mum. I won't have him running my life like he does yours. He won't change and I won't change, and that's all I'm going to say."

The one person who seemed to help him most was Father Bill, the local priest. The Church was only about a 5-minute walk away, but Colin always went to Mass ahead of her as he was an altar server, and she would watch him proudly during Mass carrying himself with such dignity as he performed his tasks. She always knew when it was his turn to ring the bell. He was always so precise. She had been a bit startled one day when he told her he had been round at the priest's house. He told her that talking to the priest kept him sane. "He's just such a good listener," he said, "And we can talk about almost anything together." After a bit, he told her that he'd been invited for the day on the priest's boat on the canal, and then came back full of where they had been and what kind of engine it had, but then John came in, and he quietly removed himself upstairs. The priest also took him to visit that Steam Railway he loved, but she knew why they always chose a weekday during the school holidays. He wanted to be absolutely sure he didn't meet his Dad there. Finally, he announced one day when he was about 17 that rather than go on holiday with them, he was going on a week-long boat trip with Father Bill, and that was that. She tried to persuade him to come on holiday with them as well, but nothing would move him from what he had decided to do, and she gave in. She was at least grateful that he had found someone sensible to spend time with, rather than roaming the streets as some young men did. Monica sighed. How sad to find out later what that priest had been doing. She often wondered if her Colin was the victim, but couldn't quite believe that he would ever get involved with something like that.

She remembered how he had come back home full of his trip on the canal. He was very clever at finding the times his Dad was out or in the garden to sit and share with her what he had been up to. He spoke of their journey almost as far as Oxford, and how much he had enjoyed jumping off to work the locks, as Father Bill steered the boat in and out of them. He even spent time explaining to her how they worked. She smiled to herself as she remembered his grasp of the technical details, and also how he had learnt more about the boat and its engine. Yes, that was her Colin, such a clever lad. She had been so proud of him. "No," she thought "I'm still proud of him. Just sad the way things turned out."

She remembered how nothing kept him away from his studies, and how pleased yet not surprised she was when he got those brilliant exam results and a place at University. But then came that fateful day when it all went wrong. Colin had come back from Loughborough for the weekend about halfway through his first term and she and he had been alone. He had said how glad he was that his Dad wasn't there, and then had said rather bitterly "I wish he wasn't my father, then I wouldn't feel so guilty." Astonished that he didn't know, she said "But he isn't your real father Colin, I thought you knew that, your real father died when you were only a baby. He's your stepfather." There had been a sudden long silence, and then for the first time he really shouted at her. "All these years, I've been feeling I should really love him, and now you tell me this. Why didn't you tell me before?" She had tried to explain that she thought he knew, but he wasn't really listening. "Well that's that," he'd said, and within minutes he had packed his things and disappeared, slamming the front door behind him. She had stood waiting to say goodbye until it was too late, until he had gone. She had run to the door then to call him back, but he was already some way away and she was too embarrassed to call out to him in front of the neighbours. She had just hoped that when he calmed down, she and he would be able to sort it out and get on as they used to. After all, until that time, they had continued to be close. It was only when John was present that he retreated into silence.

But it was not to be. He came back once with a friend in a car to collect most of the stuff from his room, and then for a long time she had heard almost nothing. After a bit she had written and pleaded with him just to let her know he was all right, as otherwise she got so anxious about him. In response, he had taken to sending her a short typed letter at the end of each Term telling her what he was studying, or what he was doing if it was before the Summer Vacation. She sighed. It had been better than nothing, of course, and just like Colin to send her without fail a brief factual report, but she had longed for more. Soon after that, Jessica had announced that she and her husband were moving to Australia, and so the comfort of at least seeing one of her children was taken from her. She had been very strong when Jessica told her, saying what a good opportunity it was for her and her husband, but when the final goodbye took place she found herself in floods of tears. Alone, apart from her husband, she had longed to see Colin face to face and get back to those friendly chats the two of them used to have in his Sixth form days. She kept all his letters in a file and would read and re-read the most recent ones.

Then one day, out of the blue, in his final year at University, a very different letter had arrived. He wrote to say that he wanted to bring Rita his girlfriend, to see her. He had named a day, and a precise time when they would arrive - 12 Noon; that they would stay for lunch and leave about 3.00 pm. When that day came, she had been almost sick with anxiety. How would he cope with the presence of his stepfather, and what would this girl Rita think of them? She'd planned his favourite food, and laid the table very carefully with every knife and fork and spoon placed as carefully as a butler would do at a royal banquet. Then she'd gone round and round tidying and dusting, so that her always immaculate house was even more immaculate, if that were possible. She wondered why Colin was bringing this girl to see them. Perhaps he was thinking of marrying her? But when they arrived,

Colin had soon explained that he'd been taken to see Rita's parents, and she had then insisted that she should meet his. "I have to do what she tells me Mum, or my life's not worth living!" Monica remembered how she had controlled her urge to say what she thought about this. That it was a pity it should take a girl to persuade him to come and see his parents. Instead, she had said "How nice of you Rita. Are you a student at Loughborough too?" Rita hadn't been shy at all but had chatted about the course she was doing and how she and Colin had met. "We were both doing a vacation job as Lifeguards at the Pool, and we started chatting when we were on the same rotation." Oh yes, Monica thought to herself, he had reported he was doing that in one of his letters, and then to Rita. "Are you as good a swimmer as he is?" And was delighted when Rita said "We're fairly evenly matched. He always beats me especially over a short distance, but over a long distance, I can wear him down. But I reckon my style is better than his!" They both laughed, and Monica decided that she liked Rita a lot, not least because she made her quiet son laugh, and soon the two of them were chatting away like old friends, whilst Colin and his Dad looked on.

After that they had come to visit quite often, and she soon discovered that after they had graduated they were living together. She found this a bit difficult since it was not the kind of thing she had done in her day, but at least she knew her lovely Colin was being looked after and seemed to be happy. She remembered too that proud day when she and John had gone up to Loughborough for Colin's Graduation Ceremony. Two tickets had arrived, which surprised her a little as she wondered why Colin was happy to have his stepfather there, and then thought "This is Rita's doing." When Colin's name was announced and he walked across in his gown to receive his degree, she wept with pride, and now she treasured his official graduation ceremony photo which had pride of place in her sitting room.

She was downstairs now doing a bit of dusting, and she looked up at that wonderful photo, and the rest of the photos up on that wall which were all of her grandchildren. There were photos of the three Australian children of course. They had been over to visit some years ago, but they were so far away, whereas Colin and Rita's Maria and Peter were nearby, and she had been able to see them regularly as they grew up, even helping now and then with a bit of babysitting. They were teenagers now, so she saw them less often, but despite the divorce Rita had kept in touch and brought them all over to see them every so often, as well as inviting her over occasionally for Sunday Lunch. Monica sighed again. "She's such a lovely person," she said to herself, "So sad that she and Colin split up."

Yes, she had seen both those babies soon after they were born. Maria had come along less than a year after Colin and Rita got married and Peter about two years later, and all seemed to be going very well. Colin became an expert on some sort of computer program and was then able to create his own computer consultancy firm. Soon they had been able to buy a very pleasant house in Coleshill with a big garden for the children to play in; how she had loved going over there to see them. But gradually she had realised that things weren't going well. Rita had always been rather less tidy and organised than Colin had liked, and gradually he had begun to put up with it less and less as his work had taken up more and more of his time. Rita had told her how he would come home exhausted by his determination to make his business even more successful, and how he had begun to be impatient by the lack of order in the house. She supposed that in earlier days when he was under less stress he would have just tidied up things himself, but now he was unable to cope with it. Rita had her parents close by, but she had also confided in Monica that she feared the marriage wouldn't last. "He just loses his temper," she said, and Monica remembered how he had done the same with her. Finally, and apparently very suddenly, Colin had said he was leaving her. There wasn't anyone else. She was glad that he had continued to support Rita and the children very generously, but there was no other contact.

That was some four years ago, and sadly soon after that, when Colin had discovered that she was still seeing Rita and the children, he had accused her of taking Rita's side against him. Once again there had been angry words. "How can you be on her side?" he said. "Look at how tidy and neat your house is. It was always like this even when I was a boy. But Rita never seems to tidy up anything. I can't live like that!" She had tried to point out that she, Monica, was obsessively tidy and that Rita really wasn't the way he was describing her. Rita might not be quite as immaculately tidy as she was, and as he was, but really her house wasn't at all bad, and she had thought he'd got used to her more relaxed way of doing things. "No!" he said "It always drove me mad, but I kept it in for years, but it couldn't last, especially when she tried to justify herself. Why can't you see that?" Her attempts to try to help him see Rita's side of things had completely backfired, and once again he had walked out, and from that day, she like Rita had heard no news of him.

So now, out of the blue, this strange woman had come to the door with Colin's mobile number. Again, she wondered why this neighbour had gone to so much bother, but whatever the reason she was determined to act on it. She decided next Sunday would be best, as that was the day when her John would be off to help on his Steam railway, and she could phone Colin and speak to him without fear of embarrassing explanations. And so that is what she did.

Chapter 9: More about Colin

Angela had wisely popped around that evening and told Colin what she had done. He had been a bit surprised to see her but even more startled when he discovered how enterprising she had been. He thought of being angry with her, as that had always been his way when people did things he didn't like, but he'd learnt new ways from his Counsellor, ways that he had used successfully in running his business. The Counsellor had taught him never to react too quickly, especially if his first thought was to be angry; instead he had to take a deep breath, look for the positive side of things and then respond. Given that Angela had achieved what he wanted, he knew deep down that he should be pleased. He was annoyed when anyone interfered in his life; but knowing that she had meant it kindly he was able, using the techniques he had learnt, to control his anger and simply express genuine surprise. "How on earth did you manage to do that?" He said "You don't even know where she lives." Angela laughed. "Well I did work for the police for years, and I've picked up a thing or two from them." She went on to explain how a short hunt for people with his name in Birmingham, and then the knowledge from Walter that the house was next to a railway line had clinched the matter.

"Of course, I remember telling him how much I loved living beside the line as a boy."

There was a slight pause, as a worried frown appeared on Colin's face. Angela knew what was troubling him. "Don't worry, I made sure I saw her when your father was out."

Colin was amazed by the way she had read his mind. For one long moment he'd started wondering how to extricate himself from the new muddle he thought she'd got him into. Now he was as quickly grateful to her again. "But how did you manage to contact her without my father knowing?" He was much amused by her slightly exaggerated account of how she and Penny had acted like police officers on surveillance, sitting in the car till the coast was clear. Little did he know that Walter had done the same to him.

He guessed that his mother would ring him on Sunday, as that was the day when his father went to do his voluntary work on the Severn Valley Railway. He was more than a little anxious about how the call would go. He had always felt guilty that he'd cut off contact with her largely because of that man. She had every right to be angry with him. He knew, now that he had got over his divorce, that she was also right to have kept up contact with Rita and the kids. They were her grandchildren after all. At the time, when the split happened, he had reacted in his usual way by getting angry and cutting himself off. It was soon after this that he had found himself so stressed out of his mind by everything, that even his work had suffered. It was then that he'd begun to see a Counsellor. He'd been reluctant at first, just hoping the Doctor would give him some Pills to help him relax, and to sleep, but the GP had more or less insisted on the Counsellor, and he was glad she had. He had pills as well, which enabled him to keep his business going, as there was no one he really trusted enough to actually run it. Then with the help of the Counsellor he had gradually got himself back onto an even footing and, indeed had begun to feel much better about life than he had before, but he still had his dark days and his even darker nights when the anger about life all welled up again. Perhaps this was why he still hadn't had the courage, or maybe the time, to get back in contact with his Mum fearing it would drag him back into the bad memories. And the longer he'd left it, the more he'd got into the habit of not being in touch. At the back of his mind, this had niggled at him, and he'd kept thinking he should contact her, but had been a little fearful of the response he might get. Angela had relieved him of all this, and now all he had to do was wait for the call, and be ready to say sorry and arrange a meeting.

He shared some of these thoughts with Walter as they did their daily commute to Sheldon. "Angela is a rather pushy lady," said Walter. "So I was worried you would be angry with her for meddling." Colin admitted how very nearly he had been. "But I realised in time how kind she was, how much her insistence that I should get back in touch was a sign of real concern for my Mum as well as for me. She'd told me about her own situation, and actually cried as she told me. So how could I be angry with her after hearing that?" Walter realised that in some way Angela was, as he had suspected, actually getting closer to Colin than he ever could, especially as he would soon be going back to Oxford. Once again he wondered, even hoped, that eventually she might succeed where he had failed, in finding out why he had made unjust accusations against Father Bill. "So roll on Sunday," he'd said, and Colin had nodded and said, "Sunday yes. I hope it comes soon because it's making me very anxious about what I should say to her?"

"Well, you don't have to say much do you? Just say sorry for not being in touch and arrange the meeting and leave it at that." Then after a pause, "But be ready to answer her questions. She'll want to know how you know Angela, so you can tell her about how you met via me, and how you are going to landscape her garden for her later this summer. You might even tell her about our trip to see the Steamtrains!" They laughed at this and Colin seemed much comforted by Walter's suggestions. It might be less difficult than he had imagined.

Walter's predictions proved uncannily correct, and the fact that Colin was prepared made it so much easier for him to relax when he answered the phone. His Mum did not need to be persuaded to have a day's shopping in Birmingham in 10 days time, so that she could have lunch with her lovely son. She said yes almost before he proposed it, and agreed to his suggestion of a 12.30 pm meeting at a restaurant he knew she would like. She knew where it was, although she had never been there, largely because she hardly ever went out for a meal, so she was quite excited about the idea. Colin had chosen a good restaurant.

not some cheap place, but not too upmarket, as anything very posh would have made her feel uncomfortable, and he didn't want that. Everything was so easily settled. "Ok. Love you Mum. See you then." And he was off the phone and online booking the table.

The following day he and Walter met again, and he was full of how well the phone call had gone. "Do tell Angela how grateful I am. I only wish I had done this sooner, but it's taken me a very long time to get over my divorce and the feeling I had that Mum had taken Rita's side. Gradually, I've realised that she had every right to want to keep in touch with the kids. They are her grandchildren after all. And whilst I stupidly cut myself off from them, she kept the contact alive."

Walter then asked a question that he feared might be too challenging. "Yes, you told me some of this before. I understand why you left them but why didn't you keep in touch?"

"Oh I don't know Walter. Sometimes I don't know myself at all. I suppose I was just so stressed out by the whole thing that I couldn't face seeing them. Actually, I couldn't face seeing anyone. How I kept the business going I just don't know, although actually it was only through working on building it up, plus help from my Counsellor, that I survived, but only just."

"So when did you last see your children?"

"I know it's terrible, but I haven't seen them at all since I left them about 4 years ago. Maria must be a teenager by now, 14 or 15 I think, and Peter's two years younger. I really should do something about them, shouldn't I?"

"Well take one step at a time. Let your Mum tell you how they are, and maybe let her arrange a meeting rather than you contacting them out of the blue. At that age, they are going to find it pretty difficult. And if I were you, I wouldn't mention this to Angela, or she'll try and sort this out too."

Colin smiled. “She’s such a kind person, isn’t she? But I think you’re right. My Mum is the right person to do this. She’s the one who they know, and I suspect they trust her, so I’ll take your advice.”

Once again, they had reached the bus stop and this personal conversation ceased. Nudged by Walter, Colin then tried to explain to him what his computer business was all about, and how many people he employed. Some of this Walter followed, but the more complex technicalities of the computer side were beyond him. “Computers are like cars for me,” he said. “Provided I can drive them, then I leave clever people like you to fiddle under the bonnet and make sure they keep running.” Colin then discovered what he had always suspected, that Walter was on Facebook and Twitter. “I hardly go on them myself. Javid is my main advertising person and so he runs our Website and our appearance on Social Media. Look up Shelcol Analysis and you’ll see how we advertise ourselves to the world. He’s quite brilliant at it. I took him on as an Apprentice at 18. He wanted to get straight into a job rather than go to University, and I’ll never regret my decision there. His loyalty to the Company is 100%.”

“Right, I’ll do that. But if you’re not on Facebook or Twitter can you give me your email address so we can keep in touch?” Colin was really pleased about this. He had so enjoyed their time together and was sad that Walter was soon going back to Oxford. “I’ll send you a photo or two of the work on Angela’s garden once I’ve started on it,” he said, as he sent Walter his email address in a text. “Ah yes,” said Walter. “But don’t worry, we’ll be coming up again in August to inspect the finished result. I really am so grateful to you for doing this, as well as being a help just round the corner if she has any more taps that need fixing. Her husband was so good at that kind of thing, and most of her other friends are getting on in years and less able to crawl around under sinks and things like you can.”

“I’m just happy I can help her. And I’ll report on that too.”

When Walter got home that morning, he looked up Shelcol Analysis on the web and was most impressed. He took his laptop to Penny and Angela. “Look at this,” he said to them. “It’s Colin’s firm. Such an impressive layout.” The girls were impressed of course, but even more interested when he explained that the Firm had a Facebook page and a Twitter Account as well, and all of them went online and linked up so that they could see the Firm’s regular Postings and Tweets. They loved the photos of Colin of course. “He’s such a handsome young man, isn’t he?” said Angela, “Isn’t it sad that his marriage went wrong? I would have thought he was a great catch for any woman. I wonder why his wife couldn’t hold on to him?” “Well,” said Walter “I know that he’s always supported her and the children since he left them, which is more than some men do. I think he almost had some kind of nervous breakdown you know. He often talks of his Counsellor and how she helped him through a rough patch soon after the divorce. I wonder if that’s got anything to do with his other problem?” “Well I wouldn’t be surprised,” said Penny. “If you’ve been abused it leaves you very mixed up in all sorts of ways doesn’t it?” “So mixed up that he accused the wrong person?” said Walter, without thinking. Then it was too late, as Angela was quick to respond. “Oh no Walter. You must have got that wrong. I understand how you might think that before you met Colin, that you might think badly of someone who has hurt someone you so like and admire, but now we know him, I find it impossible to believe that he could make up a story like that!”

“You’re quite right. The longer I have known him, the more difficult it is to believe he could behave in such a way. But Bill has always professed his innocence to me, and I find it even more difficult not to believe him.”

“Hmph! People who abuse teenagers like that, or abuse children, are very good at hiding the truth even from themselves. The reports I’ve had to write up when I worked for the police showed me this over and over again. False accusations when they happen, are made by people who are usually mixed up themselves or just like making trouble. But Colin just isn't like that."

Walter didn't argue with her about this, but knowing what she didn't know, that Colin had actually been very mixed up indeed after his divorce, he still felt deep down that it was quite possible that he had accused the wrong person. Bill had told him how he had often taken this young man who was an altar boy out on his boat, and once had taken him on holiday. He had admitted to Walter what a fool he had been. "It was about twenty years ago," he had said, "It was before we priests had realised how easily we could all fall under this kind of awful suspicion as the cases of abuse became public. Back then we often befriended boys with troubles at home, and it was only natural to invite them into the house so that they could talk through in private the things that were upsetting them. It was simply part of our calling as a priest to help them, never dreaming for a moment that we were making ourselves vulnerable to false accusations. The problem is that all the publicity caused by one or two evil priests has tarred us all with the same brush. That's one of the reasons, though not the only one, why I pleaded guilty. It was his word against mine, and I didn't want him to have to go through a trial like that, nor did I want all the publicity." It was only then that Walter had begun to understand Father Bill even better; and became even more convinced of his innocence. He remembered how Bill had told him how he had noted that occasionally Colin's bulge would grow in his trousers. He had tried to ignore it of course. "I remember as a teenager even getting an erection from the vibrations of a bus," he'd said. "It's one of the trials of being a teenage boy, especially if you are sensitive about such things, and the last thing one does is draw attention to it." Walter had been a bit astonished at how open Bill had been about such matters. He too, as a teacher, knew the trials that both boys and girls experience in different ways as they enter puberty, and how difficult some of them find this; but despite knowing Bill well as a friend, as someone who had helped him find his faith, they had never talked about sex before, and certainly not in this open and frank way. He remembered how startled he had been that a priest could be so open about such things, and had said so, and Bill had said, "You forget that we have to hear many people making their Confession Walter, and sexual things are often mentioned there. One learns to speak about these things openly in such situations, hoping to help the person cope with their sexuality without making them feel guilty. People are often surprised by how matter a fact we are about it and forget that we have heard people confess such things many times before." Walter had to admit that he hadn't thought of it like that. He had somehow forgotten that all sorts of things are shared in the Confessional.

"So did he speak about sexual things with you?" he had said. "Not that I remember," said Bill. "Maybe he did when he made his Confession, but because we priests aren't supposed to remember what people say there, I never can. It can be a bit difficult when someone assumes you can remember what they said last Christmas or last Easter months ago, but that's how it is. But I'm pretty certain sex was not an area that Colin ever talked about. Of course, although I didn't abuse him, once the accusation against me was made, I have always assumed that he was abused by someone; then keeping quiet about sex made sense, because victims of abuse can struggle even years later to speak about this sort of thing. I certainly remember talking with him about how difficult he found it to get on with his father, because I remember trying to persuade him to understand his point of view, explaining how difficult it can be to be a parent, but it was no use. He simply said it was impossible. And now I wonder if it was his father who abused him. After all most abuse is committed by married men. Anyway once he had insisted that he did not want to talk about his father, we talked more about some of his problems at school, especially with some of the disruptive boys who annoyed him and made fun of him because he wanted to study whilst they just wanted to lark around. And I remember how much better things got for him once he was in the Sixth Form. Then, we talked about the faith, of course, and about politics and life and things like that. I'd thought he would carry on going to Mass once he was at University, but something happened early on that made us lose contact. I had expected him back at Mass that first Christmas, but there was no sign of him, and I never ever saw him again."

Chapter 10: Meeting Mum

Monica reached the Restaurant at about 12.20 as she didn't want to be late, but was a bit shy of going inside, so she hovered around hoping that her Colin would soon be there to look after her. Then a voice said "Hi Mum," and there he was giving her a big hug. "Oh Colin, Colin," she'd said "It's so good to see you."

"Sorry it's been so long Mum. I got angry with you over Rita, and then had a hard time sorting myself out, and then as things got better I kept on putting off getting back in touch. Let's go in."

"Wait a minute Colin. Stand back and let me look at you." And she made him stand there in the middle of a busy Birmingham street whilst she looked him over. She noted his very smart grey suit and remarked on how nice it was as she stroked it. She also commented on his white shirt and his dark green tie, "You're still as slim and handsome as ever. With your Dad's dark hair and his Irish eyes."
"Mum! Stop it. You're embarrassing me." Deep down however he was actually enjoying her attention, but one thing she'd said had really caught his attention. "So I'm like my real Dad?" I really like that idea, but why have I never seen a photo of him?" She had anticipated this. Indeed it was partly why she'd said it, and she had come prepared. She reached into her handbag and took out a photo, handing it to him with tears in her eyes, "Here you are. Meet Paddy Riorghan, your real Dad." He held the photo for a moment looking at it in amazement, then seeing her distress took her in his arms again. "Oh Mum," and could say no more as tears came in both their eyes.
Once at the table she started to explain what she had always wanted to tell him, why there were no photos of him in the house, and no mention of him either. "He died very young and very quickly of testicular cancer Colin. I loved him to bits, but he wasn't always an easy man to live with, and his death left me very mixed up. Photos of him, even talk of him, just upset me too much, and Jessica, even though she was only 5, soon realised that asking about him made me angry with her, so she just stopped mentioning him. I'm so sorry. It was all my fault." Colin was looking at the photo again, and he said gently, "It's all history now, Mum, but I'm glad to see a photo of him. Can I keep it, or copy it?"

"Could you copy it? I'd like Jess to have a copy too."
"No problem, I'll scan it, and make copies. Have you any others?"
"Just some photos of our wedding, but they're not so good of him as this one is, but if you would like to see them I'll get them out."
"Yes please," he said, but the waiter came up then, and for a few minutes they were busy ordering things, before Colin asked, "And did my father have any family?"
"Oh yes. But they're mostly in Ireland and I just lost touch with them. I suppose we could try and get back in touch. Look, I've written your Uncle's name and phone number on the back of the photo, and I'll look out the address I had for him and other family members, but I've no idea whether they'll still be there. It was almost 40 years ago. I was told about the funerals when your grandparents died, but it was over in Ireland each time and John didn't want me to go. He said it would upset me too much. And he was probably right, and anyway I hardly knew them."
This was all news to Colin. He loved the idea that he had a family he didn't know anything about, but he was also aware that sharing all this was hard for Monica.
"Great, I would like to have all their details out, but this will only be for now. But now tell me about you. Are you OK?"
"A bit older, but I couldn't feel better today now I have got back in touch with you. Tell me about this lady who managed it for you."
"Aha Angela! She's just a neighbour who asked me about my family. I went round to dinner there because I'd met and got friendly with her cousin's husband Walter. We share a common interest in trains, and his wife and Angela insisted they lay on dinner for us after we came back from a day on the Severn Valley. She's recently widowed and was quite shocked when she discovered I wasn't in touch with you. She has a son about the same age as me. Next thing I know she's somehow found out where you live and contacted you."
Then he told her the whole story of how he'd met Walter by accident, and everything that had happened since, and how he was going to do a hard landscape job on her garden.
Once that had been explained, Colin took the next step that he'd been preparing. "And Peter and Maria Mum? How are they? I know I have been wrong to be out of touch with them for so long. Do you think they would be prepared to see me?" Monica paused to think. She knew that when she saw them they never talked about their Dad, so she

wasn't quite sure what to say without hurting him. "I really don't know. I see them quite often, but at their age they are full of the things they are doing, and I just listen and try to understand. But then if I ask them how they're doing at school I just get an OK, and I know I can't press them any further. They're always on their smartphones of course, and I think Maria is doing something to do with Computing at school so you might find a common interest there."
"It's tricky isn't it? I wondered about contacting them directly, but then I thought it might be best if I asked you to speak to them about it first, and see how they react." Monica nodded in agreement. "And I'll talk to Rita before I talk to them. She might think it better if the suggestion comes from her."
"She probably won't want me to see them," Colin said rather gloomily. "She can't think much of me after the way I've treated them all, can she?"
"Well yes. Once she'd got over the shock of you leaving so suddenly, she was very angry with you, but as time has gone by she has often asked me how you are, and was sad to discover that you hadn't been in touch with me either." Colin put his head in his hands. She could feel how guilty and agonised he was. "You just told me it was all history," she said. "And it is. There's no point in looking back at past mistakes, it is better to look forward to making things better. What you probably don't know is that she had another man in her life for a while, but it didn't work out and she had to ask him to leave. He's been a bit of a trouble to her and the children since, and so you might find that they are more happy to get back in touch with you than you might expect."
Colin was quite shocked at the idea of another man with his Rita. He knew it was silly to feel like that, given his lack of contact with them, but a bit of him, a very macho male bit, felt quite annoyed that she should want anyone other than him. He knew Rita had had other boyfriends before him. He had never been out with any girl till Rita came along. Before that, he had thought he was gay, but the more experienced Rita had soon shown him how wrong he was. Once they had got together therefore, he had been utterly enraptured by her, and still deep down she was the only woman for him. His attempts at dating other women since he left her had never got further than a drink or a meal together. He just hadn't been able to face the complications of a physical relationship. It had been talking this through with his

Counsellor that had made him share his sexual hang-ups. She had been very sensitive, and had never probed, or asked him to share further than he wanted to, but eventually she had got into the sexual area with him and had wondered with him whether sex had a part to play in his marriage going wrong.

He had found it hard at first, finding himself in tears about it all. She had been very gentle but explained that when he was ready to talk about it, talking might help. Finally, he had told her that he thought he had been sexually abused as a teenager, and she had been able to explain to him that such abuse left a lasting effect, and that this was almost certainly why he found any new relationship so difficult to face. He had struggled for some time with this, "Rita somehow knew how to deal with me when it came to sex", he'd told the Counsellor. "She took the lead and helped me along. I could never initiate sex, but when she did, then I soon became quite eager. It wasn't really our sex life that split us up. Just my growing annoyance that she didn't keep the home the way I wanted. But then as I got angry with her, I couldn't face having sex with her, which made things worse." He remembered how one time when he and his counsellor had discussed this, he had found himself weeping again and saying "Yes he abused me, he really did."

Monica saw that he was even further troubled. "Oh Colin, you've had more troubles than I realised. How have you coped with all this sadness?"

"It was bloody awful Mum. I more or less had a nervous breakdown and nearly ruined my business. I couldn't sleep and I went to the GP in desperation, and it got worse before it got better, and they even began to discuss admitting me to a mental hospital for treatment. I think I was so shocked by this suggestion that this was when I began to turn the corner, and then found with their help a way to slowly rebuild my life." He told her more about all he had been through, and how his Counsellors had been such a help to him. "I got the first one through the GP, but now I pay for a different one to see me about four times a year, and it's worth every penny. Of course I'm lucky. The firm is doing well, and I can put it on my expenses. It must be awful for other people who aren't as lucky as I've been."

"So that's why you cut off all contact. You just couldn't face it." He nodded. "Now that I know this," she said "Can I tell Rita? It might

help her more than you can imagine, and maybe even the children too."
"Yes. Why not? Now I'm more or less over it, I wouldn't mind them knowing. I told Walter only the other day. So please do tell Rita to help her understand."
"Well, you never stopped supporting her financially did you? And that's very important." "But all too easy to do. The Bank just sends the payment once a month, and I hardly notice it's gone."
Monica wanted to know where he was living, and he was able to tell her that he had his own house and where it was, but then she encouraged him to talk about his business, as she'd realised that it must be going well since he talked so easily about his own house and about sending the money. She sensed that too much personal talk might be a bit too much for him. She remembered how as a teenager, he was often happy to talk about what he was studying, or about trains or boats, but never about anything personal. He was soon trying to explain to her what his company did, which she didn't really understand, so she steered him on to tell her about the people he employed and what his office was like and things like that.
Time passed all too rapidly for her, and soon, he asked for the bill. "Let me know what Rita says as soon as you can Mum. And when you do, we'll arrange to meet again. OK?" Of course she said OK, and after a quick hug, he was striding away from her down the street, and she was happier than she had been for a very long time.

Chapter 11: Rita Remembers.

Rita wasn't surprised to hear from Monica. They were in touch pretty often by phone, and she always enjoyed Monica's visits, very occasionally bringing her husband with her. She was a bit surprised however when Monica said she wanted to talk to her when the children weren't around. "What's this all about?" she asked, a bit worried by this rather unusual request. Once Monica had explained that she had seen Colin, she understood why there was a need for a bit of privacy. Indeed, she realised that both the children were listening to her side of the conversation, so she said, "Ok. I understand. The children are here at the moment, so let me work something out and then I'll get back to you." The children loved their Nan and wanted to know what the phone call was all about. "She wants to know when would be a good time to see you both, as well as having a good natter with me when you're not around." she said. "Next Sunday" said Maria. "That's often when she comes while Grandpa plays with his trains. We're both out in the morning so you can have a good chat and then we can see her for Sunday lunch."

Rita nodded. "Yes ok but I wanted to make sure you two would both be here for lunch. Are you sure you haven't arranged to go round to a friend, or something like that?" Assurances were given that neither of them had any plans and that now they knew Nan was coming and that they would make sure they were in for lunch.

Rita's mind was racing, and she found it difficult to hide this from the children. It seemed years since Colin had been in touch with any of them. About three years actually or maybe even four? Yes, the money arrived in the Bank every month, and she'd noticed that it had gradually gone up. Colin was giving them far more than was required by law, and she knew it, and was grateful to him for it; yet his refusal to speak to any of them, to be in touch with them in any way, had always puzzled her. Something had happened to him when he suddenly left them like he did. It was as if something had come into his head that hadn't been there before. He'd been a gentle and loving partner, and a good Dad for the kids, and then suddenly things had gone wrong. It had started with him getting angry with her and the children. Then he'd become more and more distant from them, and then suddenly he'd announced to her that he was leaving and had walked out of their lives there without any real explanation.

After that, he had ignored all her attempts to contact him. She had tried by text and by email, but he'd clearly changed all his contact details, and when she'd tried to contact him at work, they had always asked who was calling, and then said he wasn't available. It had made her very angry and upset, for she knew he was doing it deliberately.

It reminded her of when they first went out together, and she had discovered that he was living in Loughborough completely cut off from his parents. Back then, she had eventually persuaded him to do something about such stupidity, by telling him that if he was serious about her then she had to meet them, and he would have to as well. But there had been no one to do the same for her, and when she got over being angry, she had just been very sad. She knew she still loved him in a way, not perhaps as passionately as she had done at first, but still she cared about someone who had meant so much to her, and the possibility of being back in touch was both disturbing and exciting.

Memories of how they first got together came flooding back into her mind. She remembered how many of her girlfriends were envious when they discovered who her new boyfriend was. They had noticed this ravishingly beautiful man more than once, but they'd all thought he was gay, because a number of the people he mixed with were, but she had proved them all wrong. How lucky it was that the boy she'd fancied at a distance had ended up working as a lifeguard in the same Pool as her.

She remembered how careful she had been just to be friends at first, because she'd soon realised how easily he backed away from anything too personal. So they chatted at the Pool, and then one day she challenged him to a race. She reckoned he would beat her on a short distance, so she proposed 200 metres, and lots of the people in the Pool had great fun taking bets on who would win. He'd been amused by the whole thing, but quietly confident that he would beat her. She remembered how right she had been to choose a long distance. He drew ahead of her to start with, but then very slowly she began to catch him up. Oh how close that finish had been, and it was a turning point somehow, for gasping at the effort he had had to make to beat her, and astonished at how nearly she had beat him, he lost his usual reserve and gave her a big hug which quite surprised her, whilst various Pool friends clapped and cheered.

It was soon after this that he first asked her out. One thing that helped was that she was doing business studies, and once she discovered that his aim after graduation was to set up his own business, there were lots of ideas they could share together. So their first time out together was just to meet to discuss further how a business like his might work. Unlike some men who treated her mostly as a body to get into bed with, Colin approached her as a real person with an interesting mind, and indeed continued to be very hesitant about any physical contact. When they first made physical contact, she couldn't quite understand why he pulled away, saying he was sorry without explaining what was wrong. She discovered eventually that he was embarrassed and even confused by how aroused he was by her. Later he would say to her, "I thought I was gay till I met you." It took him quite a long time to really relax in her company, and it was only then that one day he told her, in his typically direct way, that he wanted to go to bed with her. She had trouble not laughing at him when he also said he was worried about her getting pregnant, and asked if she should he buy some condoms. She was able to tell him that it was Ok as she was on the Pill, and even showed him the packet to reassure him. He was a gentle but passionate lover, always concerned to do it right, and never ever trying to persuade her to have sex when she didn't want to. How different from previous boyfriends! Yes, Colin had always surprised her.
When they had moved in together in their 3rd year, she was amazed at how organised he had been. "Ah yes," she thought looking back. "If only I'd realised then how difficult it would be to live with someone who expected everything to have its place, and to be exactly as he had planned it." At the time, it had just been wonderful to be with a man who didn't make a mess. She had assumed that all men were a bit like her Dad. Her Mum had warned her how untidy and dirty the male species could be, dropping their dirty clothes on the bedroom floor and forgetting to change into clean clothes, never making the bed or washing up the dishes. Colin was never like that. He not only treated her as an intelligent human being, but also took his full part in everything domestic.
Their holidays together were magic. Planned carefully in consultation with her, Colin had organised the flights and the hotel bookings himself at a time when most people still used to book package holidays through travel agencies. They would always swim of course, but they also found interesting places to visit, and he would be a mine

of information on wherever they went. He had always done his research. She remembered too with a smile how often he had managed, wherever they were, to fit in one day visiting a railway, cable car, tramway, or something else magically mechanical. That made her think of the time she had taken him to visit her grandparents in Manchester. How astonished they had been when, of all the things they might have visited, he asked if he could visit the Barton Swing Aqueduct and then proceeded to take them up the steps into the Control Tower to chat to the man who was there to make it swing when it needed to.

He was just the same when the children came. A real hands-on Dad whom she could trust to look after them as babies, and then when they got older to occupy them with games, as well as pointing all sorts of things out to them, always finding something to interest them, and also quietly controlling them when they got a little too excited about something. Rita sighed. So many happy memories until he had got to the point of setting up his own business as he had always wanted to. Then he began to change, for as he struggled to make a go of his business she and the family suffered, and her attempts to help him were rebuffed. The old days when they had talked things over together disappeared, for he seemed determined to make a go of it all by himself. He began to come home later and later, and she knew it wasn't another woman. Even at home, it was work, work and more work. He would get stressed if the slightest thing went wrong or was out of place at home, and retreated away from them, even to sleeping on the sofa downstairs. Finally, he simply announced that he was leaving her, gave her a paper with all the details of their Bank Account and Mortgage, and left.

She remembered her many attempts to contact him that followed, but she had eventually just given up on him and tried to live her life as if he had never existed. Of course it was difficult, not least because Maria and Peter were so upset, and kept asking her for information that she just hadn't got. She finally lost it with them and told them exactly what she thought of their Dad for walking out on them like that. Silence followed. Maria wept quietly, whilst Peter went off to be by himself in his room. Just like his Dad, she thought!

In her fury she had ended up getting into a relationship with Jack. He was a colleague at work who had always shown an interest in her. At the time, she had rebuffed him very firmly, but now, faced with

Colin's cruelty, she made it clear she was open to offers, and given the childcare problems, invited him round to the house. It seemed quite fun at first; sex after the children had gone to bed. But she quite soon realised that she really didn't like this pushy bloke who fancied himself too much, and thought he was God's gift to her. It meant that when she finished with him, he never gave up trying to get back with her. He was always approaching her at work, and turning up on her doorstep. Finally, she changed jobs to get away from him, but that seemed to make him worse as he followed her down the street and even tried to get physical with her. Finally, she reported him to the police, but they hadn't really been much used as he didn't appear to be dangerous, just annoying. She wondered what Colin would think if he discovered what had been going on. Interesting!

And now this phone call from Monica looked likely to bring Colin back into her life in some way, and actually she was glad, as much for the children as for her. She wondered what could have happened for him to make contact again? Knowing how he had needed her to push him back in contact with his parents while at Uni, she wondered now if there was someone out there who had done the same for her? Perhaps Monica would tell her on Sunday?

Chapter 12: Monica and Rita together

Monica arrived quite early on a Sunday morning, as John dropped her on his way to his railway line. He was always happy to do this because he knew she wasn't too keen at being left alone on Sundays, and it was easy for him to pick her up again in the evening on his way home. Normally when she was alone on a Sunday, she went to Mass and saw various friends there, but going to see her grandchildren was a priority for her, and so when that happened she went to Mass on the Saturday night instead. She wasn't quite sure why she kept going to Mass. Habit maybe, but also a sense that both her children and their families needed praying for, especially Colin. Now at last her prayer could be one of thanksgiving that finally he was back in touch, and a little bit of sorrow that it had taken her till now to tell him about his real father. Rather appropriately, the priest had talked about looking to the future rather than regretting the past. She hadn't told him what was happening to her, so she was amazed that the message seemed to be just for her.

Maria and Peter were already out, so she and Rita could sit down straightaway and she could begin to tell Rita how Colin had got back in touch. "I gave him a photo of his real father," she said. "It was something I should have done for both of them years ago, but I let my own confusion and misery about him and how he died swamp what they were entitled to. They were his children after all. Colin said he's going to try to make contact with the family in Ireland. He seems to think it won't be too difficult using the Internet." Rita was a bit startled. She had expected to hear about what Colin wanted of her, but instead here was Monica sharing with her a part of Colin's life that she had never really heard much about. She knew that John was Colin's stepfather, and that he couldn't remember his real father because he had died when he was a baby, but she hadn't quite realised that Colin had never had any more information about him than that. "So until last week he had never even seen a photo of him?" she said, and she knew from the nod from Monica that this was correct. "Wow, you must have surprised him with that. What was his reaction?" She was quite surprised to be told that he was really happy about it. Her memory of the last few years of their time together had been of a man

increasingly stressed out about everything, and likely to react almost violently to anything that upset his equilibrium.
As Monica continued with her story, she began to realise that Colin seemed to be a very changed man, that somehow he had got beyond the troubles that had weighed him down, and which she had been so helpless to support him with. She could hardly believe what she was hearing and wondered if it was just an act for his mother, whilst the angry stressed-out Colin would appear as soon as he met her. Monica didn't think so. She told Rita what she had heard from Colin, about how he only just got through what many would describe as a nervous breakdown, and how he had been helped by a counsellor to see things in a different way. "He's made some friends who are his neighbours in Marston Green," she said. "And it was one of them who persuaded him to get back in touch. In fact, she didn't just persuade him, she took the matter into her own hands." Rita was amazed to hear how this complete stranger had knocked on Monica's door, and made the meeting happen. "So he's got a new woman," she said, but was told quite firmly "No. I don't think so. She is an older woman, about my age. Apparently, Colin met her quite by accident through a man who shares his interest in steam trains. They went there together, and then he recruited Colin to do some garden landscape work for her over the summer. His wife is her cousin and they were staying there to support her after the recent death of her husband. I think she was just being a very good neighbour."
Rita looked out into her own back garden. It always reminded her of Colin, because he had done a lot of work there when they had first moved in. That was before he began his own business and everything had gone wrong. What happy times they had been, with the children toddling round and helping him. He had been so tolerant of them, even if their "help" hadn't really been help at all. "He was so calm, quiet, and friendly," Monica continued. "So sorry for having cut us off, and so keen to get back in touch. I think he feels very guilty about how he has behaved, especially with you and the children, and wants to know if you would let him see them again. I know this may be hard for you Rita, but I do hope you can work this out even if you are still angry with him. He is their father, after all."
Rita surprised herself by her reaction, "Oh this makes me so angry Monica. He hardly deserves to be called their father after the way he has behaved". There was a long pause and then she continued, "But

you're right. I can't carry on being as angry with him as I was. In fact, I realised after you phoned that I wasn't angry in that way anymore, and I really would like the children to be back in touch with him. I could never go back to living with him of course. I have too many bad memories of that, but I would like to work out some way in which he could be back in touch, especially with the children. He used to be so good with them when they were little, and before everything went wrong."

"I know," sighed Monica, "He always ran away from things he didn't like, hiding in his room and hardly speaking after he'd fallen out with his Dad, and then he did the same to you and the children. I just hope that this time he will be more reasonable. You were always so good for him Rita, but I quite understand that you would not want him back as a husband. Too much water has flowed under the bridge for that."

They talked more about Colin and lots of other things, while Monica helped Rita get lunch ready. She was delighted with the glorious welcome from her grandchildren when they arrived back home. They rushed upstairs to clean up and were soon down again and ready to eat, so it was some time before Monica felt ready to share the news about their Dad with them. She and Rita had agreed that it was best coming from her. She had wanted Rita to do it, but Rita said that they had heard so much anger from her about Colin that they might be a bit confused, whereas Monica as their Nan and Colin's Mum would be able to raise the subject more naturally. Rita kept looking at Monica wondering when she was going to say something, but to start with she encouraged the children to tell her about school and life, and as usual was amazed how much they would share with their Nan that they never mentioned to her. "Typical," she thought. Rita began to wonder if Monica would ever get round to Colin, but eventually as pudding was being served, she spoke.

"I want to tell you something rather important," she said. Maria and Peter stopped. Nan rarely spoke to them like this, in such a serious voice. They wondered what they had done wrong. Monica continued, "The thing is, that a few days ago, your Dad got back in touch with me." She was going to continue, but Peter was agog. "What! After all these years? How is he? Where is he living? What's he like?" The questions came pouring out of him. Meanwhile Maria sat silently, looking at her Mum to see how she was reacting to this news, whilst Monica tried to answer Peter's questions. Once Peter's questioning had begun to lessen, Monica took the next step. “The really important question is not what he is like now, but how would you like to meet him again? He feels really bad about having walked out on you, and realises that you are probably very angry with him, so he asked me to talk to you about it, and see what you think.” Now it was Maria who spoke, “I’m sorry Nan but I don’t want to see him. He made me so angry when he left without saying goodbye or explaining anything to us, and he has never been in touch since, so why should he think he can just come back into our lives as if nothing has happened? It was so horrible. Mum tried to be brave but she kept crying for ages, and Peter and I were just confused. We thought he loved us and then suddenly he was gone, and…..” She burst into tears and ran out of the room.

Peter was very fond of his sister, but held back his own tears to say, “Well if she doesn’t want to see him, then I don’t either.” But Monica detected a slight hesitation. “Well, even if you don’t want to see him talk to you, would you mind if he came and watched you play football?” This was a clever ploy. Peter was very proud of how well he was playing for his local Sunday morning football team. That’s where he had been earlier in the day when he had helped set up a great goal. “Oh well,” He said. “That’s different. Anyone can come and watch us, and I would quite like Dad to see me play. But what about you Mum, are you going to see him?” “Let me go and see how Maria is first,” said Rita, “And then I’ll tell you both what I think. Why not play one of your games on your mobile while I talk to her? And maybe you could make some tea Nan?”

Maria needed some encouragement before she was prepared to appear again. She’d done a lot of weeping, so Rita just sat and hugged her, and between sobs she said “You don’t want to see him, do you Mum?”, and was a bit surprised when her Mum said. “Well, I was very angry with him, just as you are, and I will never have him back, but I do want to see him, not least so he can explain why he treated us so badly. Nan says he’s had some kind of a breakdown which might explain his silence. And he is your Dad.” Maria sighed as her tears subsided. “I don’t think I could be as calm as you Mum. I just don’t think I could face it.” And Rita assured her that no one would force her to see him, if she didn’t want to, and then encouraged her to wash away the tears sort herself out and come back downstairs.

Downstairs, Rita was able to share what she had already said to Maria. She explained that she was going to see their Dad first, and talk things over with him. She would see then if he would be prepared to come and watch one of Peter's football games, but stressed that this wouldn't mean him coming to the house. She now knew how to contact him, as their Nan had given her all his contact details, and she promised that she wouldn't keep anything from them. But although she appeared calm, her mind was full of all sorts of questions and imaginings. Where could they meet? She wouldn't go to his house. But meeting in public wouldn't work either. And what would she say to him? Would her feelings overwhelm her and make her too emotional? She couldn't imagine falling into his arms even though there was a little bit of her that would like to pretend that nothing had happened, and they could go back to the way they were. But it had happened. It was too late. Longing for something from the past was a waste of time. Somehow, they had to make a very different future.

Later, after Monica had gone home, and the children were busy watching a film they had recorded, she sent an email, and was astonished that Colin replied almost immediately. Had he been on the watch for her? No, that was stupid. He probably had his smartphone beside him and had just seen her email straightaway. Yet the fact that he replied so soon showed her that this new Colin really did want to be in touch.

His email read: *I am so sorry about the way I have treated you all. Yes let's set up a meeting ASAP. I have a neighbour who Mum may have told you about and I think she might let us meet at her house. Would that be OK with you?*

Rita replied immediately**:** *Yes that would be a good idea. Let me know whether that will be OK with her.* Colin replied *Ok I will contact her now. What sort of day and time would be best?*

Rita had to think about this. If it were too soon, would he think she was too eager, think she might just fall into his arms? But if she waited too long, would he think she didn't care?

Finally, after quite a long think, she wrote:

Would next Saturday morning be OK? And got an immediate *Yes. I'll check with Angela and get back to you.*

She went to sit with the children and watch the Film, just to be with them as it wasn't really the sort of film she liked all that much, but they did, and being with them was what mattered most.

Within less than an hour, an email from Colin arrived on her smartphone: *How about 11.00 am on Saturday? The address is Merrymead, Newlands Lane, Marston Green B37 6ED. It is a private lane off Elmdon Lane and the house is 3rd on the right down the lane. Angela (Heryward) will be happy to meet you. Come early if you want to so you can talk to her and I'll turn up dead on 11. I only live a few minutes walk away.*
OK? She did a quick *OK* and that was that.

Chapter 13: Angela as Host

Walter and Penny were amazed and delighted to hear how fast things were moving in Colin's life. Walter had continued his daily journeys with Colin for a bit, but then explained that they were getting ready to return to their home in Oxford. "If you ever want a little holiday in Oxford" he said "Do come and stay with us." And Colin had said that he would sometimes, but that at present he was too occupied with reuniting with his family. Walter tried to dampen down his hopes for a total recovery of his marriage. He knew how rarely this happened.

There was usually too much pain and too many bad memories for that to take place, but he admitted that he did know one couple who had come back together again and were now well past their Golden Wedding celebration. He counselled caution, rather than trying to tell Colin the idea was impossible. "Whatever happens, don't push too hard" he said, fearful that Colin would get hurt. How had it come to this, that the man he had started to stalk because he was angry with what he had done, was now someone he really liked, someone who had become a firm friend? It puzzled him that Colin had made what he was sure was a false accusation. What had pushed such a nice person into doing such an awful thing? Of course, he knew what Angela and Penny thought, for they had made it quite plain that his idea that Colin had done this was just nonsense. The man accused was obviously guilty, and that was that.

It was just before they left for Oxford that Angela announced that she was going to host what she called a reconciliation meeting between Colin and Rita. She was full of hopes for his future and her part in it, "First I got him and his mother together." She said proudly, "And now, it is him and his wife." The whole project had brought her alive in a way that Walter and Penny hadn't seen since Tom had died, and they were glad of it. But Walter counselled caution to Angela too. Just as he had said to Colin, now he said to Angela "Don't push them too hard" and hoped she heard him, even though he feared her enthusiasm made her oblivious to his advice. Angela saw them off on the Wednesday, without any sign of the tears they might have expected a few weeks back, when the idea of being left alone had always made her weepy. Now she was full of how she was going to organise this coming Saturday, and Walter had to say to Penny that he was glad they had already arranged to go home before this event took place, as coping with Angela going on and on about it had been driving him nuts. Penny was a bit annoyed with his failure to sympathise and told him so, but she wasn't too rough on him, as she had also found it a bit much, though she wasn't going to admit that to Walter.

As soon as they had gone, Angela began a big clean and tidy up. She knew she had accumulated a good deal of unnecessary stuff during Tom's's illness, but hadn't had the heart to throw lots of things away. It was Penny who had encouraged her to begin the process before they left and had helped her bag up Tom's clothes and other personal items. Angela had found this quite hard, and there had been a few tears as some items evoked thoughts and memories from the past. That shirt she had bought him to wear on one of their loveliest holidays. The cuff links that she had given him when they were newly married, and which he had hardly ever worn. The suit that he kept for special events but had eventually been unable to wear yet never thrown away as his waistline had expanded – a bit! Such happy memories, but now just that, memories – a past that was over and done with. Leaving a load of washing churning away in the washing machine, she put all the bags of clothing in her car and headed for the nearest Charity shop in Chelmsley Wood. There were quite a few in Sheldon of course but Chelmsley Woods – as she called them – was much closer. The Woods had been a lovely place to walk in when she was a girl, and she remembered people getting off the train at Marston Green to pick blackberries there. So now she always found it strange to visit this great housing estate with its shopping centre where no sign exists of what was there before, apart from the name.

Whilst there, she did a bit of shopping in readiness for Colin and Rita's meeting at her house on Saturday. Some special biscuits to go with the coffee, and some chocolates as a present for Rita to take back for the children. She day-dreamed about a great reunion where they actually did fall into one another's arms and all was forgiven; and although she knew she was going over the top to think like that, it was hard not to have it as a tiny hope for the young man she had taken such a liking to. When he had phoned last Sunday and asked if her place could be the venue for the meeting, she had said yes instantly, and had been having silly romantic thoughts ever since. She couldn't help it, despite Walter's warning to be cautious. She had seen wonderful reconciliations on the TV that had brought tears to her eyes, and the idea that one might happen under her own roof really appealed to her. She was determined to spend the three days ahead, making the house sparkle.

She hardly slept on Friday night and got up early desperately trying to think of more things she could do until Rita arrived. She had even got Rita's phone number from Colin and had asked her to come early so they could get to know one another. It had been a strange conversation, as she explained that she was the woman who had button-holed Monica on her doorstep and begun the process that had now led to this meeting. "I just think you will be more relaxed if you come early" she'd said. And Rita, intrigued to meet this woman, had agreed. Angela was pleased when she arrived to find that she was as attractive as Colin. How could these two beautiful people have ever fallen out with one another? It was such a tragedy! And she wondered what she could do to put it all right.

Rita was so easy to chat to, especially as she wanted to know the full story of how she'd met Colin and how she'd done her detective work to find Colin's Mum. "It was a bit like a film." Angela said "With us like the police on surveillance until the right moment." Rita couldn't help laughing, as Angela actually made the story more like a Film than it actually was, adding touches of humour, of how they had skulked in the car, and how she had then leapt out and run across to talk to Monica before her husband returned. Rita sighed, "You know, I'm always sad that John has to be left out of all this. He must be told before long, and then he'll have to face the fact that Monica has been deceiving him. It's one more thing about Colin that I could never understand, why he hates his stepfather so much. He's always been very kind to me and the children, perhaps even kinder since Colin left us. He's even taken them to see his precious railway, although what startled him was that Peter wasn't interested, whilst Maria was enthralled, and plied him with questions some of which he couldn't answer. Peter loves his football and his swimming, but he just isn't interested in trains. I think Maria is more like Colin than she realises. She loses me when she talks about what she is doing in Computer Studies, and she's very keen on detail, on getting things just right, just like him. And that's the news I am going to find most difficult to tell him Angela, that Maria is refusing to see him."

Angela was saddened by this news but picked up immediately on the positive side of it. “So Peter will see him?” she asked. “Well sort of” was the reply “I got him to agree that his Dad could come and watch him play football, and I’m hoping that this will lead to a breakthrough for them. But I’m not sure whether Colin will be prepared to watch a game he doesn’t like, standing with other Dads shouting advice at their sons! It’s not really his scene at all.” “I think you’ll find him very keen to do anything to mend things.” said Angela. “But what about you?” “Oh, I can’t take him back Angela. He hurt us all so much you know, and though I am not angry the way I used to be, it doesn’t mean that things can ever be the way they were.” Angela had been prepared for this. “Well. There’s no need to think that far ahead. Just meet him now and talk things through a bit. He’s actually been through an awful lot of soul-searching and trauma in the last few years, and maybe you should ask him to tell you about it. It might make it easier for you to understand.” “So has he told you?” asked Rita, amazed that Colin would have opened up to someone he had known for such a short time. “Only a little bit here and there” was Angela’s reply, unable to share what she knew of the abuse case Colin had been involved in. She knew that in a way she had been breaking police rules when she’d told Walter, but if she hadn’t they wouldn’t be where they were now, and Colin would still have been entirely isolated and trapped in the pain of his past.

It was at this point that Colin arrived. It was all rather awkward. He didn’t know what to say, and Angela had to take the lead by bringing them into the Sitting Room and sitting them down facing one another, and pouring out some tea for them. “Now I’ll leave you” she said. “And I won’t interrupt unless there’s a fire. So stay and talk for as long as you like.” Colin was very quiet and left Rita to say thank you. And Rita realised that, just like the first time they had met, she needed to do the running. But part of her didn’t want to. Why should she help him anyway? She sighed. “Come on Colin. Can you please say something? Why did you walk out on us like that? Why did you then cut off all contact with us? I really need some answers.”

“I’m so sorry” he said ‘I thought I was going mad. I just couldn’t cope, and I thought it was the situation at home. So I left, but then life got darker and darker and I couldn’t sleep and hardly ate anything. It was the people at work who kept me going. Luckily the business had reached the stage where they could take over much of what I had been doing. I should have delegated things to them much earlier, but I was so fixated on making it a success. If it hadn't been for them, I think the whole thing would have crashed round me. Julian made me go to the GP, and Wren handled all the phone calls and stopped anyone from contacting me." Rita nodded, so now she knew why. They had been protecting him. "The GP put me on pills to calm me down and help me sleep, and I ended up sleeping and sleeping and hardly going out of the house. I'd got the house ready you see before I plucked up the courage to tell you I was leaving. I'm so sorry that I hid it all from you. All you got was me getting angrier and angrier about everything didn't you?" Again she nodded. She realised that a few affirmative nods would keep him going, even though she wanted to interrupt with all kinds of questions. "The GP referred me to a Counsellor, and Julian and Wren came round and checked up on me, and actually took me there the first time because I didn't want to go. There was a moment when they threatened to call the GP to force me into a mental hospital if I didn't, so then I gave way. And once I met her and she got me talking, I was able to tell her things that I've never told anyone else ever, and then gradually I began to feel better, although I was on anti-depressants for quite a long time, and you know how I hate taking pills. But I think it was the Counselling that helped me most. Actually, I now pay to see a Counsellor every other month, though not that one. It just helps me to keep my head clear and to manage my anger. But all this took some time you know. She took me back to my teenage years, and we looked at why I had become so angry. Eventually I told her that I'd been sexually abused." There was a shocked silence, and this time Rita could not keep quiet. "What! Oh Colin no" she said. "How awful for you, and you never felt able to tell me, to share it with me in any way?" "I'd locked it all away" he said. "I didn't want to think about it, so I just erased it from my conscious memory. I thought I'd succeeded, but she showed me that it was still there and that I needed to bring it out into the open." Up till now he had kept his head down, but now he looked up at her. "Of course, you don't know about the Court Case do you?" he said, realisation dawning. "Victims in such cases have their identity hidden, so hardly anyone knows. I'm not sure whether it helped me, Rita, or made things worse. The Counsellor thought I should report it to the Police. In fact she told me she had to if I didn't. So I did, but I made such a mess of it, trying to tell them something I didn't want to remember. I still feel guilty about what I told them because I wonder if it's really just in my head, but in the end it did make me face up to myself and realise that lots of my anger came from there, and that I had to let go of it. Once I'd got through that, she then started to encourage me to reconnect with you, but I lacked the courage to face your fury, so I kept putting it off. Then I met Walter just walking to work, and he introduced me to Angela who is his wife's cousin, and she just did what I should have done ages ago, contacted Mum, and through Mum you, and so here I am." Rita found it hard to take all this in. She hadn't expected this, as this wounded man poured out his story. He was almost like a different person, and yet he was still the Colin she had once loved. He looked up at her. "I don't expect you to take me back Rita. That would be asking too much. But I would like to be back in touch with you and the kids, if that's possible?" She had been meaning to be hard on him, but once she realised that he knew she couldn't take him back, it all became easier and she was able to say quite gently, "You're right Colin. I don't think it would work for you to just come back. At the moment the children hardly want to see you. I think it will take time, and we'll have to think of things you might do with them. You would be great to talk to Maria about Computer things, but at the moment she is just very, very angry with you and refuses to see you at all. But I did persuade Peter to let you do something that you might not like…" She paused as he looked questioningly at her. "You see he has become football mad and plays for a local boys' team. He's really very good, and when I suggested that his Dad might watch him play, I hit the right note, and he said yes." Colin looked startled, but then he grinned. "That will be torture of course, as you know only too well, but torture is probably what I need. Some sort of punishment. And standing on the edge of a football field will certainly be that. So when's the next game?" "Next Sunday morning?" she said. "Ok. But would he like to be taken out to lunch afterwards?" Rita smiled. "Probably, especially if it's McDonalds. I'll ask him" "McDonalds!" sighed Colin. "One more bit of torture for me, but lovely for him." And so it was arranged.

Chapter 14: Colin's Children

June weather can be lovely, thought Colin grimly, as he stood by the football pitch coping with the steady drizzle. Rita had brought Peter in the car, although he could have walked, so that he could stay dry till the game started and she could take Maria on to do some shopping of the kind that Maria loved and Peter hated. They met as arranged, so that Peter could be happy that the man he was now meeting was his Dad, although Rita knew it was more for Colin's sake, worried that he might not be able to recognise his own son. Actually, although Peter was much bigger than the 8 year old he remembered, he was glad that he seemed just the same, even though the greeting was just "Hello Dad" as he rushed off to join his team. "Typical twelve year old" said Rita, handing Colin a key to their front door. Colin didn't dare tell her he still had his old key, and she didn't tell him that if he had it wouldn't have worked as she'd had the lock changed. "Just take him in so he can change" she said. "We might be back, but I doubt it." She knew that Maria, sitting in the car and pretending not to look at her Dad outside, must decide for herself whether to extend the shopping to make sure they weren't in, or speed it up so that they were.

Colin had never been keen on football at school. He had always preferred individual sports, where you didn't have to worry about other members of the team but could just get on with winning by yourself. The school hadn't given much opportunity for that kind of thing, which is why he'd carried on with the Swimming Club that he'd joined when he was about 9, but he'd had to play football of course, and knew enough to follow what his son was doing. There came a point, as Peter would later tell him had happened before, when Peter skilfully passed to another boy who then scored a goal. Dads around Colin, especially the Dad whose son had scored, were ecstatic. Colin was quietly elated, as the Dad in question spoke about Peter. "That Bransted boy is just brilliant" he said "Just like Beckham from my day." It was a great compliment, as Colin knew well, and was able to tell Peter at the end of the game. "I was so proud of you," he said. "But I didn't tell that Dad you were my son. Didn't want to boast too much, but it was a wonderful feeling." Nothing could have pleased Peter more, and he now began to go through the game in detail for his Dad,

whilst all Colin could do was nod and say yes every now and again, quite unable to really understand what he was talking about.
When they got back to the house, Peter sped upstairs to change, whilst Colin waited below. Then he heard the front door and knew Rita and Maria were back. He heard Rita say "You could at least come and say hello." Maria peered round the door "Hello Dad" she said, and then fled up to her room. "Well that was better than nothing" she said. "She knew that you would be here at this time, and she could have kept us shopping longer but she didn't. She was clearly curious to see you." "Should you go up to her?" Colin said "No. Well at least not straight away. She's a big girl and she needs her own space. I'll go up once you and Peter have gone, or she'll come down."
Peter was soon down and raring to go for his Burger and Chips treat. His Mum was into healthy food most of the time, so his Dad's offer of lunch at McDonalds was just stupendous for him. Rita laughed to herself as they left, for she could hear Peter going on at Colin about how pleased he was that he was taking him out for this treat, as she knew it was her suggestion that was being so successful. Colin was pleased to discover that he could have a Veggie Burger and Salad whilst Peter munched away, but between munches he did get Peter to talk, although it was mainly about football again, with Colin making encouraging murmurs to keep him going. When he eventually asked him over the Ice Cream what he was doing at school Peter was far more reticent, but admitted that he hated English but quite liked Geography, but this clearly had more to do with the teachers than the subjects. Colin then asked him about the Swimming Club and found him a bit more enthusiastic about this, but talking to his son was much harder work than he had expected.
So when he drove home that afternoon, Colin was far from happy. Was this to be his future, desperately trying to get his children to talk to him, to share with him their lives? He had heard from other fathers how difficult it was, but had somehow thought he would get on better than them. He sighed, realising that if he had begun the process immediately he had left Rita, it would have been a lot easier as there would have been an ongoing relationship; instead it was like starting something completely new. Yet he also knew that if he had tried it earlier he might have been too fragile to cope. He sent a text to his Mum telling her what had happened as he knew she would be pleased,

and she was, replying almost immediately but saying that John wasn't very well, and she was going to get him to the Doctor in the morning. Meanwhile Rita was coping with an over-enthusiastic Peter, annoying his sister by going on about how marvellous Dad was, mainly because of the great food he had just been allowed to eat. "Can't you remember how he walked out on us?" she said. "Can't you remember how sad Mum was?" But much to her annoyance, Peter said he did remember, but the past was the past, and now he wanted to enjoy the fact that he'd got his Dad back. With that remark, he fled to his room before she could carry on the argument, and so she turned her fury about his lack of concern onto her poor mother. "Why can't he see how he is being taken in by all this?" she said. "Just because Dad watched him play football and then took him for his favourite lunch, he now thinks all can be forgiven." Rita sat down beside her on the settee for Maria was almost in tears, "It's no good just feeling angry about the past, you know. I'm angry with him too, but he is your Dad, and I have now discovered that soon after he left us he had a nervous breakdown and almost had to be taken into hospital. Of course, I'll never get over the way he left us, and how he cut off all contact instead of explaining things to me, but I am beginning to be able to forgive him a bit now I've heard more of all he has been going through." But Maria wasn't convinced. "I'm sorry Mum, but I think you're crazy to feel sorry for him. He was the one who walked out on you, on us, not the other way about. I'll never be able to forgive him. And then to tempt Peter with McDonald's was just horrible." Rita wondered about telling Maria it was her idea, not his, but decided not to. She might well want to suggest an equally devious way for Colin to tempt Maria at some future date, and she didn't want her then to suspect some kind of plot. "Let's leave it for the moment," she said. "And see what he decides to do next time he contacts us." "Maria was horrified, "Us! You haven't given him my Mobile number, have you? I don't want him to contact me ever!" She was relieved to hear that no such information had been given. Colin only had her Mum's number and email address, as well as her Nan's. "This all happened because of your Nan, you know Rita. Your Dad contacted her and they met in Birmingham and he took her out to lunch. It was she who wanted him to get back in touch with us. He's her son remember? He's her little boy, even if you find it hard to think of your Dad like that, and with Jessica in Australia, the idea of being close to at least one of her children is very special for her. And

then of course, as you know, she loves both of you and wanted you both to be back in contact with him too. So maybe we should think what we might do to make her happy?" "Oh God, that makes it worse," said Maria through her tears. "I love Nan to bits, but how can I ever love him, or even see him when I am so angry with him?" "Why don't you phone her and talk to her about it." Rita suggested "You often do phone her on a Sunday afternoon when she isn't with us. Maybe that would help?" "But what would I say to her?" Maria said "It all makes me feel so horrible, and I don't want to upset her." "Ok" said Rita. "Perhaps it's time you did something to take your mind off it. Maybe your homework ?"
Maria actually loved school and was easily persuaded that this was a way she could forget her anguish over her Dad for a bit, and over her easily persuadable brother, and went on up to her room to sort of work, but also to talk to her friends over the Internet. Rita stayed on the settee, emotionally exhausted coping with her anguished daughter. She had had to stifle her own anguish in order to help Maria, but it was still there – her bitterness against him wasn't going to go away that easily. She sighed, and then decided she would phone Monica instead.
But she soon realised that Monica was too worried about John to talk much about Colin. "He's in so much pain since he had lunch that I almost phoned 999, only he wouldn't let me. I've told him he is going to see a Doctor in the morning whether he likes it or not. He's just sitting watching the TV with a hot water bottle on his stomach. It's just not like him you know Rita. He's normally out to his shed or out in the garden doing something or other. I'm so worried. Oh yes. Colin sent a text to say he'd seen Peter, so I told him about his Dad too. It's so worrying." So Rita found herself gently supporting Monica rather like she had been supporting Maria. It was not a very satisfactory phone call, and it left her even more exhausted. "It never rains but it pours," she said to herself quoting her Mum's favourite saying.
Meanwhile Colin had popped in to see Angela, because knowing how hard this meeting with Peter might be, she had more or less told him to report back to her. She had put it more gently, of course, asking him to come and see her because she was longing to hear how things went. She was glad that she had, because Colin was almost in tears as he related his struggle to talk to his own son. "It was all so one-sided," he said. "Me asking him questions and trying to drag some answers

out of him. I'm exhausted." Angela was full of sympathy and was sad to hear that Maria was still refusing to see him. "I was so full of hope." he sighed. "But now I wonder if it was all worth it. Why should I bother? I know a few Dads in my situation who have just given up, but I suppose I'd better go on with it?" Perhaps he was hoping that Angela might not pressure him to carry on, but if he did he was sadly disappointed. "Being a parent is hard." She said "And being a parent at a distance is even harder. You must just keep going." He went home knowing she was right, but pretty depressed about the whole situation. It was made worse, or better, by Rita's response to a text he'd sent about next weekend. "Sorry Colin, but we've got things on then. Let's arrange something for the one after?"

Waiting even one week to see if he could do better next time would have been agony, but waiting two weeks just prolonged the anxiety, the turning round in his head of what he might do next, or what he might say the next time he and Peter met. Then he thought of Walter, the expert on kids this age, and he phoned him straight away. Walter listened carefully, and explained that it was very difficult for children of Peter's age. "They are not really children anymore, but they haven't yet worked out how to be grown up, how to have an adult conversation, and especially with their parents." He too encouraged Colin to keep on seeing Peter however hard it might be, and then having heard the stress in Colin's voice, he suddenly said "Why not come down and see us in Oxford next weekend, rather than sitting there worrying about it?" Colin was a bit hesitant at first, but Walter told him he could give him a mini-tour of Oxford and a chance to visit the Watercress Line, so he agreed.

Chapter 15: Oxford

Colin left work early on Friday just after lunch to get down to Oxford before the Friday traffic got too bad. He was sitting down having a coffee with Walter and Penny by 4, and was very glad to be there. "Thank God for the SatNav" he said. "I would never have found you without it. And how strange that I live in Marston Green and you live in Marston!" He was soon telling them the details of his time with Peter, saying how hard it had been for him as he tried to get him to talk. "I wanted to hear how he was getting on at school. But he hardly shared anything worthwhile." Walter was encouraging. "It sounds to me like a good start," he said. "He'll have been really chuffed at you watching him play football. Then feeding a lad of his age his favourite food was a brilliant idea. They never like talking about school, and many of them are embarrassed when they have to come with their parents to a parent/teacher evening; so although the conversation may have been hard work that's only to be expected. In fact I think you did a lot better than you made out." "It was all Rita's idea," admitted Colin. "I hate football and I never eat in places like McDonalds." They all laughed as Colin described some of the food he had seen around him, and the cars queuing outside for takeaways. "It's a different world." he said. "But their Veggie burger was better than I expected!"

It was a lovely summer afternoon, so they went for a walk before dinner, ending up going over the Rainbow Bridge and into the University Parks. Walter told an old story about how one of the sites they passed used to be a nude bathing place and what happened when some girls came past in a punt. "Most of them covered their private parts" he said. "But one old don covered his face. I am known by my face he said, not by my genitals!" And they all laughed. Back at the house, they were soon sitting down to a good meal and Colin was really relaxing and enjoying himself much more than he had expected to. The house was a simple semi but seemed to be full of books, and Walter soon had a book out to show Colin something of what they would see the following day when they were to go to the Watercress Line. "Then on Sunday we'll give you a little Tour of Oxford and have lunch in town." he said. "But you won't mind will you if we leave you here whilst we go to Mass?" Colin was surprised, for he had somehow forgotten that they were Catholics. It was Angela of course, who back in Marston Green had unwittingly misled him by saying that they had gone to Church rather than gone to Mass

Without any hesitation he said "Oh actually, I'd like to come to Mass with you. I was brought up as a Catholic, but haven't been to Mass since I left home, so it will be a bit of a jog down memory lane." Walter was pleased. He didn't, of course, tell Colin that he already knew he was a Catholic, but it was always nice when a visitor or a friend asked to come to Mass with them. "It will mostly be like you remember it." he said, "But there have been a few changes to the words we say, so I'll have to give you a quick rundown on Sunday morning."

Colin was a bit flummoxed by the idea of changes. He had always thought that even though he never went, the Church would be there for him just as it had always been if he ever felt he needed it. He looked a bit worried, but Walter noticed immediately and assured him that mostly it would be just like he remembered, so not to worry, and then he said innocently "So did you carry on going to Mass right until you left home, or did you stop going earlier?" "It's my Mum who is the Catholic." Colin said. "My Dad, my stepfather." He emphasised the word 'stepfather'. "He only came with us on big occasions like Christmas. But Mum never missed a Sunday and I guess she's still as regular as ever, at least I can't imagine her not going, unless she was really ill. But I was very fond of the priest who was there at the time, so I served at the altar and used to go and talk to him about things. He even used to take me for trips on his boat." Suddenly he paused, as if it had hit him where he was going with this line of thought, and Walter knew why. "But that's so long ago now" he said. "So much has happened since, and I lost touch once I went to Uni." Penny, knowing the fuller history that he had almost got into, helped him by changing the subject. "Walter doesn't have any of your background," she said. "The poor man fell for this Catholic girl and gradually got sucked in, and now he's a much better Catholic than I am." Colin was fascinated by this. He had been surprised to discover from Angela that Walter and Penny went to church, but now, discovering from Penny that this intelligent man, whom he felt he knew quite well, had decided as an adult to become a Catholic really amazed him.

"I'm not sure I believe anymore" he said. "I sort of feel there must be something, but I'm not sure what, and the faith I was taught was full of stories that I just can't believe in. So I reckon if I am still a Catholic, which I suppose I am technically, then I'm a pretty bad one. Didn't you find it difficult to believe all that stuff Walter?" Walter gently explained a bit about not taking all the stories literally. "It's like your computers" he said. "I remember when I first wanted to record some music onto my computer, and the silly machine offered me the terms Rip and Burn. I was horrified because I didn't want to rip up my precious CDs nor did I want to burn my Computer, and I had to consult one of our kids who just couldn't understand what my problem was. Just get on with it Dad he said, laughing at me, you'll find it's all right. But to start with, I still found it difficult as those terms stared up at me. Why can't I just copy and paste? I said to myself, but rip and burn it had to be? In the same way, we talk about God being up in heaven, but since God and heaven are not physical, the words 'up' and 'in' are no more accurate than rip and burn are." "Wow" said Colin. "Now that's sounds a bit like the sort of things Father Bill used to say to me, but I didn't listen very carefully." Walter wondered whether to bring up the fact that they also knew a Father Bill, and let Colin discover that it was the same one he had known, the one who was now in prison because of him, but he decided that was a step too far.

The trip to the Watercress Line was great fun for both of them as they talked about trains, regional variations, and all sorts of technical things that would bore most people silly. So it was the following morning at Mass when something more significant happened. The Church was packed to the doors with an amazing mix of people clearly from all over the world. "This is Oxford" Walter explained. "And the Hospital is just up the road, so what with hospital staff and two Universities it would be odd if the Church wasn't full." They had got there early to make sure they had seats, and Colin found that Mass was almost just as he remembered it, apart from that odd word change. The sermon wasn't brilliant, but they sang some hymns he knew well, and he felt quite at home. He'd said that he felt it would be hypocritical to go up and receive Communion, and Walter had agreed with him but said that if he wanted he could come up with them and ask for a Blessing, but Colin decided to stay put. It was after Walter and Penny had returned that Colin suddenly said, "I'm sorry. I'm all right, but I'm just going outside. See you there." And he was gone.

Outside Colin sat on the low wall that surrounded the Car Park and gradually calmed down. He knew why he had fled from Church. It was that Hymn during Communion. He suddenly realised that he was almost in tears, and no way he was going to cause a scene. Looking around him, he was rather surprised that so many people seemed to be outside, and he gradually realised that they were all talking Polish. He knew it was Polish from two of the people in his office who had taught him a few words so that he could say "Good morning" to them in their own language. The fact that the boss was prepared to learn such things had really pleased them, and he had been pleased too. When Walter and Penny came out, they showed their concern. Penny put her arm round his shoulder which was rather comforting, and asked him why he had got upset. "It was that hymn" he said, "Soul of my Saviour". It was Father Bill's favourite Hymn. He was always humming it, especially when we were on the boat together. In fact I would often sing along with him, and people on the canal bank would look at us as if we were a little mad. But then I went off to Uni, and lost touch for years, and then...." There was a long pause. Once again, Walter and Penny knew what had happened, but he didn't know they knew, and they didn't know what to say without giving away this knowledge. It was very awkward.

After a short silence it was Colin who solved their problem by changing the subject. "What are all these Polish people doing here? Do they always stand outside instead of coming into Mass?" Penny explained that they were actually waiting for the next Mass which was in Polish, and all became clear, as more and more of them were turning up. As they made their way through the crowd and walked to the Bus Stop, they realised that Colin was struggling to contain his distress. Again they knew what it was but didn't know what to say. Eventually Penny made an attempt. "Are you all right Colin? Would you prefer to go home rather than take this trip round Oxford?" "You two are so kind to me" he said, "But I don't deserve it. No. I've never seen Oxford, and going there will take my mind off other things. So let's keep to our plan."

Arriving in the City Centre, Walter led them first to the back of the University Church. Around them were many of the most famous Oxford buildings and Walter explained how the University was run from the Church in its first few years and pointed to its first Library. Then turning around he told them to ignore the famous circular building that appears in so many of the photos. "That's a modern 18th Century addition to the Library" he said. "But beyond it over there are the 15th Century Buildings which are also now part of the Library, and what we are about to walk into now is the 17th Century Bodleian Quad. In a way we thus see much of the history of the University all here in one place." Colin was suitably impressed as Walter held forth on all this history. It was rather like when they went to visit a Railway. He knew the technology whilst Walter knew the history. They went next into the Sheldonian Theatre and climbed up inside to get a good view of all of Oxford and the surrounding hills. "So are all these buildings part of the University?" Colin asked, and Walter launched into a long description of how each of the Colleges was independent and yet part of the University as well. Colin began to feel that he had heard enough history for the day and hoped there wouldn't be much more. But Walter knew Colin well and took them to the building next door. "I think you'll find this interesting" he said, as he took him into the Museum of Science to see amongst other things Einstein's Blackboard.

Penny wisely sat in the sunshine outside waiting for them. It was a long wait, and as she watched all the people passing by, many of them tourists from all over the world, she wondered whether this was the best way they could help Colin. She had always been sceptical of Walter's belief that Colin had made a false accusation against Father Bill, so she had been surprised by Colin's expression of great fondness for the priest, provoked by that familiar Hymn. If he was so fond of Father Bill, why did he make that accusation? Perhaps that was the problem? They had become too fond of one another? But then surely once he had turned on him and brought him to Court he would think about him with anger? But there had been no anger in what he had said. His face had lit up at the memory, and then clearly sadness had flooded in, almost as they had seen, overwhelming him. If Walter was right. If a false accusation had been made, then why had it been made? What had pushed Colin into accusing a man that he was clearly so fond of? It didn't seem to make sense.

As she thought through this, Penny remembered that most people, over 95%, were not abused by celibate priests, but by members of their own family. Was there someone else who had abused Colin who for some reason he couldn't accuse, so that in his confusion he had blamed the priest? But why the priest? Was there actually something there as well? She shook her head as she realised she had come round in a circle. If the priest wasn't guilty, why had he pleaded guilty? Walter had talked to him about this, but she couldn't remember what he had said as she was so angry at the time. It was a puzzle that she needed to talk through with Walter.

By the time Walter and Colin emerged, she had given up her puzzling and gone back to people watching – always a fascinating thing to do in a town like this. Colin was full of the fascinating things he had seen. "Such interesting history" he said, and then stopped short as he realised he was implying that the earlier lecture from Walter had not been quite to his taste. Walter laughed. "Yes, I know that you only really like history that relates to your interests. Trains or Computers are fine, but old libraries are a bit stuffy. We'll have to take a trip to Bletchley Park to see the early Computers there next time you come. Let's go and eat."

Over lunch Walter explained about the early computation done at Bletchley Park which had helped win the war, and Colin said that there had to be a visit next time.

Colin was rather quiet after this, and so Walter eventually steered the conversation onto Colin's children saying, "I brought you to this Pub deliberately in the hope that Peter and Maria are into the Narnia Stories or the Lord of the Rings." Colin was a bit puzzled until Walter explained that this was where the authors met and over a few pints and encouraged each other to write the now famous stories. "The sad thing is" Colin said "That I don't know whether they are into things like this or not. I walked out on them more than five years ago, and a lot has happened to them since then."

"Well, try them out when you next see them. They may well have seen the films, even if they haven't read the books. It will give you a new thing to talk about."

Colin didn't respond as enthusiastically as Walter had hoped. He sensed that the Hymn in Church had brought back some very mixed memories, and that he was struggling more than he let on. They took him back home, pointing out a few other Oxford sights on their way, and after a cup of tea, Colin set off for home, leaving them wondering how much help they had been. Penny sighed. "I spent quite a lot of time thinking about him while you were in the Museum. I am now wondering if you are right. How could he still be so fond of Father Bill if he had actually been abused by him? But then why did he accuse him? I am now wondering if he projected onto Father Bill the abuse that he suffered at the hands of someone else. He is clearly a very troubled man still." Walter nodded and then infuriated her by falling asleep in front of the TV!

Chapter 16: Colin's troubled mind

Walter and Penny were right about Colin. The memories evoked by that Hymn had really shaken him, and once alone in the car, they came out even more clearly. Did he love Father Bill or hate him? He had thought he hated him, but now he wondered about himself. Why had he so many good memories mixed up with bad ones? The Hymn tune kept going round and round in his head, so although he normally didn't have music on when he was driving, he decided he just had to have something to divert his mind. He arrived home to his empty immaculately tidy house, and felt very alone. He had a bite to eat and checked his emails. They were all connected with work, except for one from Walter, which made him even sadder. He couldn't be bothered to reply straightaway, he would reply later. Apart from that one email the lack of any others brought out how alone he felt. He tried watching a bit of Sunday evening TV next, but soon turned it off in disgust and decided to watch something he had recorded earlier – on trains of course.

He went to bed but couldn't get to sleep as ideas of what he might or might not do about Father Bill went round and round in his mind. The next thing he knew, it was the middle of the night and he woke to find himself shaking. A dream was still vivid in his mind. He was trying to find his room in what was maybe a Hall of Residence but the stairs he took always led him to the wrong floor. Again and again he retraced his steps looking for the right staircase. He opened one door only to find himself in the boiler room. He tried to ask for help, but everyone seemed to ignore him as if he wasn't there. He was getting more and more desperate as every attempt to find the right way led him nowhere that he wanted to go. Eventually he found a tiny hole in the wall and squeezed himself through it almost suffocating in the process, and suddenly he had no clothes on and all sorts of things were being done to him.

Why was he so mixed up sexually? Was he really a homosexual? Were his memories all false? Was it all in his mind? Had he been accused unjustly? Why did his children and his wife hate him so much? How could he cope with endless McDonalds with Peter? Maria would probably never forgive him, never speak to him again. He was a failure as a father. How could he escape from all this? Why did everyone turn against him? Why had his mother deceived him all these years? Why was his stepfather, as he now knew he was, such a hateful man? Why did his real father die? He began to think of the easiest way to kill himself. They didn't really need him at work. He had trained them so well that they could do without him. They didn't really like him anyway. They were only nice to him because he was the boss. Perhaps he should jump in front of a train? But that wouldn't be fair to the driver. Throw himself off a high building? Yes. Maybe that was the answer.

Then he began to go through the same dark thoughts again. He remembered sex with various men at Uni before he met Rita. It was never very satisfactory and they often forced him to do things he didn't really want to do. He tried to remember the great sex he'd had with Rita to try to stop the confusion in his mind, and all he could remember was the way she made him angry. He tried to think about the good times with Father Bill, but all he could remember was being looked at as they got ready for bed. Simply being looked at had given him an erection. That tune was going round in his head again: "Soul of my Saviour, sanctify my breast.." Arggh why wouldn't it stop? He tried to think of the fun times with Maria and Peter… but now they hated him for walking out on them. Mcdonald's for Peter was a bribe, and he didn't really like him anymore. He tried to think of his mother, but then the anger welled up again, as he remembered how she had always done whatever "that man" as he called him, wanted and that everything she had done had been surrounded by that one big lie about who his father was. Perhaps he should try and contact his father's family, but they probably wouldn't want to meet him. Even Walter and Penny were just being kind. They didn't really care. Do-gooding Catholics!

Finally, realising that he would never get back to sleep with all this going round in his head, he got up and went downstairs and made himself a hot chocolate. He couldn't get the thought of suicide out of his head. It seemed as if all those times with the counsellor counted for nothing. He had now ended as mixed up as before. He sat in an armchair with a rug pulled up round him and sipped his drink miserably. Then he just sat there in the semi-darkness, wondering what to do next? He dozed on and off, but the dark thoughts were still there, and once he woke and found he had been dreaming of a computer programme that he tried to fix, but it kept getting back at him, behaving in utterly illogical ways. He said to the people watching him that he would soon fix it, but the more he tried the worse things seemed to get, and gradually they were all walking out in disgust with him as again and again he said that he had almost solved it, and yet knowing that the problem seemed to be getting worse. He woke up in a sweat. He tried to think rationally about the dream. He knew now that what he should have done was simple. All he had needed to do was to turn it off, but in the dream he was unable to work out how it turned off, or something like that. Such a nightmare.

The morning light came early as it was summer, but he was so exhausted he went back to bed. He was woken by the phone. It was Julian from work. "Are you all right Colin?" He groaned down the phone that he was not very well and wouldn't be coming in and put the phone down. Then he just lay there feeling miserable. Eventually he had to get up to go to the Loo, and he forced himself to change into some clothes. Standing there looking at himself naked in the mirror, something he hardly ever did, he saw only a miserable sack of a man, even though he knew that he was actually good-looking. "What's the point of me having good looks and money, a lovely home, and a successful business, if I cannot be happy?" he thought. Ideas of suicide came pouring back into his mind. Perhaps he should go to that multi-storey Car Park not too far away? He had heard of others dying there.

He went downstairs and had a coffee, but couldn't face eating anything. He tried to remember what his counsellor had suggested when he felt like this. Do something active, go for a run? A great idea, but he just couldn't get himself to do it. He sat on the sofa. He lay down on the sofa. He put the TV on, zapped through the Channels then turned it off in disgust, and just lay there feeling sad. The day seemed to go so slowly with his mind going round and round with his dark thoughts. Perhaps he dozed off now and again. He didn't really know. It began to get dark. He had some more coffee, and tried to eat something but didn't get very far. He remembered those sleeping pills, so he took one and went to bed. He slept, but in the early hours he woke again with the same thoughts as before. Same routines repeating themselves, and though the morning light came flooding in, he was still in the dark. The day, the second day wore on. He just sat there.

Finally in the late afternoon or maybe it was evening, he wasn't really sure, someone rang the doorbell. He couldn't face answering. He just

hoped they would go away. It rang again but he just couldn't be bothered. Then they started knocking and a familiar voice from the office called out to him "Colin. It's me Julian. Please open the door." He groaned but dragged himself up dishevelled with two days of stubble and let him in. Wren was with him. She took one look at him and went into the kitchen with her shopping bag whilst Julian just sat down saying "What's up then?" "Oh I don't know. Suddenly, I seem back to where I was years ago. I don't see the point of going on." "Well we do" said Julian. "You made our business, you are our inspiration and our guide. You are like a father to us all and we've all wondered what was wrong." Colin sighed. "It's kind of you to say all this, but you know the business could easily go on without me now. You are all so efficient."
"But that's only thanks to you Colin. It would be so easy for it all to lose its flair, so easy for us all to stop providing the kind of service to our customers that you have always demanded of us. You just don't realise all that you mean to us, how good you are at gently but firmly encouraging everyone, never losing your temper, and always helping if someone is struggling with a problem. They know they can always come to you, and they know that you are always nearby, and that stops them from slacking. We need you." Colin was quite startled by this. He and Julian had a very male relationship with one another where you showed you were fond of your mate by always being a bit rude to him. He didn't know that Julian had learnt from the last time. Wren had given him a lecture while they were driving over. "If he's gone into depression again, I don't want you just being cheerful with him. You have got to tell him how much he means to us, and it must come from you. I'll go and cook some food. He's bound not to have eaten anything, but you must tell him in no uncertain terms how important he is for us and for the business."
Colin suddenly realised that sounds and smells of sizzling were coming from the kitchen. "What are you doing?" he said, even though he knew the answer. A voice came from the kitchen. "You've time for a quick shower and a shave, so get on with it." Startled by Wren's commanding tone, Colin simply responded almost automatically. Rita used to treat him like this and he missed it, and now without thinking too much, he did what he was told.
They all sat down to eat together and after a bit Wren began to talk about work. There was a problem, she said, that they weren't quite

sure how to solve. Some were suggesting one approach, and some another. What did Colin think? It was a clever move. Colin was never more happy than when he was faced with some problem that had nothing to do with him. He asked for more details, and Wren immediately stopped eating, went over to her bag and fished out her laptop. It knew Colin's wifi code from old, and she was soon able to pass the Laptop over for him to look at, satisfied to see him so quickly absorbed. She went back to her food. Colin had already eaten his, wolfing it down as if he hadn't eaten for days, which she guessed he hadn't. She had timed this very well and soon a technical discussion was going on which would have left most people completely bemused.

Having come to a decision about what should be done, they realised it was time to go, but this was a problem. They remembered the last time when he had said he would come to work the next day and then hadn't made it. Wren looked at Julian questioningly. They had discussed this too on the way over. Should they stay the night? But had decided it would be wrong to completely take over his life. But then much to their surprise, the doorbell rang. Colin looking puzzled went to answer it, saying as he left them that he had no idea who it could be. They heard him talking at the door – a voice was asking if he was all right because he hadn't replied to an email from three days ago, and they heard him reply that he'd not been very well but that his friends from the office had turned up to rescue him. They thought she was going away, but then they heard him ask her to come and meet them and he came back in with a lady that they didn't know. "This is Angela my neighbour" he said. "I told you about my project on her garden later on this summer when I have my break. She came to see if I was all right. I didn't know I had so many people who cared about me, so perhaps you better meet one another?"

There was the usual handshaking, and then Wren said she was going to clear away the dinner and would Angela like a coffee. She found to her surprise that Angela had followed her out into the kitchen carrying some of the dirty plates. She shut the door and whispered "Is he going to be OK?" "I'm not sure" was the reply. "Last time this happened, he kept saying he was better but then went down again."

"Right, I'll check on him in the morning and if he doesn't get to work, we can decide together what to do next."

"I'm so relieved you're close by Angela. Let's exchange phone numbers." So they did, and then Angela went to clear other things from the table.

Colin went to sleep quite easily that night, but woke in the early hours and yet again found all those dark thoughts running around inside his head. He tried to get back to sleep but after an hour of tossing and turning he decided to get up rather than lie there feeling suicidal. It was still dark outside but rather than sit in the house feeling sorry for himself he decided to go for a walk round the local streets. He walked down Elmdon Lane first till he came to the Airport Gate and the enormous dark bank beyond that shielded the village from the worst of the noise. Then he turned and walked back again past his house, on and over the railway bridge, and into the Village Centre. All was quiet of course as he walked up to the Station and crossed by the Footbridge. He waited there for a bit. Perhaps he should stand in front of a train. It was easy to get on to the Platform and he would be on the track. It would be a quick end. But then he thought of the chaos it would cause to the railway, the delayed trains, the frustrated passengers; he knew too much about railways and loved them too much to finish his life doing this to them. He didn't think he would see a train at this time of night, but then he heard a distant sound and waited until a freight train roared underneath him. He walked on home on the other road, hoping that he had tired himself out and that he might forget his thoughts and get a bit of peaceful sleep.

Back home, he slumped on the sofa, as the idea of going back to bed with all those dark thoughts frightened him, so he sat there watching as the dawn gradually turned his windows from dark to grey and then to white. What good was another day if his life was so empty, so pointless? He made some tea and had some cornflakes, automatically tidying up as he finished whilst listening to the News on the Radio which was depressing as usual. It was far too early to go to work even if he felt like it. He slumped back down on the sofa, and tried to look at some emails on his phone, but put it down in disgust. He just couldn't face it. So he just sat there, knowing how stupid it was to feel sorry for himself, and yet unable to break the cycle of despair. His head drooped on the cushion.

He was jerked awake by his front doorbell being rung again and again. It took him a moment to realise that he had fallen asleep. He pulled himself up to answer the door. It was Angela. "Sorry Colin, but Wren phoned me to say you hadn't turned up for work and I could check on you. So here I am. Can I come in?" He let her in somewhat reluctantly, and yet he was comforted that someone cared about him. She was about the same age as his Mum which felt right. He assured her that he'd had some breakfast but hadn't felt up to work. Angela looked at him sympathetically. "You're still pretty depressed aren't you? Still feeling bad about your family I suppose." Suddenly he could feel the tears welling up, and before he knew what he was doing he was weeping profusely. He tried to stop but he couldn't and almost without realising it, he found himself in her arms shuddering with the misery within him, as it poured out of him in a torrent of tears.

Angela let him cry. She knew how tears could heal, but then as they subsided, she gently suggested that he needed something to do, something to take his mind off the misery. "Why not go away somewhere for a few days holiday? Go and see one of those little steam railways in Wales that you've never visited.

"Yes you're right. Too much sitting around is no good for me at the moment. I need something to do, something constructive that is different from work."

"Well, there is my garden project," she said tentatively "You were going to do it later in the summer when you had a holiday planned, but you could always do it sooner?" There was a moment's hesitation and then he said "You know, that's a very good idea. But I'm not sure that would be fair on them all at work." "Why not phone them and see?" she said. So he did, and was soon assured by Wren and Julian that they could cope, especially as they could always consult him if something came up that required his decision. And so it was agreed.

Chapter 17: The New Beginning

Colin was transformed. He asked her to wait for him back at her house whilst he showered and changed into some clean gardening clothes, and soon after this he arrived at her door armed with his Laptop and a Measuring Tape. She held the end whilst he measured and marked the plot. She was a bit bemused by some of the measurements he wanted to make but assumed he knew what he was doing. He wanted to go home, but she suggested working on his Laptop on her Dining Room table promising to leave him in peace so that he could concentrate on drawing out his plans. She popped in once and gave him the coffee he'd asked for, but wisely did not try and see what he was doing, nor ask any questions. When lunchtime arrived, she told him she was making something for both of them, and he seemed quite happy to accept her hospitality. He explained over the meal that he was now ready to show her a number of alternative plans, and so once she had cleared the table that is what they did.

What he showed her was a bit beyond her understanding, but he was so very patient at explaining things that she gradually began to guess which of the plans was his favourite, even though he insisted that she should choose. It was fairly obvious when she did choose that her guess had been correct, as her choice clearly pleased him. "We'll need to go to a Builders Merchant tomorrow to get the right stuff. Would you like to come with me?" Angela was only too happy to agree, as she was really enjoying seeing this young man (as she saw him) coming back to life. That afternoon, she watched him from the window as he began to tear up the old crazy paving, and all the weeds. The old paving was piled up in one heap whilst he took the weeds off in a wheelbarrow to her weed dump. It really couldn't be called a compost heap! He stopped work at about 4 o'clock when she took him a cup of tea, but he refused to stay for dinner. "You've given me one good meal," he said. "It's best if once I'm home and showered, I just have a bit of bread and cheese and then relax. It's been a busy day hasn't it?" She was pleased to see him clearly so content. He wanted to use his car in the morning, but was persuaded to accept her car instead. "Best we use my big car," she said. "See you tomorrow at 9.30."

Back home, after a welcome shower and a bite to eat, he decided to phone Rita. They'd agreed that he should do something with Peter every other weekend, and now he was feeling so much more positive, he felt ready to discuss what that might be. Rita was glad to hear from him because although she had decided he must make the running on this agreement, she had been hoping he would phone soon, as Maria was driving her mad moaning about a computer problem that she knew Colin could help her with. Colin certainly had the knowledge to help, "But how can I help her if she won't talk to me?" he said. She had her reply ready. "I think she's so desperate that we might just persuade her. Let me make the offer to her and see what she says." "What about the weekend?" asked Colin. Her answer was a wise one. "Let's see if we can get her talking to you first and then we can decide."

A few minutes later, the phone rang. It was a number he didn't know, so he answered quite formally "Colin Bransted here." "It's Maria." said the voice. "Mum thinks you can help me with this problem with my Computer, but before you say anything, I want you to know that just because I've phoned you it doesn't mean that I am not still very angry with you. I don't think you realise how much you have hurt and worried Mum and us, and you can't expect to come walking back into our lives as if nothing has happened." Colin did not attempt to defend himself. He knew he was in the wrong and he told her so. Maria wasn't satisfied that easily, and he was subject to another strict telling off, where all he could do was murmur an odd "Yes" or "Sorry" or "No" as appropriate. Finally, much to his relief, because it had been a real grilling, she suddenly said, "Right, I've said all I want to say, so now let's see if you can help me with this problem." The discussion became very technical, and Colin soon realised, much to his surprise, that she basically knew what she was doing, and together they soon had the problem sorted. "That's really great. Thanks Dad. Bye." And she was gone.

Colin wondered whether to phone Rita again. He waited quite a long time, his anxiety building, but just when he thought that he couldn't wait any longer, the phone rang and he saw it was her. "Well that went well," she said. Colin actually laughed. "She gave me such a grilling Rita. I thought she'd never stop. It was tough just listening to her, but I think it actually did me good. I certainly deserved it."

"Yes, you did. I was listening on the other side of the door and was proud of her. You've got to remember that she's not the little girl you knew when you left us."
"And she's so bright. I'd expected I would have to give her much more help, maybe even take over remotely, but she'd almost got the answer as to what to do before I could suggest it."
"What's more, Maria has agreed that you can come to Sunday lunch. Now that is a breakthrough! She says that she won't be nice to you, whatever Peter says, but in her own words 'She will tolerate your presence.'"
"But are you sure that's all right with you? I could always take Peter out again."
"No Colin, now we've got her at least accepting your presence. We need you to be here, so that all of us can get a bit more used to you, and not find things so awkward."
Colin was really delighted by this reply "See you at about 12 then. Bye now."
Angela picked him up the next day as arranged and he was able to tell her all about the phone call with Maria and the plans for Sunday. She gently enquired how his night had been and was delighted to hear that he'd slept well. "All that hard work in my garden paid off then," she said, "And some more to come today." He was relieved to hear her add, because it had been worrying him a bit. "And please don't worry about spending as much of my money as is necessary, because I don't like skimping on things." They were soon at the Builders Merchants choosing paving and all the other things they needed, and they returned home where he spent another day, quite like the first, clearing the ground in preparation for tomorrow's deliveries.
He spent the next two days deep into the project, watched over surreptitiously by Angela, who took secret photos through her windows. Penny and Walter had been in touch asking how Colin was, and delighted to hear the good news, so she sent a couple of her secret photos of Colin at work to Penny. She showed them to Walter who was equally enthusiastic, and they were both pleased to hear that he was going to have lunch with his estranged family on Sunday. "I do hope it works out for him" said Walter. "But I fear that it may not be as easy as Angela thinks. He's clearly a very troubled person. While he's busy in that garden it will probably be all right, but I worry about what will happen to him next."

Lunch on Sunday was rather more difficult than Colin had imagined. It was one thing being a family all living together and chatting about this and that as one does, but this was much more artificial, and he found himself trying to make conversation and not being very successful. Peter was more interested in wolfing down his food, and then going off to play on his Computer. He didn't like being questioned about things like school, and got away as soon as he could. Actually, things became a little better after he'd left, because Maria asked him whether he'd been down to the Severn Valley Railway recently, and he was able to tell her about his new friend Walter and the trip they'd taken together not long ago. "I used to love going with you before you left us," she said bluntly. "Why don't we go again soon?" Colin then made a bad move. "Ok," he said. "Let's ask Peter when he would like to go." "Typical," said Maria. "I have a sexist Dad who thinks only boys are interested in Trains. Why don't you wake up and move into the 21st Century?" Colin was startled. He wasn't used to being attacked by his children, and then Rita started laughing. "She's quite right Colin. I can tell you now that Peter won't want to come with you. He may be a boy, but he is not interested in trains, only football." Colin then had to apologise for being stupid, and was a bit astonished when Maria said "Yes. You are stupid. I told you that the other day, but never mind, I'll let you take me, even though I am a girl. When shall we go? Next weekend?" Colin hesitated. Did he really want to spend the day with this teenage girl who kept telling him off? Maria was noted his hesitation.

"So you don't really want to take me do you?"

"No, no, I just need to get over the shock of coping with all the flak you are giving me. Will I get more on the day?"

"Yes you probably will. And you deserve it. But I will try not to be too cruel. Do you think you can cope?"

Colin sighed. "I'm not sure I can. But I will try my best not to shame you too much. Will that be all right?"

"Ok. Next Saturday then."

Rita now stepped in. "Hang on a moment. Your Nan and Grandpa were coming over. But he's not well so they've cancelled, but I thought we ought to go over and see them. Can't you do the Sunday?"

Now it was Maria's turn to sigh. "Oh no, I'm meeting a friend then. I love Nan and Grandad, but I don't see the point of visiting them if he's ill. You wouldn't go would you Dad?"

Here was another problem Colin now had to face. She knew he wouldn't want to see his Stepfather, but saying that, and then maybe explaining why, when he didn't really know why himself, was just too much for him. There was a long silence.
In the old days Rita would have rescued him, but instead she sat and looked to see what he would say next. Finally Colin forced himself to speak, stuttering at first, as he tried to find words to explain himself. "Yes…. you're right… uh. .. I … well you see.."
Maria was not impressed "Why can't you just say that you just don't like him? I think he's lovely, and I think you're mad to have a Dad like him, and not like him or want to see him."
It was another dose of teenage cruelty, but by this time Colin had an answer. "He's not my Dad. He's my Stepfather. My real Dad died when I was a baby."
Maria was astonished. "What! Why have you never told us this?"
Colin frowned, "I suppose it's because I just didn't want to talk about him at all. He just made me so angry trying to control my life. I was brought up being told to honour my father and mother, and I'd always felt guilty that I couldn't like the man I thought was my Dad. And when I did find out, when I was not that much older than you, that he wasn't my real father, I was so angry that my Mum hadn't told me that it made me even more screwed up about it."
Maria was now much more sympathetic. "Well I would hate it if suddenly Mum told me you weren't my real Dad," and then she looked at Rita, "He is my real Dad, isn't he Mum?"
"Yes, of course he is. I only have to look at you to know who your father is. But I think you are right that perhaps a visit to your Grandad will be too much for him, so I think it would be OK for you to go on that trip with your Dad … your real Dad!"
Maria was pleased, and everything was arranged, but then she brought the conversation back to the news that she had a grandfather she had never heard about. "So who was your real father Dad? What was he like?" Colin then explained the little he knew of his real father, and then showed her the photo of him that his Mum had given him only a few weeks before. "Your Nan only gave me this photo a few weeks ago. So I've only just discovered that my original name was Colin Riorghan. And on the back are the contact details from way back of his family in Ireland. But they probably moved years ago." "So have you been in touch?" she said. "I'm probably missing out on loads of

Irish relations that I've never met." "I think that's harder than you might think" Rita said to her. "Finding someone from an old address and phone number from 40 years ago could be a long and difficult search."
Maria looked scornful. "You don't know much about the Internet, do you? You can find all sorts of people there. But anyway, why not start by trying that phone number?"
Rita looked at Colin. "Well Maria, you may be right, but can you imagine how difficult it is going to be? Imagine someone phoning you up out of the blue and saying I think I'm your nephew." But whilst they had been talking Maria had been fiddling with her phone, and suddenly they realised what she had been doing. She had rung the number Monica had given Colin. "Hello" she said. "I am trying to find my Dad's relations, and we were given this number. His name is Colin Bransted." There was a pause. "Well he lives in Birmingham and his Dad died years ago, when he was a little boy. I think his Dad's name was Riorghan like yours?" Another pause and then "Yes, that's right. That's my Dad. Would you like to talk to him? It's your Uncle Sean," she said, handing him the phone.

Colin didn't really have time to think. "Hello" he said "I'm Colin. Are you sure you're my Uncle?" Rita and Maria could only hear one side of the conversation which was pretty frustrating. It seemed to go on and on with Colin answering all sorts of questions about himself. Then Colin said "Are you saying I have a cousin here in England? Where did you say? .... "Bicester? Where's that? ..... "Oh right." "Could you give me her contact details? "Marion Plestowicz? ... Sorry how do you spell that? ...Oh Marianne I see. Did you say Keble Road? Bicester? ... Where's that? ....Amazing. ...I was in Oxford the other weekend. ....Yes, I will make contact. ....Thanks so much..... Yes, it's wonderful to be in touch. ....Sorry it's been so long. My Mum only gave me your details a couple of weeks ago and I didn't think you'd still be living in the same place." There was a long pause. Rita could see Colin struggling with his emotions as he listened to what his Uncle was trying to say, and responding with the odd "Mm". or "Yes." Finally he said "I think we're both finding this difficult. Let me give you my details and then you or your daughter can contact me again at any time." After giving his details to his uncle, there were long goodbyes and then he sighed again and he gave the phone back to Maria. “That was so difficult. At the end he was talking about Pat, that’s my Dad, and crying, and I didn’t know what to say. My Dad was his little brother.”

Chapter 18: Angela and Marianne

Colin was rather surprised at how easily Maria had taken control and got him in touch with his real father's family. He told Angela about it, and she laughed at his lack of knowledge of what teenage girls can be like. His time working on Angela's garden had meant that she had cooked him lunch every day during that fortnight and they had sat and chatted over all sorts of things. Angela had been determined to get him to talk about why he had been so depressed. She was sure that the main reason must be something to do with him being abused as a teenager, and she hoped that eventually as he got to trust her more, he might be able to share some of the pain with her.

In a way she was right. Colin had never really been able to talk about this to anyone, apart from official people like his Counsellor and then to the Police. He had never felt it right to share this with his mother, as he was sure she would have felt very guilty for not protecting him in some way, and he had never told Rita. Perhaps he might have got more help if he had faced a Court Case, where he would have given evidence, but because Father Bill had pleaded guilty nothing like that ever happened.

Meanwhile, given that Colin's Gardening Project at Angela's was going well and Colin was clearly feeling so much happier with himself and the world, Angela decided to ask him the question that she had so far avoided raising, even though she wanted to. Eventually she decided now was the time, and during one of her lunches when they talked of many things, she launched into this rather more tricky subject. "I hope you don't mind me asking you this" she said, "And please say if you'd rather not talk about it, but now that you seem to have thrown off your depression, I just wondered whether you have any idea what triggered it?" Colin looked at her for a moment, wondering if he was up to sharing this kind of stuff, and then began to explain a little of what he thought might have sent him into that downward spiral. Much of what he shared she expected to hear, about how he felt he had failed as a husband and a father, but she was surprised when he went on to tell her how he hated being such an angry person. She had always known him as a someone who was very gentle and polite, and when he began to describe his moments of raging anger, she could hardly believe what she was hearing. "But you're such a gentle person Colin. Are you really that angry underneath? What caused all that anger." She had hoped this might lead to where she wanted it to lead. It didn't, but it did mean that Colin's pent-up feelings about himself could be poured out on her. "You know, I used to have no idea," he said. 'But now I think it was what my stepfather did to me that is at the root of the problem. You see, he was and is a bully. He was always telling me precisely what he thought I should do, and as a little boy I accepted that this was normal.

In fact, to start with I liked the way he interested himself in everything I did, in the way he took me into his shed and taught me things, and took me on trips, but gradually I began to resent the way he constantly checked up on everything I was doing. He would interview me every day about what had happened at school, and I never knew what to say. He insisted when I was about 12 that I go for extra tuition in English. This was quite helpful to start with, but then when I said I didn't want to go anymore, he tried to insist I carry on. It was then that I simply shouted at him in a way I'd never done before, and retreated to my room seething with anger. I suppose I was about 15.

After this, I never spoke to him unless I had to. It was, as my Counsellor got me to admit later, a very extreme reaction, but not that unusual for a teenager. I coped by retreating into my studies, especially computing, and going off to the one place he never went – to the Church. For years therefore, I almost forgot the anger that was there, until Rita and the children began to annoy me with their untidiness and lack of order. As I got more and more irritated with them, I suddenly realised to my horror that I was actually seething with anger, just as I had been with my stepfather, and later I realised too late that I had begun to behave with them just the way he had dealt with me, and I was horrified. At the time, all I could think about was how to get away to somewhere where I could control my anger… so I got it all organised and ran away from them. Of course, once I'd done that, I then realised what a failure I was, both as a husband and a father, and I spiralled down into depression, and then began to think of suicide as the only solution."

Angela wasn't surprised that he hadn't mentioned the abuse, although she was a bit disappointed. "So you reckon it all goes back to the way your stepfather treated you?" she said. "I'd thought it might have been caused by the Church?" It was a bold move, and she wondered for a moment if she had pushed it too far, for Colin's brow furrowed; but then he said, "Some years ago I would have said it was that." He didn't say what "that" was. "It was certainly what my first Counsellor thought. But lately, and partly helped by the Counsellor I use now, I've realised that it is actually my stepfather's treatment that is at the root of the problem. She says that I need to work out what to do about this, but all I have ended up doing when I think about him and me is to descend into sadness and self-pity." "Might it not help if you got back in touch with him, as you have with your mother?" she said. "I told you how sad it was for me that my son and husband didn't get on, and how angry and confused he was at the Funeral."

Like so many people, Colin rarely thought about death and so explained with some certainty that his stepfather was as fit as a fiddle, and there was no chance of him dying. Anyway, for him, death was something that happened to other people. Little did he know that as he spoke to Angela, his Mum was watching her husband with increasing fear as he unsuccessfully tried to cover up his pain. Anyway, Colin went back out into the garden promising Angela that he would think through what she had said, and he did, mulling over it in his mind out in the bright sunshine. When Walter and Penny came up for another visit, to inspect the new garden, Colin made sure he was there to give them a conducted tour almost as soon as they arrived, but on Saturday, Colin was able to have a longer private talk with Walter whilst the girls had gone shopping.

Walter had always wondered if the abuse had been committed by Colin's stepfather, knowing and believing as he did, that although Father Bill had pleaded guilty, he hadn't actually done anything to Colin. But, as with Angela so now with Walter, Colin talked of the bullying nature of his stepfather. Clearly, Walter thought, the stepfather was guilty of psychological abuse if nothing else. Colin then went on to tell him the news about getting in touch with his real father's family, and how he now knew he had a cousin living in Bicester. "Well why not come down and stay one weekend" he said. "And then you could visit them either on the way down or the way back." Colin had thought that was a great idea and it had at last made him pick up the phone and dial that number in Bicester.

He hated phoning someone he didn't know, and so was much relieved to discover when his cousin answered the phone that she'd already been told about him and was delighted that he had got in touch. "I do remember your Dad" she said. "Such a lovely man, but I was only a girl when he died. I remember how upset my Dad was that his little Paddy was no more. We all came to the Funeral. It was very sad, but I don't think I met you as you were only a baby." "I'm a bit more than a baby now," said Colin. "Anyway, the point is that I'll be down your way in two weeks time, staying with some friends in Oxford, and I wondered if I could pop in?" "Oh Yes," she said. Why not come for Sunday lunch? And I'll see how many of the family I can get to come and join us."

Colin was a little flustered by this, wondering what this meant, so he asked "How many of you are there?" "Well now" she said "We've got four sons and they're all married with children. But now I come to think of it they might be a bit too many to face on a first visit. Perhaps a bit too much for you?" Colin's "Mm" was taken as agreement and so she went on. "So maybe we'll stick just to my brother and his wife. You see, they've got grown-up children too and I know that like our kids, they all want to meet you, so I think we should stick to us two cousins and our partners first don't you… Unless you would like to meet them all?" Colin said that he thought her plan was best. He had been brought up in a quiet household without many relations, and since his sister was in Australia, the only children he knew well were his own. The sudden discovery of this big Irish family was quite startling.

The next weekend had been his time to go and see his kids, and was he glad that this time he could tell them that he had been in touch with his cousin, because Maria had been asking if he had done this every time he had seen them, and even Peter was interested to hear he had Uncles and Aunts he had never heard of before. Maria wanted to know much more about where they lived and how many children they had and what their names were and what did they do, and was a bit irritated that he had found out so little. "Give me time," he said. "Once I'm down there I'm sure I'll be told all the details and be shown photos, and then I promise I'll bring back a full report." Maria had to admit that that was fair, and Peter just wanted to know if any of his cousins played football and which Team they supported. Colin promised that he would find that out too. The rest of the time with them went really well, and he returned home really quite happy and looking forward to the trip the following weekend.

His visit to Marianne went really well. She had greeted him with a great hug, and said how much he looked like his father, showing him a photo on her wall of their two Dads together. He had been right to expect lots of family photos. In fact, he had never seen a house with so many photos up on the sitting room wall, and he was very moved to see the one with his Dad and his big brother centre stage. She had immediately introduced him to each photo, and after a bit he'd asked if he could take the photos so that he could show his children their relations as they had been asking about them. She was delighted by this, and in this way he was able to take a note on his phone of all their names, and what they were doing which he would never have remembered otherwise. She had told him to come by 11.00 "So that we can have a little quiet chat before the others turn up," she'd said. Once they sat down, he realised what she meant by a chat. "I wanted to explain why we never got in touch with you. The point was that my Dad was so upset by the death that we were told never to talk about it. I think he found it all too painful, and so we did what we were told, and then because we'd never been in touch we just never got round to getting in touch. If you see what I mean?"
Colin had wondered about this, perhaps feeling a little resentful. "But when I phoned your Dad, he couldn't have been more pleased?" "Ah yes," she said. "Because he felt guilty about not contacting you all these years, but couldn't pluck up the courage to do it. The death was a long time ago, and he's an old man now, and your call was like his little brother coming alive to him again. When he phoned me, he was in tears you know, and I cannot remember the last time he cried. Even at the Funeral, whilst we were all weeping, he kept his grief in. I suppose he knew that he had to be strong to support all of us." After a while she changed the subject. "What about you Colin? How are you? Are you happy?" At first, he had told her the happy things, about his successful Computer business and things like that. "And the family?" she said. And in a moment, he had begun to tell her all his troubles. She was wonderfully sympathetic and, as with Angela, the sharing somehow relieved the pain, and even made him feel less guilty about the long estrangement with his stepfather. Soon after this her husband arrived with her brother and his wife, and the two women went into the kitchen whilst the men sat round and discussed the sort of things men discuss. Colin was rather glad that Peter had asked him

about football, and took careful note that Aston Villa was the family Team!

Chapter 19: The Stepfather

It had been a Monday that Colin's stepfather John had been taken to the Doctor's Surgery, but only because Monica had insisted and had phoned to make an emergency appointment. Then she had stood over him when the Doctor phoned back. When he tried to downplay his symptoms, much to his surprise she took the phone off him, and gave the Doctor a more honest account of the pain her husband was in. She then gave the phone back to John, a bit surprised at herself for being so assertive. After asking a few more questions, the Doctor said that she wanted him to come in later so he could be given a proper examination. And so there he was, feeling pretty foul, and in more and more pain.

He was the sort of man who had never been ill, never seen a Doctor. He had always been in control of his life, quietly but forcefully dominating his wife and his children, which was one of the reasons Colin had clashed with him as a teenager. He had never actually abused them physically, but the Counsellor had certainly told Colin that it sounded to her like psychological abuse – more subtle but just as damaging to those who endured it. She had actually told Colin that his rebellion was probably inevitable, and that had certainly made Colin feel rather better, although he still felt guilty for turning on his mother. Monica had always seen her John as a loving husband who looked after her with great care. She accepted that he was a bit of an old-fashioned husband – as she saw it – who wanted everything done his way, but she knew that provided she accepted the way he wanted things to be, then her life was a pretty happy one. The one thing that made her sad was the way he and Colin clashed. When it first happened, John shouted at Colin in a way she had rarely ever heard him shout before. There was, she remembered, one time way back when he had shouted at her and frightened her, but once she had said sorry for what she had done, he had taken her in his arms and told her how much he loved her, and after that she had known better than to do anything that might upset him. Colin's defiance had absolutely astonished her. She thought he would give way as she had done, and go along with what John wanted. Instead, he had shouted back and told John he was a bully, and defiantly gone off to his room, threatening to leave home, and John had been so astonished that he

hadn't taken it any further. "He'll calm down eventually," is all he said to her, and when Colin remained defiant, the result was a silent stalemate.
John had also been amazed by Colin's response. He wondered what had got into the boy, for he had never had anyone defy him like this. Quietly he had climbed the ladder at work, and with his skill at any practical task he was faced with, and his polite but firm way of asserting his opinion, he had ended up eventually heading "The Works Department" (as he still called it) of the local Council. It had been the same at home, where he'd hardly ever had to shout to get his own way, and on the few occasions when he did feel the need to shout, his family had quickly and quietly obeyed him, always avoiding doing anything that might upset him. Of course, if anyone had asked him why he had shouted, he would have said that every now and then it was necessary to express oneself forcibly to make sure things got done the right way. He had learnt, although he probably would never have admitted this, that most people like a quiet life, and that provided he was careful, he could get his family and those at work to do things the way he wanted them done and (he thought) be all the better for it. He didn't realise he was a bully. He thought of himself as a good-living man who knew how things should be done, and by explaining carefully but firmly his views, he made sure that life for everyone ran smoothly and efficiently.
Now he tried to play down the pain in the back of his stomach and a few other symptoms. The Doctor, much to Monica's annoyance, had been taken in, and had simply given him a Prescription. They visited the Chemist on the way home and he began to take the medicine. He did find that this gave him a little relief and tried to hide from her that he was in fact still in quite a lot of pain. Monica soon saw that things were still not right. She had cancelled their visit to see Rita and the children, simply telling them John had bad gastro-enteritis, but the following weekend she realised that she could not let him go on suffering and they were soon at the Doctors' again.
This time, the doctor insisted on making a phone call while they were there and got him an emergency appointment at the hospital. He kept saying that he would soon get over it, and they really shouldn't make all this fuss, but here too he found that he was being treated as firmly as he normally treated others. The Doctor, and Monica, were very kind, but very insistent. The word cancer was not spoken, but he was

no fool, and he realised it was looming in the background. He did however insist that no one should be told anything until the tests had been done.

Just over a week later, they had the result. Pancreatic cancer. They explained that there was little they could do and that he only had a few months left. Monica shed some tears, and he comforted her as best he could. Even now, he would not make a fuss. “Death has to be accepted when it comes,” he said. “Remember there’s no mortgage on the house, and you will have a good pension. You’ll manage better than you think.” It was just like him, Monica thought, to have it all organised. She remembered the chaos she’d faced when Paddy had died, and she had been left with two little children. In her desperation, it was Paddy’s workmate John who had helped her through that tough time, organising the funeral, sorting out her finances. Then eventually he married her.

Once again, she found herself going against what John wanted. He didn’t feel the need to let the children know, but she insisted. First phoning Australia and weeping quite a lot as she shared the news with her daughter, and then phoned Colin. It was this second phone call that she was most worried about. How would he react? Would he come over and see John or would he simply blot it all out? She was quite surprised by his reaction. His main concern was for her. “How are you coping with this Mum? I’ll come over tomorrow afternoon and see you. I want you to know that I am here for you whatever support you need.” Then she wept over him, because he was being so kind. All the ways she had failed him by standing by John were swept away as her lovely lovely son surrounded her with his compassion. She was glad she had made these two calls whilst John was sleeping upstairs. The painkillers had inevitably led to an end to his ceaseless activity. He had struggled out to his shed a few times but soon gave up. Monica had discovered that she was beginning to take control.

When Colin came round the following afternoon, he gave her a big hug, and she wept again. Then, he sat her down and let her tell him what was happening. She was able to reassure him that there were no problems about money but that she had been so used to his Dad doing things that she found it all a bit bewildering. She knew how to access their bank accounts online and was able to show Colin and share the passwords with him. “Just in case,” she said. “And Colin, will you come upstairs and see him?” There was a slight pause but not a long one "Yes OK Mum. Let's do it now." John was astonished when he was woken to find Colin there beside him. "How're you doing Dad?" he said in a way that he had never heard Colin use before. "What are you doing here?" he said rather more brusquely than he meant to. But Colin didn't rise to this, simply saying "Sorry if I surprised you. Just came to see how you are." "Oh, I'm managing," he said still with a touch of aggression, "I hate being like this. You will look after your Mum won't you?" He knew deep down that he ought to be more gentle, but it wasn't his way, and even now he found it hard to be friendly to the son who had defied him all those years ago. He was even more irritated when Colin told him that Monica had already been given Colin access to the Bank Accounts saying gruffly "So you've written me off as dead already, have you?"

As his hackles rose, Colin remembered the advice Walter had given him when he had shared with him his stepfather's problem. Walter had suggested that Colin needed to step away from his teenage relationship with that man. He had once heard of a piece of good advice that a priest had given to a friend of his who couldn't get on with his parents. The priest had said "Stop trying to make it right. It has happened to you, but it is in the past and there is nothing you can do now to change it, so wrap it up in a parcel and hand it over to God." Of course, Walter hadn't always expressed it to others in a religious way like that, but he'd often used the basic idea, that in order to move on from an historically bad relationship you have to let it go. You have to stop endlessly worrying about it. This was the advice he had now adapted to share with Colin.

It was this wise advice that helped Colin now. He had simply decided to ignore his father if he became aggressive. John hadn't really changed from the bossy person he had rebelled against all those years ago, but now he just changed the subject. "I took Marie to see our Railway last weekend Dad. We had a picnic at our favourite place by the river. Great memories eh!" Monica was amazed at Colin's sensitivity, the way he ignored the aggression, and diverted his stepfather onto a neutral topic. Soon, John asked Colin which engines they had seen, and they were soon into technicalities that she couldn't follow. After a bit she realised John was finding it hard to keep going. "I think it's time you took your next painkillers" she said. He took them obediently like a little child, and even thanked Colin for coming to see him.

Downstairs Colin and Monica talked for some time. She had persuaded him to stay for a meal, and they chatted while she cooked. When the meal was ready, she asked him to go up and ask his Dad whether he wanted to come down or should they take a tray up to him. "I'll come down" he said, and he struggled downstairs. He didn't eat very much and was very quiet. After a bit he said he thought it best for him to go through the Sitting Room. Once he'd gone, Colin asked his Mum how she would cope when he couldn't get up and downstairs anymore. 'Will they take him back to the Hospital," he said. "Or into a Hospice?" He was told that she wanted to look after him at home, and the Hospital had said that they could bring in a special bed and send in nurses if that's what she wanted. Colin needed convincing that this was the best thing to do. "Do you really think you can manage that? It will surely get more and more difficult. And he can't be an easy patient." Monica laughed, "Well I'm still fit and strong, and I know John would prefer to be at home, so that's what I'm aiming for." Colin went in to see John again before he left. He had the TV on, but appeared to be asleep, so he slipped away without saying goodbye.

John hated being ill and in pain. He just wasn't used to it, and some weeks later as the pain got worse, the idea that there was nothing he could do to put things right became more and more difficult for him. He tried to tell his wife what to do, but then much to Monica's surprise, he held on to her one day and started weeping uncontrollably. She had never experienced anything like this. Paddy had kept up with his Irish jokes almost to the last. John seemed to have descended into darkness. "You know I'm praying for you," she said, and was surprised that as he continued to cry, he thanked her. He had never been much into church. He had come for special occasions of course, like Christmas and the children's First Communions. He had said to her a number of times, "You do the praying and I'll do the practical side." And anyway, he often went off to visit his precious railway on a Sunday. Steam trains were his religion! But now, as the weeping subsided, he said how sorry he was he hadn't come with her to church more often. "Can God forgive me?" he cried. "Oh yes" said Monica "God is love and he forgives us all the time." "Well, I wish I could be convinced this was true, given the way I've ignored him all these years." Her attempts to reassure him on this were not very successful, so finally she said gently, "Would it help if our Priest came round to see you?" "But I'm not a Catholic," he said "Why would he do that?" She said she thought he would, and later on she phoned Father Jake and told him what was happening. He was concerned to hear how ill her husband was and that he only had months to live. Once he knew that, his response was immediate, "I'll come round tomorrow after Mass. About 10.30? OK?" "I did explain that he isn't a Catholic Father, didn't I? "Yes. Don't worry about that. Anyone can be prayed for, and then we'll see what he wants to do." Monica wondered what that meant, but didn't feel she wanted to take up too much of his time by asking, so she simply accepted his offer. "God bless you Monica," he said as they finished their conversation. She went up to tell John, but he was asleep again and she didn't want to wake him, but later when he woke up she was again amazed at the way he accepted it. "That's very kind of him," he said. "What did you say his name was?" She explained that his real name was Jacob, but that everyone called him Father Jake and that she thought John would like him. "He's very ordinary and down to earth," she said. "Not like some of the old priests. But he's very prayerful. He says Mass with such reverence, not gabbling it off like Father Dooley used to, more like Father Bill. I think you'll like him,"

Chapter 20: Father Jake

Father Jake put down the phone and pictured Monica in his mind. It was the way he always prayed for people, there and then, straightaway, just in case he forgot them in his prayers the next morning. Although since she had told him her husband John only had a few months to live, he was unlikely to forget this prayer. He had been at Holy Trinity long enough to know the names of all those who came to Mass regularly, but he was pretty certain that he had never really had a long conversation with Monica Bransted. When he first arrived, he made a genuine effort to learn everyone's names by greeting them at the door on Sundays. This allowed him to greet her and many others by name after Mass. That, however, had been the limit of their contact, and so he knew little about her and had no idea whether she had any family close by. Monica had told him her address, and he knew that was no more than a 10-minute walk, especially if you cut through and avoided the main roads, though he might take the car if he had to go on somewhere else after seeing them.

He loved his work as a priest. The regular times of prayer every day, including the Daily Mass, meant such a lot to him. There were always a dozen or more regulars at the weekday Masses, so he had got to know them pretty well. However, Sunday was a much more strenuous time with two Masses in the morning and another in the evening and more people to greet than it was possible to give much time to. That was the frustrating part, and so when he had the chance to visit someone at home, he was always glad to do it. This was where you could get to know people better and really listen as they shared their lives, their thoughts, hopes and regrets. People asked him why he was so good at it, and he always used to laugh and say, "Because I'm nosey! I just love finding out things about people." Indeed, occasionally, his questioning had taken him too far into people's lives than they were comfortable with, and he had had to back track. Mostly however, they just appreciated a priest who was genuinely interested in listening to them, rather than simply preaching at them. And so Father Jake knew he was popular, and he hoped God wouldn't hold that against him.

When he arrived at the house the following morning at about 10.30am, Monica ushered him into the Sitting Room where Mr Bransted was sitting in an armchair. "John," Monica said. "This is Father Jake. I'll leave you two by yourselves to have a chat. Would you like a cup of tea or coffee Father?"

Jake said, "Coffee please," and sat down in the other armchair in the room. "So Monica tells me you've got Pancreatic Cancer. Are you in much pain?" asked Father Jake.

John liked the fact that he got straight to the point, and he explained that it wasn't always easy, but the pain relief they had been giving him usually helped, though it left him very sleepy.

"And you wanted to have a chat with me?"

Now John was a bit embarrassed. He explained that he rarely went with Monica to Mass – which Father Jake knew, although he didn't make that knowledge obvious. "So I don't quite know why I want to talk to you, Father. I've tried to live a good Christian life, to be a good husband and a fairly good father – well, stepfather actually – but when you're faced with death fairly soon, you begin to feel the need for something more." He was relieved that the priest didn't go straight into some religious stuff but simply asked him about the family. John found this fairly easy going. He could talk about his daughter in Australia and her children, and about Colin, and he was able to explain that his relationship with Colin wasn't very good. "But since I've been ill, Father, he has been to see me, and we got on reasonably well. I think I was a bit gruff with him, but he still said he'll come next week. I'm so glad we are talking to each other again. There was a long time when even if I saw him we never spoke, and since he left his wife a few years ago, we haven't seen him at all, even though he doesn't live far away. We see Rita and the children, of course, over in Coleshill, but until I became ill, we hadn't seen him for years." Monica could have told Father Jake that this wasn't quite true, but she wasn't in the room, and John didn't know that she and Colin had been in touch for more than just a few weeks.

Father Jake was used to hearing about family breakdowns like this. There were more of them than most people realised, and he was able to sympathise, which put John even more at ease. Soon, John was telling him how well he and his son had got on when Colin was a boy. "He used to love our regular trips to the Severn Valley Railway, and we had great times together. In fact, that's what we've been talking about a lot when he visits. It's great to know he still goes there sometimes, and he's recently taken my granddaughter." Father Jake's reply astonished and pleased him. He had found a priest who was a fellow Steam train enthusiast, and they were soon talking away, sharing each other's experiences, when Monica came in with the coffee. "We're talking Steam Trains," John said, beaming at her.

Jake grinned, "I'm afraid it's one of the obsessions I don't usually share during Mass Monica. I've found a fellow fanatic."

Monica laughed. "I can see you're getting on fine, so I'll leave you to it." She was pleased but a little surprised at how well the two of them were hitting it off, and she might have been even more surprised if she had stayed in the room because John was asking this priest how he knew so much about the construction of these engines.

Father Jake explained that he had actually studied engineering at university, and only after that did he decide to become a priest. "I worked for a couple of years in engineering, but then I began to think more and more about being a priest."

"How long did you have to study after that?" asked John.

"Oh, another six years," was the answer, which left John almost speechless.

It was soon after this that Father Jake began to steer the conversation back to the reason John had asked to see him. He soon discovered John's fear that God couldn't love him because he'd never really bothered about him. "I'm not even sure I believe in him, Father. Maybe in a sort of vague way, but I've never had the kind of faith that Monica has."

"Everyone's faith is different," Father Jake replied. "There isn't a standard way of believing, even if some have tried to pretend there is. And even if there have been times, many times, when you didn't really believe in God at all, God was still with you."

"But don't you Catholics believe that unless you're a Catholic, you're heading for Hell?"

Father Jake replied very carefully, "Well, some Catholics have interpreted things that way, because we say that there is no salvation outside the Church. But nowadays, we would be much more careful about saying who is in the Church and who is not. Being a Catholic certainly helps people get closer to God. We call it being assured of salvation, provided they take it seriously. But remember, there have been a lot of so-called Catholics who have done some pretty awful things, so just being a paid-up member who goes to Mass doesn't necessarily guarantee you anything."

"Ah yes" said John. "All those priests!"

"And some Bishops," said Father Jake. "If you have ever been to a Medieval church with a Doom Painting, you will have seen Bishops heading for hell."

John liked this priest who called a spade a spade. He had no time for people who pretended to be religious. His Monica had never been like that. She went to Mass without any fuss, and she had been a good wife and mother. It was because of her that he was now prepared to talk to Father Jake. “So you reckon I’m Ok with God, do you, Father?”

“Ah well,” said Father Jake, “That’s between you and God. I can help you by talking about things and praying with you. I can also tell you that I think you’d be even closer to God if you became a Catholic, but none of us can be guaranteed a place in heaven. As Jesus once said, ‘No-one is good but God alone.’”

John looked sad, “But there’s no time, is there? Monica and I once talked about this, and she explained to me that becoming a Catholic takes a good six months of learning all about it, but I haven’t got six months.”

“Monica is right,” Father Jake replied. “But when someone is dying, then all the rules are put aside. If you want to be a Catholic, I can do it almost immediately.”

Now John was really startled. “What! Just like that, without you checking up on what I believe and what I’m like?”

“When people are dying,” said the priest, “All that matters is that they want to be close to God.”

They talked on for some time like this. Father Jake didn’t want to rush things too much. He had discovered that John had at least a few weeks or months, and he sensed that John didn’t want it too easy, that whilst he had his wits about him, he wanted to talk things through and learn a bit more. He was happy to be told that rather than tire him out, Father Jake would come back in a few days' time, and then they could talk through it in a bit more detail. He was a bit taken aback, though pleased when the priest said he would say some prayers before he left. After a few short prayers, Father Jake began to say the Our Father and John joined in, and as they got near the end, the priest guessed he would finish the prayer the way non-Catholics did, and so quietly joined in with him as he said "For thine is the kingdom, the power and the glory, for ever and ever. Amen."

Monica had stood in the doorway and joined in, too, and was now able to have a brief chat with him at the front door as she saw him out. "I'll come back on Thursday morning at about the same time, Monica. He says he wants to ask me a few more questions before becoming a Catholic, but I didn't want to tire him out too much now." Monica looked puzzled. "When someone is dying," Father Jake said gently, "We just receive them without the normal preparation."

"Oh I see, of course, I should have known," she said, tears coming into her eyes, "Thank you so much, Father. I can't tell you how much this means to me."

"Of course," he said. "Bye now." And he drove off home pleased that he had had such a positive response from both of them, and in a bit of a hurry as someone else was due to see him back home at Midday.

Later, John told her how much he liked Father Jake. "You never told me he was a qualified engineer."

"Is he?" she said. "Well, I never knew that, but I did come home from Mass once and tell you how he'd preached about finding God in some of the great bridges of the world." John hadn't remembered that. He'd probably been told it over Sunday lunch when he was too busy thinking about the latest project he had got going in his shed or his greenhouse. What happened in Monica's church hadn't really interested him at the time.

"Bit strange to think of finding God in a bridge," he said. "But I think I could find God in a Steam Engine."

"Well I'm not surprised at all by that," she said, laughing. "I always said that railway was your religion."

“Pity more priests aren’t as down to earth as he is,” he said. “Then maybe more people would go to Mass.”

“But we don’t go to Mass for the priest,” said Monica. “We go for God. There are lots of good, lively, caring priests like Father Jake and Father Bill, but there are also others who, though not bad, are just remote and boring. But they are there to say Mass for us, and so we appreciate that and ignore the fact that some of them are less good than we might like.”

John was astonished at his wife’s eloquence on this matter. He didn’t think he would be able to tolerate a lazy or boring priest. He had always expected high standards from all those he worked with at the Council, and those who worked under him knew that he wouldn’t take slackness and low standards from any of them. It was precisely why he had ended up in charge of them all. “Good thing Father Jake’s one of the good ones, isn’t it?” he said, pleased that he would see him again soon.

Chapter 21: Mulling it Over

By the time Walter and Penny visited Angela again, Colin had been to see his stepfather many times and watched him getting weaker. He had been rather pleased at the way he had dealt with his stepfather's aggression on that first visit, and how, since then, they had been able to talk to one another in a reasonably civilised way, mostly about the Railway. Looking back on it, he realised that the reason why he'd managed it so well was down to two people - Angela and his newfound cousin Marianne.

He was pleased, however, that he had other things to talk about with Walter. First, there was a necessary view of the new garden and a discussion about which plants to put in, and then there was their already planned Railway trip. This time, it was to be to the Great Central Railway, for Walter had been surprised that when Colin was at University in Loughborough, he had never visited this Railway. Colin had to admit it was odd, and had suggested that his mind was so fixed on the Severn Valley Railway that he failed to notice another Steam Railway right under his nose. It was another happy trip, but it gave Colin a chance to talk with Walter about some of what he had recently been experiencing. He had got home from his visit to Marianne, and her family was quite elated by what he had experienced. Suddenly, he had an enormous array of Irish relations, and it made him think of himself in a new way, especially since they were all so delighted to see him and make him one of their own. He was particularly moved to see that photo of his father in such a prominent place in the house and to hear them point out how much they resembled each other. He had to take notes to keep up with the numerous family members they mentioned and went home buzzing with all the new information.

It was as he shared this with Walter as they drove to Loughborough that he suddenly realised that this, too, was helping him with his hang-ups about the man he'd called "Dad" for so many years. Now that he had met his real Dad, even if only through photos and family memories, the "Dad" he had struggled with no longer mattered as much as he once did. Walter was glad to hear that his advice had worked, and that some kind of a relationship had been re-established. Of course, he still wondered if this was the man who had abused Colin, for it was clear that he had certainly abused him psychologically, if not sexually. "I'm so glad that this is happening to you, Colin, jettisoning all that past baggage and all that resentment and anger; it must be such a relief for you." Colin had to admit it was, and that Walter's advice to think about his stepfather as a bossy old man who you might deal with as you might deal with a difficult customer, had worked out well.

He knew now that the main reason he had managed it was because he'd had to deal with quite a few difficult customers, especially men who thought they knew more about computers than he did. He'd learnt early on not to get angry with them because that just drove them away, which was hardly a good way to run a business. So he knew he could control his anger and divert their aggressive behaviour if he wanted to, and that was how he'd begun to cope with his stepfather. He explained to Walter that this had been a life-changing moment for him. Then they'd had a great day on the Grand Central with lots of railway talk, but it was the talk in the car going there that had helped him most.

Meanwhile, his first visit to Rita's for lunch after he had been to visit Marianne had gone brilliantly. He had found telling them all about their new family quite exhilarating. Peter was thrilled to discover that they supported the Villa just as he did, and even began to ask questions about all these relations who had such good taste in their Football Team. Maria was very impressed that Colin was able to bring out his phone and show them the photos and tell them the names of all these new relations. Rita saw how moved Colin was when he showed them the picture of the two brothers, one of whom was his Dad, the children's real grandfather. They all noticed, even Peter, how alike they were. Back home that night, Colin felt really happy that all this had happened, that somehow it was not he alone who had found his family but that it was for all of them. He had also phoned Angela after he had got back from that visit to tell her how interested the children had been – he almost treated her like a second mum now, and she was so pleased for him.

At work, Colin had taken that photo of the two brothers, enlarged it, and put it on his office wall, and since it was an open office, he then had to explain to all his colleagues who the two men were and why the photo was so special for him. All these things brought everything together in a new way, like a jigsaw puzzle where one struggled to work out where certain pieces fitted, and then suddenly found that they all fitted together, and the picture was complete.

Yet Colin still found it a hard battle. He knew only too well how easily his anger against his stepfather boiled up every time he prepared to visit him. He faced a struggle with himself each time. He often felt physically sick as his anxiety rocketed. Why should he bother? Let him die. But at the same time, bolstered by his new family, he remembered Walter's advice. The pain is all in the past. Forget it and move on. His love for his mum helped, because he had no difficulty in spending time chatting to her as he arranged the next visit. But as that visit came nearer, he had to remind himself again and again of Walter's, *"Forget it. Move on."* Yes, the night before the visit was often a bad one, as he rehearsed in his mind all the cruel things he would like to say to him, all the accusations he would like to fling at him, but he'd realised that it was all pointless, for it just brought up to the surface an anger and bitterness that had never made him happy. He would rehearse Walter's advice *"Treat him like a difficult customer,"* and thinking this usually brought him a kind of peace that finally lulled him into sleep. Of course, that didn't mean that it was easy the next morning. The angry thoughts would keep popping into his head, making him feel bad again. He would struggle to cope with them, but then he would think of his real Irish dad and his real live Uncle and his cousins, and he would get out his phone and look at the two of them in that photo; and he would find himself talking to them. At work, too, he was able to look at their photo on the office wall, and supported by their presence, he was able to arrive at the house after work and be calm and kind to the man who, in the past, had driven him almost demented.

Driving home after these visits, he often wondered how he was managing this man who had been such a bully and made him so angry in the past? He knew the anger was still there, creeping around and within him, ready to swallow him up again. He knew that part of him was glad that this man was dying, that soon his mother would be free of him and his control over her. He found himself remembering the many times when he had seen his mother quietly submitting to this man's overbearing tactics. He could not remember any time when she had stood up to him, either on her behalf or to defend him. She had often sympathised with him in private after that big bust-up, but she had always admitted that she couldn't criticise him to his face the way Colin wanted her to. Now he thought he understood her, now he knew that he had always loved his gentle mum, and that his anger had been all for that man, the man he still called Dad; yet he realised that as a teenager he had been angry with her as well, and he felt guilty that he had cut himself off from her. Anyway, now he had begun to understand rather better how difficult it had been for her, and that made him even angrier with John. But somehow, he managed not to show the anger he still felt for his stepfather when he visited them and was actually rather pleased at his self-control.

It was another long talk with Walter in the garden that took them both a step further. Angela had told them that she had no idea what plants she wanted for her new garden that Autumn, so provided they didn't give her too much work, they must work it out between themselves. The new Patio looked great. On the left, it opened onto a path and a strip of lawn, but alongside the house and off to the right, Colin had created a new bed. It then curved round and along the right-hand side of the patio with two breaks to walk through into the rest of the garden, joining the path from the back door. The bed then continued round and across the far side of the patio till it met the lawn. There was, therefore, a great deal to fill with plants, as well as a sort of oval bed in the middle. Angela had been dubious about that, as she thought it might block her view, but she had been told firmly that breaking the view so you couldn't see everything at once would be more effective. It encouraged you to walk around to see what was there.

Walter and Colin, using a plan on Colin's Laptop, mapped out the plants they wanted to buy and where they would be placed, but then, on a mild Autumn day, they had plenty of time to walk around the rest of the garden and chat. Colin shared about the battle he had to face every time he saw his stepfather and how much Walter's advice helped. "I just keep remembering that you told me to treat him like an awkward customer, and it actually works, even if I still get angry about him at other times. Mind you, I think partly that I am just getting angry with myself for letting him off so lightly rather than giving him a good talking to."

"Hmm," said Walter, "I can imagine. But it wouldn't do any good, would it? It would probably just make your mum unhappy, whilst your stepfather sounds too ill to do much more than wither under your attack."

"Yes, he would certainly wither if I went for him," sighed Colin. "But part of me really wants to make him wither, and yet I don't. It's very confusing. Half of me is proud I keep my cool, and the other half is angry that I do!" Walter laughed. "We're funny creatures, us humans. Such a muddle of different thoughts and feelings. That's why so many people find prayer difficult."

"Prayer," said Colin. "What's that got to do with it?"

"Lots," replied Walter. "Most people who pray complain that they can't concentrate, that they get distracted by lots of thoughts swirling around inside their heads. I used to find that really difficult, until Father Bill explained that sharing all your muddled thoughts with God was probably a better way of praying than prayer using thoughts that are composed and proper." He paused, aware that he had always avoided mentioning Father Bill until now. He wondered in the pause whether Colin had noticed the name, realising that now he would have to be less than truthful with Colin.

Colin had noticed and looked straight at Walter saying, "Father Bill? Do you mean my Father Bill? How do you know him?"

"Ah! Yes, it is your Father Bill," said Walter. "Once I found out where you lived until you went to uni, I realised that the Father Bill I knew in Oxford was once the priest at your local church, and I realised that you would have known him."

"Known him…" said Colin. "We were really close friends. He helped me so much when I stopped speaking to my father. He became like a second father to me whilst I was in the 6th Form. But then I lost contact and then…."

There was a long silence. Colin sat down suddenly on one of the Garden seats on the Patio and looked down at the ground. Walter sat down too waiting, until Colin said, "So you know what happened to him?"

Walter replied with great care, "Well, I know that he was accused of sexual abuse and went to prison. In fact, I have visited him there. I know he pleaded guilty, even though he told me he had never actually done anything." There was another long silence. Colin kept trying to start saying something, and then kept stopping. He continued to keep his head down. Eventually, Walter attempted to help him. "Let go Colin. You might as well tell me your side of the story."

Colin sighed. “I feel guilty about him..... guilty that I dropped him when I went to uni. That I never kept in touch... guilty that I...”. Again he stopped. “I’m sorry Walter. I don’t think I can talk about this anymore. It’s... it’s... I let him down. I failed to be his friend. Remember how upset I was when we had to sing his favourite hymn when I came to Mass with you? Oh I can’t tell you why. I think that if I did, I might lose you as a friend just as I lost him.”

Walter felt he could go one step further. “Actually Colin, I think I know what you are still struggling to tell me. It’s quite a coincidence, isn’t it? You see, I found out some time ago that it was you who made that accusation, but I didn’t say anything because I didn’t think it was right for me to bring it up, unless you wanted to. But I think now is the time. You see, as I’ve got to know you better, to know you as a kind and caring person who doesn’t normally make false accusations, I have had to revise my view about you as the accuser. Now I guess.... but of course, I may be wrong ... that in the midst of your nervous breakdown.... when your mind was confused... perhaps encouraged by a counsellor searching too hard for answers, you thought he had abused you?”

Colin gave a great sigh. “I’m so glad you know Walter. I kept wanting to tell you. It never went to a full trial, you know. He pleaded guilty and it made me even more convinced that I was right. That it did happen. Only months later, as I got calmer and looked back, I began to realise that in my confusion, I’d muddled up what actually happened with what happened in my mind. But then it was too late. What could I do?”

At last, Walter had got there. All his work over many months had paid off, and he could say, “Now this is out in the open, I think we need to talk it through further, and one of the things I want to do is explain why Father Bill does think he is guilty, because I think that may make you feel a lot better about it. But not now. There isn’t time, and it needs to be private. Penny and Angela may appear at any minute.

Could I come round to your place this evening, so that we can talk it through?"

Colin was a little reluctant, but Walter was persistent, and so eventually, he said yes.

Chapter 22: Father Bill

"First, I need to explain to you, Colin, how I got to know Father Bill?" Thus, Walter started his story. "You see, when I married Penny, I wasn't a Catholic. In fact, I wasn't a Christian of any kind. But I loved her, and she wanted a Catholic marriage and wanted the children brought up in the faith, so I went along with all that, and then went along to Mass with her every Sunday to support her and the children. My God, I endured some awful Homilies! Priests droning on about how we should be good and kind if we wanted God to love us, and sickly sweet stuff about Mary and "Flowers of the fairest", and the like. Then Father Bill arrived, the Father Bill I now know to be your Father Bill. He was like a breath of fresh air, and I found myself listening to the interesting things he said about God, and the nature of prayer, and lots more. He was so interesting, in fact, that I would often ask him questions at the door, which delighted him but infuriated our children, who wanted to get home as quickly as possible. So one day, he said, 'Look Walter, why don't you come round some time and we can talk through all this,' and so that's what I did.

"Well, talking to Father Bill was an eye-opener, I can tell you. I remember how he asked me what I thought God was like, and when I said I didn't think I believed in God, he asked me what kind of God I didn't believe in. I fell for his trap because I started going on about God up there somewhere, and after a bit, he stopped me and said, 'Well I don't believe in that kind of God either.' I remember how much I argued with him, telling him he must do, or why he celebrated the Ascension with all that talk of Jesus going up to God in heaven and the like. His answers to this and to all my other rather ignorant challenges really brought me up short. I had mistaken the imagery for the reality. As he said, and I remember this example well, 'If I told you my heart was broken, you wouldn't take me literally and send for an ambulance, would you?' After a few meetings like that, it wasn't long before I asked him if I could become a Catholic, and we began to meet every week and talk through every aspect of the Catholic faith. And of course, in the process, I got to know him very well indeed. Eventually, I became a Catholic, and by now, he had become not just my friend but a friend of our whole family, often coming round for meals and family celebrations and the like.

"I tell you all this, Colin, because when he was accused of abuse, I was one of the first he turned to for support. I was the one with whom he shared his decision to plead guilty. I was astonished at first, even angry that this good priest, my good friend, had done such an awful thing. And then he said something that seemed very strange to me. He said, "I didn't do what I am accused of, Walter. You must believe me. But I think if I faced a trial, they would find me guilty anyway, so what's the point. Nor do I think it fair to put my accuser through it. So I am pleading guilty to save him and me from a lot of pain." I argued with him then, telling him that if this man was accusing him unjustly, then he should stand up to him and declare his innocence. "Yes", he said. "That's just what my lawyer said." And then he told me that although he wasn't guilty, he didn't consider himself innocent either. I remember now how confused I was. To my mind, either he was one or the other, and I said so, but he shook his head and said that maybe one day, if he felt it right, he would try to explain it to me in more detail."

Now came Walter's lie. He took a deep breath and continued. "So you see, Colin, it was only after I met you that I then pushed him to give me that fuller explanation that he had promised." It wasn't all a lie. Father Bill hadn't told him all before he met Colin, which is why the more he got to know Colin, the more difficult he found it to think of him as making false accusations, and the more confused he became trying to work out why Father Bill had insisted that he was guilty. And it was true that only then had he asked for the full explanation. He breathed a quiet sigh of relief at getting through that necessary deceit. Now, he could continue.

"So Colin, he told me that you were a teenager who he had got to know first helping him at Mass. He explained what a great altar boy you were, and how he'd got to know you better and better, as you always arrived first in the church, and how you and he would talk, and how he then discovered you had troubles with your father at home, and how one day he'd offered to take you out for a trip on his boat; and how one trip had led to another because you both enjoyed it so much, and you soon knew more about his engine than he did. At first, as you know, these were day trips. All went well. But you probably know Colin that he became very fond of you. He loved being with you, and eventually he suggested that you and he might go on a boat trip together – a week's holiday after Easter on the canals. I remember him saying what a great mistake that had been. It was before all the publicity over priests abusing children and young people, so he quite innocently put himself into a totally compromised position. There you were, the two of you, on the boat together, sharing a cabin for a whole week. He told me how good-looking you were…".

Colin started to protest, but Walter stopped him. "No Colin, I have to tell you truthfully how he thought about you. You were a good-looking young man of 16, and he found it impossible not just to like you as a person, but to admire your body as well. It was only at this point that he admitted to me that although he had always lived as a celibate and not had sex with anybody, his sexual desires had always focussed on men, not women. Now, there you were, happily undressing before him in that little cabin you shared. He also admitted that he had lied to me when he had told me earlier that he had avoided looking at you, for that was not true. He hoped you hadn't noticed. He then explained about the time that you probably remember, the time when you fell into the canal. I'm sure you remember that?" Colin nodded. "Of course, he wasn't worried about you drowning, because he knew you were a good swimmer, but you came out of the water shivering with cold, and he made you undress, and then he got a towel and rubbed you down."

"I know what happened then," said Colin. "I got aroused by what he was doing to me, and he suddenly gave me the towel and said finish off. Then he left me in the cabin and went up on deck, and I did 'finish off.'" He paused. "After that, I wanted him to do it again. I used to tempt him by deliberately stripping off in front of him. I caught him looking sometimes, but usually, he looked elsewhere. I made it worse for myself by always asking him if we could go on the boat again, and he always gave way, and I hoped something would happen. Then I went off to uni, convinced I was gay, and had some very bad experiences where I was abused, although being over 18, it didn't count. And I blamed him for it all."

"Ah yes, that makes sense," said Walter. "Actually, it was also hard for him. He was already in love with you, and now he found himself unable to resist thinking of you sexually. Indeed, he told me that although you never had any kind of sexual contact with one another, he certainly abused you in his mind. He used to long for those moments when he could see you naked, and his fantasies were full of what he would like the two of you to do together. I'm sure you know what I mean?" Colin nodded, and Walter went on.

"So you see now why he couldn't say he was innocent, even though he wasn't exactly guilty? He felt he would be lying. He applied to himself the teaching of Jesus that if a man looks at a woman lustfully, he has already committed adultery with her in his heart; and that it must be the same for two men. He also knew that if it had come to a full trial, there was no way he could deny that incident with the towel on the boat, and no way to prove he was innocent. He knew too that the prosecution would have been bound to ask if he'd had sexual feelings for you, and he wouldn't have been able to lie about that either. And then how would anyone believe that he didn't actually do anything? As he said to me once, 'Nowadays, the idea of controlling your sexual desires, of living a celibate life despite your desires, is viewed with hilarious laughter or utter unbelief. Indeed, most people think that it is actually unhealthy to live like that!' Of course, his lawyer had tried to persuade him, as I did, to plead not guilty, but he wouldn't be persuaded, partly, as I said earlier, because he just didn't want to put you through all that trauma. You see, he still loved you, or at least he was still fond of you, and he wanted to spare you any extra pain. He told me to read "Death in Venice," and then I might understand."

Colin sighed, "I suppose I knew what he felt about me, and like the idiot I was, I became more blatant. Oh, I don't know what I wanted. I suppose I wanted to be loved by someone like him, and part of me thought that might include sex. And then there were fantasies. Then there was the bad sex I had with men at uni, which left me very confused; and then along came Rita, and I discovered how heterosexual I could be and how much more comfortable I felt with a woman than with a man. That was great for many years, but then, when my relationship went wrong with her, I fell into confusion and depression, and the counsellor who was given to help me pushed to one side my feelings of guilt about my anger towards Rita and the kids. Instead, she spent a lot of time probing into my sexual hang-ups. I remember how she explained that there might well be some sexual incident hidden in my past, and that this was what had made me angry. Eventually I said, 'If that bloody priest hadn't given me an erection, I might not be so mixed up.' And once I had told her, she insisted I must tell the police, and on it went from there in a way that I couldn't stop."

Colin had said all this, looking down at the floor, but suddenly, he turned and said, "But what can I do now Walter? How can I put things right? Should I go to the police?"

Walter had worked out the answer to this some time ago. "Father Bill wouldn't want you to do that," he said. "He wouldn't want you to be put through more trauma because you would be accused of perjury, of wasting police time. But maybe what he would like is for you to contact him, perhaps write to him, or even talk to him, to clear the air. But that's my idea, not his, and I'm not really sure what he would think, so I think the next thing to do is for me to arrange another visit to him in prison and I'll tell him what has happened and ask him what he would like you to do. That's probably the best way forward, don't you think?"

Colin nodded, "Sex is such a strange thing, isn't it? At least for us men. So many muddled and confused desires all pent up within us. Rita kept me straight. She gave me a way to focus my lust on her, and I loved it, but even then, there were times when the lust in my mind strayed, even if I remained actually faithful."

"Ah," said Walter, "Father Bill tells me that this is one of the things that really troubles men who are trying to be faithful Catholics. We know that we should be faithful, but our sexual desires are often too much for us, especially when we see sexual scenes on the TV or on the internet. He said that some men cope by not mentioning it at all, even in the Confessional, whilst others end up mentioning it again and again. He said that he tells such men that the more they worry about it, the worse it can become. He told me what he tells them, just to mention impure thoughts and actions and then move on to more important things, like anger and greed and selfishness that so often hurt the people we live with and work with."

"I did make my Confession to him a few times," Colin admitted. "But I never dared to mention sex. It was always about my dad, and how I hated him, and how I let down my mum and had rows with my sister, and things like that."

"Probably much more important," said Walter "Though I think it's a pity more young men don't face up to their sexual desires, rather than either repressing them or over-using them. Easy access to pornography on the internet doesn't help because it is actually manufactured sex rather than something real. But most people don't realise this. It's not helped by this modern obsession that your sexual desires define who you are. I remember one Sixth-Former who shared with me how confused he was about his sexuality. Was he gay or straight? I listened and sympathised, and then one day, he came and said it was ok now, as he had sorted it all out. I'm afraid I told him he was probably kidding himself, that male sexuality is never really sorted out. I didn't tell him this, but I've known gay men who, at 40, discover they can be straight, who suddenly find a woman, marry her and settle down to a heterosexual life, whilst others, having lived a straight life, suddenly find their desires leading them in a different direction. One man I know got so confused and guilty about leaving his wife and children for a male lover that, eventually he committed suicide! Father Bill says the Church is to be blamed for much of the guilt that people get landed with. I remember him saying to me, 'Too many Pelagians, Walter, preaching that unless you are good, God won't love you, whereas Jesus teaches us, and so does the Church officially, that God loves us whatever we are like; and it is because he loves us that we try to be good. But we also know that he will still love us even when we fail.'"

"Oh I like that", said Colin. "But do you think Father Bill will be able to forgive me after I failed him so badly?"

"Oh yes, I am sure he will, not least because he thinks it was to a large extent his fault. You will remember what a lovely man he is, and even in prison, he tells me he has been able to use the time positively. He tells me that the atmosphere is not pleasant, but he has a lot of time to himself, to say his prayers and to read. He told me how little time he'd found to read when he was running a parish. I think what he dreads is what he will do when he is released, because the Church will never allow him to practise as a priest, and that was his life."

"No, no. I can't allow that. It's all my fault. I must tell the police."

Walter sighed. "That wouldn't do any good, Colin. The Church would never reinstate him now, even if you declared him innocent. They have to be so strict nowadays. And also, it would be the last thing

Father Bill would want you to do. I can hear him saying that very firmly indeed. He would not want you to ruin your life for him…."

There was a long silence, and then Walter continued. "What would help him would be to know how well you are doing, how successful you have been. That would make him happy."

"Successful! In my work, yes; but look at the mess I've made of my marriage."

"No no. Father Bill would be pleased to know that you are trying to do something about that now, pleased that you have always supported them financially, pleased that you are now trying to get to know your children again. He has seen many failed marriages where the wife was left nearly penniless, as the man went off with another woman, and the children no longer ever saw their father. He would be glad you are not like that."

Chapter 23: The New Man

Monica was very pleased when Father Jake came around two days later. John had got worse and was in pain, but the drugs they were giving him helped, though they made him sleepy. She was surprised at the energy he showed in getting himself up and dressed to see the priest, but knew it wouldn't last. He told her to get him his Christening Certificate that he'd looked out from amongst all his carefully filed documents, and she did. Then, when Father Jake arrived, she explained how much worse he was. "Mm," he said "I don't think we better wait." Monica was startled but somehow relieved that her John was going to get the kind of help that meant so much to her. "He's found his Christening Certificate to show you. He seems very determined, which I suppose is a good thing, isn't it?"

"Yes, it is," he said as she took him into the sitting room and left him there.

"Right, John," said Father Jake. "Monica tells me you have found your Baptism Certificate. May I take a look at it?"

"We always called it a Christening. Is it the same thing?"

"Probably." He took a quick look at it and saw that John had indeed been through a proper Church of England Baptism, so there was no need for him to be baptised again.

"Let me explain what we are going to do, John. First of all, you are going to share with me anything that you regret doing, anything that weighs on your conscience."

John wasn't fooled. "You mean you want me to make my Confession? Good. I definitely want to do that. Then what?"

"Well, I will then briefly take you through the meaning of the statement of belief that you are going to make, and provided you are happy with that, then you will make it, and then I will make you a member of the Church."

"Is that all?" asked John. "Aren't you going to pray over me?"

"Oh yes. I will already have said some prayers for you as you are received into the Church and anointed you; then I will say special prayers for you as you face your illness, at which point I will anoint you again with oil on your forehead and this time on the palms of your hands, and then I will give you Communion."

"How can you do that? Without a Mass."

"I have brought a Host from Church, that's a piece of the consecrated Bread from Mass. You probably know that we call this bread the Body of Christ because we believe that Jesus is present in a special way within it. Is that all OK?"

"That's great. The full works eh!"

"There's just one more thing. After you've made your Confession, which is private of course, it would be nice if we could then invite Monica in to join us and pray with us. Is that OK too?"

"Nothing better. It's her faith and love that has brought me to this, so she ought to be here with me for the main event!"

John's Confession included a lot about how he had treated Colin. Some of what he said was a kind of self-justification, and Father Jake gently explained that it was best to say where he thought he had gone wrong rather than trying to explain why. John found himself in tears as he shared how he felt he had failed his stepson. "I was always fair but firm with him, Father, and it all worked well to start with. He was a good lad, and he was polite and did what he was told, and we did things together and had a good time, but then it all went wrong, and the firmer I was, the more defiant and angry he became. Then, he refused to speak to me unless he had to. It was awful. If I raged at him, or if I tried to reason with him, he just walked out of the room. If I followed him, he would just walk out of the house. Once I tried to chase him down the street, but Monica followed me out and stopped me. She told me not to make an exhibition of myself. I went back in, but then I shouted at her. I shouted at her a lot, and then I used to go off to do things in my shed. Perhaps I was too hard on her Father? She took it all, and was always a good wife. She knew how I wanted things done, and she was very good at keeping up to the standards I expected of her. But she refused to do anything about Colin. It was the only time she defied me, and I finally gave up trying to persuade her. I wasn't very helpful about Church either. I would moan about the way she went off to Mass, and sometimes I tried to persuade her to do something else on a Sunday; but then she just went off on the Saturday evening instead, so that she could come with me on the Sunday wherever I wanted us to go. I think I have been very selfish Father, and it is only in the last few weeks, as I have seen her looking after me, that I've realised how much I've taken her for granted. And I used to mock her when she said she was praying about something. I used to say, 'What good would that do?' Now that I am in pain, I feel supported by the fact that she is praying, and in my own way, I've been praying too. My prayers are very selfish, so I suppose that's wrong really, isn't it? But I just need help, and apart from her, only God can help me." There was a pause. "Is that OK? Is there something else I should say?"

Father Jake reassured him, but then asked him about his relationship with his son now. Were things any better? John was able to tell him how Colin had come to see him and chatted to him in a friendly way in the last few weeks. "He seems a different person, Father. It was amazing."

"And did you tell him you were sorry about the past?"

"I never thought of doing that. I'm not sure what I would say. Do you think I should?"

"Well, it would probably make you feel better. That's clearly the big thing on your mind, isn't it?"

"Yes. You're right, but how to say things right? He was wrong too, but I would hate to make him angry with me again."

"Well, there's no point trying to justify what happened back then, or to work out who was in the right and who was in the wrong. All you can do is say sorry for your part in it all. Perhaps you could write out what you want to say and just give it to him to read. That often works."

John pondered on this for a few moments, and Father Jake just sat beside him, watching his mind work. Finally, he said almost reluctantly, "Yes. I suppose I could do that. I suppose it would be a lot easier for him as well as for me." And then, as he became more confident, he said, "Right, that's what I'll do."

And so the Confession ended.

Father Jake now went on to briefly explain what John was going to say he believed in. "Basically, you are going to say that you believe there is a power or a force underlying the Universe, the power we call God the Father. Then you are going to say that you believe that we meet that power in Jesus, so we call him God the Son, and then you are going to say that you believe in that same power working in all of us, and we call this God the Holy Spirit. One God that we meet in three ways. Is that OK?"

John was a little puzzled by the Holy Spirit. "How is this Holy Spirit working in me then, Father? I always thought of God as somehow separate from me, a power that I might call on to help me, not that I did much of that. I preferred to go and make something in my shed or mend the car or do some gardening."

"Simple enough," said Father Jake, "In all those practical things that you did, you had within you the skill to do them, didn't you? Not everyone can do their own car repairs, can they?"

John nodded, thinking of the many people of whom he was pretty scornful, who never even looked at their car's engine.

"That skill is a gift of the Holy Spirit. Just as some people can play the piano and others are good at football, and yet others like your Monica are good at looking after people. All of us have different gifts, and it is God, the Holy Spirit, working within us, that gives us whatever talents we have. God works in all of us whether we realise it or not."

If he had been in less pain, John might have got into a longer discussion about this, but now he nodded meekly, and Father Jake realised it was time to get on with things. Monica was called in to join them, and in a few brief minutes, John was made a member of the Catholic Church, given his First Communion and received an Anointing to prepare for his death. Monica was in tears, of course, but tried to hide them from her husband, thinking they would upset him. But John knew they were there and reached out to hold her hand. "All done then," he said. "I think I need a sleep." And they left him quietly dozing in his armchair.

Father Jake sat at the kitchen table while Monica made some tea. She had insisted that Father should stay, and had baked a cake; and having taken a cup of tea and a piece of cake to John, she sat down to thank him for all he had done. Father Jake stifled a groan as he saw the cake. He loved cake, but he was offered it far too often, which made his fight to stop his waistline expanding all the more difficult. Monica could see how much he was enjoying it, and once he had eaten it, which happened all too quickly, she immediately offered him another slice.

“No Monica. I mustn’t. It was lovely, but one slice of cake is all I allow myself if I am to stop getting any fatter than I am already.”

“But you’re not fat, Father. Go on. Have just one more piece?”

And Father Jake sighed and gave in, knowing that the next time he made his Confession, gluttony would once again feature on his list of sins. And that he would now have to go for an extra long run tomorrow to work off those pounds.

He went on to more serious matters, assuring himself that Monica had enough support as she cared for John. She told him of all that had been set up to help John, and that they had promised extra support if she needed it. “Make sure you ask for it, Monica. Don’t just soldier on and leave it too late. Sometimes the extra support they can offer you can take longer than you think to materialise. and then things can get difficult.” He didn’t want to say too much, but he had seen this happen far too often, where the promised help and extra medication had failed to arrive quickly enough, and the pain for the patient and the carer had become almost unbearable.

He was about to leave when she said, “I suppose I won’t see you again Father until the Funeral?”

“Oh no Monica. I will come again next week and give him Communion again, and every week until he dies.” Then Monica shed a lot more tears, and he comforted her as best he could, staying much longer than he had meant to.

Afterwards, she went in to see how John was. “I heard you crying,” he said “He’s a good man that priest, isn’t he? I feel much calmer now, and somehow, the pain seems easier to bear. But there is one thing I want you to help me with. I want to write to Colin. I want to say sorry.”

Monica was astonished. "But I am sure he knows that now, John, given how many times he has been to see us. Why do you want to bring up the past?"

"Because I don't want any more misunderstandings, Monica. I want him to know, absolutely, that I am really sorry. Father Jake suggested I tell him, but I don't think I can face that, so then he suggested writing a letter. Then the next time he comes, before you bring him in to see me, I want you to give him the letter to read. OK?"

Once Monica realised that this was a suggestion made by Father Jake, she accepted the idea more readily. She knew the technical word for what the priest had proposed. It was John's penance. So she brought him pen and paper, and with great care, he wrote down all he felt. Once he had finished, he asked her to take it away and put it in an envelope ready for Colin's visit. When she came back, he was fast asleep.

Chapter 24: Visiting Ireland

Colin was not surprised that he didn't sleep well the night after Walter had shared with him what he knew of Father Bill's thoughts. He felt incredibly guilty that he had put the man of whom he had been so fond into prison, and had, in effect, destroyed his priesthood. Once again, he was awake in the early hours feeling wretched and alone. He went downstairs as he usually did, for he hated lying in bed feeling awful. Indeed, his counsellor had said to him, "Don't lie there letting those negative thoughts go round and round in your head. Get up and do something to take your mind off them." So that is what he usually did, although, as usual, he was not very optimistic that it would make much difference.

But then suddenly he thought of his real father, and taking out his phone, he opened up the photo that Marianne had given him and began to talk to him, and to his father's brother standing beside him; and as he did so, he realised that a new idea was getting into his head. He had met his cousin, and now he must meet her father, his Uncle Liam. That was the thing to do. Making that decision certainly took his mind off the bad thoughts that had been plaguing him, but there was not much he could do at 4 in the morning, apart from going on the internet to see how best to go to Dublin, soon realising there were plenty of flights from the local Airport. His mind raced with ideas and plans, and what he might say to him, and as he drooped, he realised he was falling asleep. He woke two hours later feeling much better and, after a shower, was off to work at his usual time.

Faced with quite a lot to do, it was nearly lunchtime when he was able to go out for a walk and phone his Uncle in Dublin. "It's Colin," he said. "You'll have heard that I've met the family, but I wondered if I could come over and see you. I wouldn't put you to any trouble. I will book into a hotel, but I would like to meet you face to face." His Uncle was absolutely delighted but would not think of a hotel. "We have a spare bedroom and you are family," he said "When would you like to come?" Colin hesitated for a moment, and then, plucking up courage, he said, "Would you be free this weekend? I could get a flight on Friday afternoon and then get one back on Sunday evening. Or if not this weekend, any weekend you are free."

There was no hesitation on the other end of the line. "Hang on a minute," he said. And then he heard him say to his wife, "He wants to come this weekend. That's ok isn't it?" Colin heard the "Oh yes." There was no reluctance there then. He knew he was going to get a grand Irish welcome. "I'll book the flights now," he said. "Is there a way to get to you from the airport?" "No no. We'll meet you off the flight. Just let us know when the arrival time is, and we'll be there." And it was agreed. Back in the office, the flights were soon booked, and a quick text message was sent to Liam, as his Uncle insisted he was to be called. "Just call us Liam and Debbie," he said. "No Uncle and Aunt needed."

Back home, Colin sent a text to Angela to tell her that she wouldn't see him this weekend. Almost immediately, she phoned him back. "What a lovely idea, Colin," she gushed. "Let me take you to the airport." He tried to resist her offer, explaining that he could easily afford the parking fee, but she was determined to get her way, and he soon accepted her offer. It would certainly be easier to be dropped off at the Terminal. Friday came quite quickly then, and before he knew it, he was on the plane heading for Dublin, looking down on the North Wales coast. He had been a little worried about how he would recognise his uncle but had been assured that they would hold up a big sign saying RIORGHAN. In fact, that was the first thing he saw as he walked into Arrivals. The welcome was almost overwhelming. It wasn't just his uncle, but his aunt and two other cousins all hugging him at the same time, with his uncle and aunt both in tears. He found himself weeping too, as they hugged him and hugged him in a truly Irish fashion before taking him home. "I don't cry very often," said his uncle, "but you are the spitting image of Paddy. It brings back so many memories."

Once at the house, he was shown to a comfortable bedroom and, after a quick freshen-up, was soon downstairs, where a meal was almost ready. The room was very conventional and a little old-fashioned, with a kind of cream wallpaper with red decorations on it and a rather old brownish carpet, but on the wall in a prominent position was the same photo of his Dad and Liam that he had seen in his cousin's house in Bicester. He went straight to it and was joined by Liam. "It's the same as the one in Bicester." "Yes," said Liam, "but I have had it off the wall and had a proper copy made for you. Here it is."

Colin took the large, precious envelope in his hands and drew out the photo. "This is going straight up on my wall at home." And tears came to his eyes again. There was another hug from Liam, and then Debbie called them to come and sit down for the meal.

His two cousins here in Dublin were full of questions for him, and he was glad to find something in common with each of them. He had thought he might meet a very traditional family where he might feel uncomfortable about the failure of his marriage, so he was relieved to discover quite quickly that his cousin Patrick – named after your Da, he was told – was also divorced like him. His other cousin Bridie worked in the world of computing, and they had to be encouraged not to talk too much jargon that the others couldn't understand. Liam (as his uncle again insisted he be called) had a big photo album ready. "Straight after we've eaten, I'll show you loads more photos of me and your Da, and then tomorrow we'll go to the farm."

"The farm? What farm?" asked Colin.

"Did you not know that your Da and I grew up on our family farm? It's southwest from here, about an hour's drive nowadays on the motorway. Took much longer in the old days."

Colin was astonished and yet delighted. Already, he was learning so much more about his father, and the idea of visiting the farm where he lived as a boy was really exciting. The photo album was full of pictures from the farm and of his father as a boy and then as a teenager, and he had to admit they were right. He could see how much they were alike. He was soon asking for more information. "So what was he like? Why did he come to England?" And his Uncle Liam did his best to explain

He discovered that his father was quite a wild young man who wasn't at all good at being told what to do by his rather traditional parents. He wanted more out of life than could be offered on a farm, and so when he was 18, having earned enough for the fare, he was off to England. They already had family and friends in Birmingham, so that's where he headed, soon getting jobs on building sites and earning far more money than he could have ever got in Ireland in those days. Uncle Liam sighed, "Eventually, I followed him. He was the adventurous one, but once he was there and settled, he kept pestering me to come and join him, and so I did. And it was there I met Debbie. She was just finishing her nurse training, and here she is today, still putting up with me over 40 years later."

"And what about my mum? How did he meet her?"

"Ah well now. You know your Da was rather a one with the ladies, and so I sort of lost count of the different girls he took out, so your mum was one of the crowd to me, until she fell pregnant."

"What!" Colin was quite shocked at the idea of his respectable mother having sex before she got married, "I never knew that. But did he marry her before Jess was born?"

"Well, I told him he should. He wasn't easily persuaded, but in the end, he gave way, and they got married when your mum was about 4 months pregnant. The priest wasn't too pleased to be pushed into a hurried marriage, and Paddy told me they both got a right ticking off. But he was a realistic man, and so that's what happened."

Colin was soon to discover that far from settling down, his father led his poor mum a merry dance. "She loved him so much," his Uncle said, "that she put up with all his shenanigans. Debbie and I used to go round to see them and find that he was out again, but I don't want you to think that he was a bad man Colin; he was just very lively. He could never sit still for long, and loved to meet his mates at the pub. But he was very bright you know, and just being a labourer didn't satisfy him. Soon, he was doing bits of work on the side, and then as more and more of that kind of work came in, he set up a business by himself, and was soon working all hours so that your mum hardly ever saw him. But because of that, of course, they were never short of money, and that's why he managed to buy that house. And then you came along, and then…" Liam tailed off into silence, so Debbie took up the tale. "For ages, he refused to believe he was ill, and, anyway, said he was too busy to bother about such things. That was his downfall. If he had gone to the doctor sooner, they might have been able to operate, but when he finally went, it was too late."

"So how did Mum take it?

"Monica was just marvellous. She nursed him at home, and he always managed to be cheerful and keep cracking jokes even when he was in pain. And John, your stepfather, was a great help to your mum, especially after Paddy died. She almost lost the house. He hadn't any insurance, of course, but John stepped in, told her it was a loan, and then about a year later, he married her. And then we gradually lost touch. The problem was that every time she saw us, it made her cry, as she remembered Paddy. And then John suggested that meeting us was too upsetting for her, so that was it. No contact ever since then, until you phoned us a few weeks ago. It was like a voice from the past. And then when we saw you today…" Now her eyes filled with tears.

"Oh aye," said Liam, now recovered. "I couldna believe it when I saw you. Paddy, come back to life!"

The next day, they set out for the farm. "One of our cousins runs it now," said Liam. "And he's really looking forward to meeting you and showing you round." The journey was rather dull, but once they turned off the Motorway, Colin realised that they were heading deep into the Irish countryside. It was very green! The Farm lay up a track off the road. Liam explained that a lot of the Farm Buildings were new, but the house, though modernised was basically the same one he and Colin's Dad was brought up in. He was taken up to see the bedroom that his Uncle and his Dad shared, and then out into the fields with Liam, reminiscing about some of the things they did as boys. "Your Dad led me into all sorts of crazy adventures," Liam said, grinning. "Our Mam and Da were always tough on me, me being the eldest, but Paddy managed to get away with murder. Ay, those were happy days!" They were given a slap-up lunch, and when Brendan, his cousin, realised he was a computer expert, he was whisked off to the farm office to help him with a "Bit of a problem" – as Brendan put it. Brendan had thought that Colin would just sit down and solve the problem but was told politely but firmly that that was not the way to do things. So they sat together whilst Colin told him what to do. It took longer of course, but Brendan was well pleased at how much he'd learnt.

Back in Dublin, Debbie explained that she would be going to an early Mass the next morning and was surprised that Colin wanted to come with her. "Not many young fellas like you at Mass these days," she said, "Especially the early one." Colin wasn't surprised at that but was taken aback at how short the Mass was. Twenty minutes and they were out and walking home, and Colin wondered how the Irish managed to say the familiar prayers so fast. What it did was give him time with Debbie, who could tell him more tales about his dad, some of which he stored up to tell his children. He knew Peter would be particularly delighted that his grandfather Paddy was a devoted supporter of the Villa. Sunday lunch was another feast that Colin found hard to do justice to, and then soon they were driving him to the airport for his flight back home. Colin found that he was a little bewildered, even overwhelmed by all the information he had been given, and as he pondered on it he began to think about the part his stepfather had played in all this. Ok, he'd been a tremendous support to his mum, but it was also his fault that until a couple of months ago, he hadn't even known that a real father, other than John, actually existed. It made him angry to think how his mother had been more or less forced into forgetting all about Paddy by that man. How could he be kind to him now he knew so much more, even if he was dying? A muddle of emotions was welling up inside him, and he was very glad that Angela was there to pick him up, and he was able to explode about things to her. "You mustn't go straight home," she said. "You are all worked up, and you won't sleep. You're coming to me for a nice supper and a glass of wine to help you unwind." It was a blessed relief.

Chapter 25: Memories of Paddy

When Colin paid his weekly visit to see his mother and dying stepfather, he managed once again to overcome the stress he always felt, buoyed up by all the good memories of his trip to Ireland. Of course, he didn't mention any of this to John, knowing that he had tried to blot out the Irish connection from their lives; but once he went in to sit with his mum, he was soon sharing it all with her. She was interested to hear that he'd been taken to see the farm.

"Ah yes," she said, "Paddy often spoke about what fun he'd had there as a boy, and how often he got his poor brother into trouble."

"Mm, Liam told me that too, but it didn't stop him loving his little brother to bits. He and Debbie were so pleased to see me, and you know what Mum, they both cried over me when they met me at the airport. They told me that I looked like him, and then couldn't stop weeping. They kept hugging me and crying at the same time. It was a bit embarrassing, but it was lovely too. They told me that he led you a merry dance too!"

"Yes he did Colin, but I loved him so much that I just couldn't be angry with him. I just kept busy looking after Jess, and then you came along, and then before I knew it, he was ill, and I had to nurse him, as well as look after you two. Even then, even when he was in pain, he would make me laugh rather than admitting how ill he felt. Always the charmer right till the end."

Her eyes filled with tears. She reached out and took his hand in both of hers. "And yes, you do look very like him Colin. I never dared to admit it before. Perhaps it was too painful for me, and John was always telling me to move on instead of weeping about the past. But also, you are different, you are much more careful and methodical than he ever was."

"That's your doing Mum. Teaching me to organise my life and to work hard at school. I don't expect my dad was much good at that!"

Monica laughed "No he was not. It was his brother Liam, the Uncle you've just met, who organised the business and kept the books straight. But once Paddy became ill, Liam just couldn't do it by himself, and he went back to working for someone else. He hadn't got Paddy's drive. And there again, you are like him."

"But why was he cut out from our life, Mum? You shouldn't have forgotten him like that; repressing all that sadness cannot have been good for you. Why couldn't you stand up to that man?" Colin gestured angrily towards the other room

"No, Colin, I never could. To start with, John was so kind and helpful. I was so numb with it all. I could hardly think straight, and he took me to register the death and see the Undertaker, and then he came round regularly and helped look after you and Jessica, and then we got married and he ran things his way. I'd got so used to relying on him and taking his advice, that I just couldn't find the strength to oppose him in any way. I remember I did once try to disagree with him. I think it was something to do with you children – I felt he was too strict— but then he got so angry with me. I just crumbled and never argued with him again."

"Yes. That was the way he treated all of us. When I was a boy, I knew that if I wanted him to take me to see the Steam Trains, I had to behave properly at home. If I didn't, if I put a foot wrong, I got shouted at and sent to my room, and that was the end of the Trip that I'd been so looking forward to. Looking back now, Mum, with the help of my counsellor, I know that it was a kind of abuse, and that's why one day I blew my top at him, and .... well, you know the rest."

Monica was silent for a minute. Then she sighed and said, "I suppose you're right. It was only when he became ill a few weeks ago that I finally found the courage to stand up to him. I simply told him he had to contact the doctor, and to my great surprise, instead of telling me I was wrong, he did. I suppose it shows how ill he already was."

There was another silence, and then she said, "Haven't you noticed how different he is? I don't think it is just that you are making an effort with him, I just think that all that pain, or knowing he is dying, has taken away from him the need to control everything."

Colin thought for a moment. "Mm, yes, I suppose it has. Perhaps that's why I am managing to control my anger with him. But it's still there Mum, lurking in the corners of my mind. At times, it can be really difficult, but I have a new way of dealing with it. Do you know what I do?"

Monica shook her head, puzzled by his question, and so he went on. "I have printed out two copies of that photo of my real dad and my Uncle Liam. One is up on my wall at home and another in the office, and I talk to him."

Monica looked startled for a moment. "But that's a wonderful idea Colin. Paddy would love that. He always talked to St Patrick if he was worried about anything. He used to say, 'Well, he dealt with the snakes, so he can deal with any troubles I have too!'"

Colin laughed. "Liam said he was always getting into trouble, or getting him into trouble. So that was his solution, to let St Patrick deal with it!"

Monica smiled as more memories came to her "Yes, always in trouble, and always laughing. His customers loved him for that. He was deadly serious about his work as a builder of course, which is why his business was so successful, but I think they also liked him because he was always cheering them up with his Irish banter."

"So did he never get depressed? Not even when he was dying?"

"No, not even then. I kept crying and so he kept cheering me up, right until the end. Even when the priest came to give him the Last Rites, and he was in a lot of pain, he joked with him, saying he needed the full works because there was no other way he would get to heaven. And he died with a smile on his face."

She paused, and she smiled. "Do you know Colin…this is the first time that I've ever told anyone about him without crying. Looking at you it's so easy to remember him alive and funny and loving. I love that you talk to him, and I'm sure he's smiling back at you. Remember, when you get depressed, he'll say to you what he used to say to me, 'Cheer up. Things could get worse!'"

They talked on about this for some while, and then Monica said suddenly, "I think now is the time to give you John's letter." Colin looked puzzled, and so Monica added, "He said he had things to say to you that he couldn't say face to face, and so he wrote this letter. I think he was scared you would get angry with him."

"Scared? Of me?"

"Well maybe I mean that he didn't feel well enough to face the way he thought you might react. You can be as fierce as him you know, Colin. Maybe even fiercer."

Colin sighed and simply took the letter that she was now holding out to him. He could feel her trembling even though they did not touch one another. There was a long silence as he read it, and then read it again whilst Monica looked on anxiously. Finally, he looked up at her and said, "Have you read it? Do you know what it says?"

"No, I haven't read it Colin. He wanted me to read it, to approve it, I think, and I sort of said I would, but when I took it away, I began to think it should be private between you and him, and so I folded it up without looking at it."

Colin sighed again. “Well you can look at it now. It’s very sad really. He says he is sorry for anything he did in the past to upset me. He says he thought he was doing everything for the best, but now realises too late that much of what he did was wrong, and he asks my forgiveness.” There was another long pause, and then he said, “Why has he done this? Was it something you said to him?”

“Oh no Colin. I think it was Father Jake’s idea. I think he told him he should apologise to you, and he then decided to do so with a letter.”

“Father Jake? You mean the priest from our church? But how does he get into the picture?”

So then she told him what had happened, how when John knew he was dying, he had wept over her and finally asked if he could see a priest. She explained how quickly Father Jake had come and, after two visits, had received John into the Catholic Church.

Colin was astonished. Like Monica, he had thought that it took months to become a Catholic, and so Monica explained to him what Father Jake had explained to her, that when someone was dying, the usual rules don’t apply.

Finally Colin said, “I’m having trouble taking all this in, Mum. I feel very confused, even angry, that after all he did to me and to you in the past, he should be accepted into the Church just like that.” He paused, waiting perhaps for Monica to answer, but when she remained silent, he added, “And how does this letter fit into all this?”

“Well, I think Father Jake asked him to make his Confession, and when he did that, he said he had to say sorry to you in some way?”

“Ha! In other words, this is a letter he wrote so he could get into heaven. Classic! I’m sorry Mum, but I think I’d better go before I start saying things that might upset you. Just remember I love you and will never cut myself off from you again, but as for him… I'm not so sure."

"But he's dying Colin."

"Yes. And that's the only thing that stops me giving him a piece of my mind."

Colin drove home with all sorts of fierce thoughts swirling around in his mind. *Why should that man, after all he has done, be forgiven… by me .. or by anyone else?* Resentments from the past welled up and almost drowned him. Arriving home, he tried to get to sleep but found himself back in his dark place, tossing and turning, so he got up and sat on his settee filled with his usual dark thoughts.

He was so alone. Nobody really cared about him. He had messed up with Rita. He had no real relationship with his kids. Peter wasn't interested in a dad who didn't know anything about football. Maria was a teenager busily growing away from him.

Then, suddenly, he remembered his real dad, and he sprang up to look at him in the photo Liam had given him now up on his wall. He told him how sad he was. He told him how angry he was. And as he did so, he remembered what he'd just learnt was his dad's favourite phrase, "Cheer up. Things could get worse." And much to his surprise, he found himself laughing. It was 2.00 am, but suddenly, he thought that if he went back to bed, he might get a few hours of sleep. And he did.

Chapter 26: The Office

Colin was not at his best the following morning. Once awake, his angry thoughts immediately began to swirl around in his head; thoughts about his stepfather, and what he would like to say to him, and his fury that he couldn't because the man was dying, and anyway, it would upset his mum. He longed for someone to talk to about this. If only Walter had been around, but he was down in Oxford. As it was, he sat on the bus wondering why on earth he was bothering to go to work. Arriving in his office, Colin walked in, flinching at the various untidy desks of some of his colleagues. Normally he'd learnt to cope with this, but Wren knew something was wrong as he looked around as he arrived and sighed. She made a sign of drinking a coffee to Julian, who went off quickly to get one, which Colin received with a pale smile and a weak thank you.

Colin's office was separated from the rest by glass screens, allowing Wren, the office manager, to see him trying hard to concentrate. However, when there was nothing immediate to respond to, he often sat with his head in his hands or got up to look at the photo he had brought in, which was now on his wall. She bided her time. She had never really discussed his personal life with him before, even though she and Julian had acted to support him through his dark periods. So she sat there worrying, knowing that someone had to act to try and prevent another depression coming on; and wondering what she ought to do. Finally, she decided to go in to see him, using the excuse that she wanted to discuss an issue of concern about one of their customers. They had a brief discussion, and then taking a deep breath she plunged in saying gently, "Something's wrong Colin, isn't it? Do you want to talk about it?"

Colin sighed and then responded, "Thanks Wren. It's my damn stepfather. He's dying, but that's not the problem. The problem is that he's written a letter to me saying sorry for the way he treated me when

I was a boy. I suppose I should just accept it, but it has brought up all my anger about what he was like with me, and I can't get rid of it."

"Oh. I see. Was it really bad?"

"Well, basically he was a bully. He was fine if I did precisely what he wanted me to do, but whenever I wanted to do something different, whenever I did anything that he thought was wrong, he used to shout at me, and go on and on at me, or send me to my room, until I submitted and said sorry, and then he would give me a lecture on how I should behave."

"But didn't your mum stand by you?"

"No, not really. She was scared of him too, and until yesterday, that's something I didn't know, so now I'm doubly angry, angry with him for bullying her, and angry with myself for blaming her all these years, assuming that she was on his side."

Wren had sat down to listen. She nodded sympathetically and just let him continue.

"My friend Walter tells me to treat him like one of our difficult clients. You know what they can be like! And I've managed that most of the time, but that letter has brought back into my mind all my resentment at the way he treated me, and I'm having real trouble processing it."

Wren nodded again, and Colin began to pour out his story to her. The story she had never heard. She sat with him for almost an hour, astonished that this normally quiet, controlled man could have so much emotion inside him. She had always thought of him as a brilliant boss, but rather less than human, except when he had his bouts of depression, and then he never talked; but now, as he poured out his feelings, she met someone very different. Finally, one of their colleagues plucked up the courage to interrupt them with a request for some help, and they went their separate ways.

Wren didn't take long to share some of this with Julian. He'd been such a support to her when she had gone through her divorce a few years earlier and was still very much an anchor, especially when her son was away at University and she was alone. Indeed, she and Julian had got into the habit of eating together at his place once a week, and it suddenly dawned on her that they might ask Colin to join them. Leaving him to go home to be alone again and drop back into depression seemed such a sad thing to do, and not good for the business either. Julian was soon persuaded. He was always happy to cook for people, and so it was agreed that they would ask him, or rather prompted by Wren, that Julian would ask him.

Julian had been rather hesitant at first. "Go on," she said, "You can tell him it was my idea." So he knocked on the door and went in. Colin welcomed him with a "Hi Julian," assuming he had some kind of question about work, so he was more than a little surprised when Julian said, "Er. Wren told me you were feeling a bit sad, and so we wondered if you would like to come and join us for dinner this evening at my place….. rather than go home to an empty house?"

Colin looked puzzled. "You and Wren? Well, I didn't know. But I wouldn't want to get in the way of your relationship."

"Oh no, no," grinned Julian. "It's not like that. You see, my partner has to be away on business a couple of nights most weeks, so I've got into the habit of inviting her round since she's all alone during term time."

Colin looked even more puzzled. "Term time? What's that got to do with it? And isn't it a bit difficult for your partner to cope with you entertaining another woman every time she is away?"

Julian sighed, "You really don't know much about us, do you Colin? Wren is divorced, and her son is at university, hence she is alone during term time. And my partner is a man, not a woman."

"Oh," said Colin. "Sorry. I didn't know ……. but I do now."

There was a long pause until Julian said, "So, will you come to dinner then?"

There was another pause. Colin was clearly working through all this in his mind, and then he said, "Well yes, thank you. I will, but where do you live? How can I get home?"

Julian reassured him that Wren would run him home in her car. "She doesn't drink, so she is a great taxi driver."

And so it was agreed.

That evening, Colin found himself impressed with Julian's house. It wasn't neat and modern and tidy like his place. Instead, it was full of interesting books and objects. It had Persian-type carpets on the floors and old-fashioned-looking lamps dotted around each room. Despite all the stuff he might have called clutter, he was pleased to see how clean it was as they sat around the big oak table in what might be called a kitchen/diner and chatted while Julian cooked. Hanging on the walls were loads of cooking implements of all sorts and an impressive array of knives and saucepans. It all looked very professional, and the smells from the cooking soon proved that he was not going to be disappointed.

"Well," Colin said to Julian, "I'm certainly learning a lot about you tonight. Do you do all the cooking, or do you share it?"

Julian laughed. "Oh, I wouldn't dream of letting Chris cook. He's a disaster. But he is good at other things."

The conversation that continued as Julian cooked was lovely for Colin. There were no issues that he had to worry about, no people who might get offended, just good friends eating together, or at least three people who were becoming good friends. He found himself relaxing and laughing in a way he hadn't done for ages. Yes, he had good chats with Walter and Angela at times, but they were the same age as his parents. This was somehow different. And his old friendship with Rita had been destroyed by his own stupid anger and intolerance, so that when he saw her, they spoke mostly with the children or about them.

Colin discovered all sorts of things about his colleagues that evening that he had never known before, even though they had supported him recently when his depression had threatened to return and overwhelm him again. At a certain point, he actually said to them, "How come I have worked alongside you all this time and yet hardly knew anything about you?"

They laughed it off, and Julian said, "Well, it's Wren's job to do all the HR work in the office, not yours. She knows more about all of us than you would ever dare to, and she does it so naturally that nobody notices. It's your job to run the business efficiently, and you do that brilliantly."

Colin laughed, "But I couldn't do it without my brilliant staff, could I, and I wouldn't have such a brilliant staff if Wren didn't help me choose them and then look after them."

Wren butted in then, "Now stop it you two, or you will make me far too big-headed. If you heard what my son says about me sometimes, you would hear a very different story."

This led to a discussion about Wren's son, Jeff. Colin remembered that Wren had brought him into the office a few times when he was younger, but now discovered he was studying English and Theatre Studies at Warwick and wasn't the least interested in computers, except as a useful way to study the subject and the people that fascinated him. This then led to a discussion of their favourite actors. Wren told them who Jeff most admired – an actor at the Royal Shakespeare Company that none of them had ever heard of – and from that, they got on to discussing actors they had heard of and their favourite Films. Colin then discovered that he and Wren were both admirers of Tom Hanks, and, whilst they ate Julian's delicious food, a long discussion followed about which was his best Film.

It was a very happy evening, and when Wren jumped up and said, "Come on Colin. I must drive you home," he didn't really want to go, saying, "I haven't enjoyed myself so much for ages. Thanks so much."

Julian agreed. "Why not join us each week? We'd love that, wouldn't we Wren? We have enjoyed getting to know you better. Normally we think of you as the boss behind the glass screen."

Colin's face fell.

"No, no. You're a really good boss, indeed a great boss, but now we have been able to get to know you in a different way."

Colin smiled. "Well, if you think you can put up with me, and really want to get to know the boss better, I would love to make it a regular thing. See you tomorrow at work."

On the drive home, he and Wren chatted about this and that, and he was home before he noticed. He leapt out of the car with a quick "Cheers" and then, too late, felt he ought to have thanked her a bit more, but she was gone. As he let himself into the house, he wondered how he could have explained exactly what the evening had meant to him, for his mind was filled with good thoughts and memories rather than the dark thoughts that had dominated him for too long. *Why had I never made any attempt before to get to know them as friends rather than colleagues?* he wondered. Perhaps he had been too professional, or perhaps he had been too obsessed with his own thoughts and worries…? He went and talked to his picture of his dad on the wall, but this time, he was telling him some good news. "Mum said you were always full of fun. Perhaps I should look for a bit more of you in me?"

Chapter 27: The Friendship Develops

A few weeks later, after a number of happy evenings, where the three of them had grown a lot closer, Colin was surprised when Wren said, "Colin?" in a rather less confident way.

"Hello... yes?" was his reply

"I hope you don't think I am being pushy, but I wanted to ask you to do something for me."

"Ask away then."

"I've told you about my son Jeff."

"Yes."

"Well, he wants me to go and watch him in a play he is putting on. It's one of those trendy modern dramas that never makes sense to me, but I must go and support him."

"And?"

"I wondered if you would come with me .... just for moral support.... I need someone to talk it through with afterwards, so he won't dismiss me as a total idiot as he usually does."

"Oh my. He sounds like my Maria. Her dad, that's me, of course, is a stupid moron who she just about tolerates. And she's only 15! I dread to think what she will make of me when she is 20 like Jeff."

"I thought you would understand. So will you come? It's on a Saturday night but I've already worked out that it's not a weekend when you see your children."

Colin was slightly surprised by the fact that she'd worked that out before she asked him, but then he thought to himself, "I shouldn't be surprised. She is so organised. That's why the office runs so smoothly." Then he said, "Yes sure. It sounds quite fun, kidding Jeff that you are not quite as out of touch as he thinks you are."

"The problem is Colin. He might read a bit more into it than that! If you know what I mean?"

Colin didn't know what she meant. He always underestimated himself. Wren knew that when Jeff saw this very slim handsome, not quite 40-year-old man with her, he would immediately think his mum had finally found her new man. He had often told her she ought to get out more and meet someone new. He had even recommended an Internet Dating Site to her, but she had always resisted the idea. She was actually rather frightened by the idea of meeting a strange man, even though it would be in a public place. Although she had never told her son this, Wren, like many women, had coped too often with men touching her inappropriately, and she hated it. It was why she had become friendly with Julian. Because he was gay, she felt safe with him. She struggled now to find the words to explain this to Colin.

"You see, Jeff will think you're my boyfriend. He'll put two and two together…"

Colin really laughed then. "Oh I see! And make five." There was a slight pause. Wren wasn't sure what to say, but Colin saved her embarrassment.

"Well, I'm glad you warned me, but I think I'll cope alright. To be forewarned is to be for-armed, as the saying goes. Otherwise, I might not have realised what he was getting at. I'm such an innocent you see. Only Rita. No one else really. And she made all the moves to start with. You see I thought I was gay, and so did she. It took us quite a long time!"

Wren didn't quite know what to say. Over their weekly dinners, Colin had shared with them some of his present problems, but he hadn't told them much about his past, except that he had rowed with his stepfather as a teenager and never got on with him since, but while she pondered on this, Colin was already asking her for a bit more information on where they were going and what they would see, so she had no chance to ask him about the personal things he had just shared. *Not that I would have asked him,* she thought.

She told him instead a bit more of what her Jeff was doing, and the amazing facilities at the university's art centre. "Lots of the productions are professional. Music as well as Drama. But what we'll see is part of Jeff's studies. The students have to perform as well as study. And," she added anxiously, "it's a very high standard, but the problem is that the plays are all a bit avant-garde, if you see what I mean."

Colin looked somewhat puzzled. "I'm not sure I do, but never mind, it will be interesting to do something different, and then your Jeff can explain it to me, and you can nod as if you understand, and it's only me who is the idiot."

They decided to make a day of it. Wren was shocked to find that Colin had never been to Stratford to see Shakespeare's Birthplace, so they headed there first. Wren suggested Lunch at the Rooftop Restaurant at the Royal Shakespeare Theatre with its wonderful views of the River, and really good food. She wanted to pay, but Colin insisted they share the cost. Afterwards, they made their visit to the Birthplace. Colin wasn't that interested in history, but as Wren enthusiastically told him about Shakespeare's life, he was fascinated more by her enthusiasm than by the actual subject. "My goodness," he said, "You're like me with my Steam Trains. I'll have to take you there next."

Wren didn't know what to say. So there was to be a next time? What did that mean? Was he just being friendly or was there more to it than that? She had to admit to herself that she really would like it if they became more than just good friends. But she hid her thoughts by continuing her lecture as they toured the various rooms and the garden. Then she took him on to Ann Hathaway's Cottage. Colin was amused by the wife that Shakespeare spent most of his life keeping away from and by the story Wren told of what they think Shakespeare got up to in London.

Then came the meeting with Jeff, because once he'd heard from his mum that she was bringing a man with her, he had suggested they should come for a cup of coffee and a bit of cake at about 4 pm at the house he shared in Coventry. Wren was glad about this because it gave her a chance to spend a bit more time with him. She would never have imposed herself on him without being asked. Of course, she knew why they'd been asked. Jeff wanted a chance to meet and assess the man!

Colin was very glad Wren had warned him that he should expect an interrogation, and she was right. The house had a shared kitchen diner. It was a bit of a mess, as student kitchens often are. Colin tried not to wince as he surveyed the unwashed crockery on the draining board and various items that seemed to have been popped randomly in different parts of the room. He had to quell his desire to offer to do some washing up. It reminded him of his own experiences at Loughborough, where he found himself regularly doing other people's washing up. They had the place to themselves since the other students were either out or in their rooms, although one did appear once to get himself a drink and sort of say hello.

They sat round the slightly scruffy table with their mugs and plates. Wren breathed a sigh of relief that Jeff had made enough effort to actually go out and buy some cake and, rather more important, to actually provide clean plates. The conversation was a bit awkward to start with. Colin broke the ice by saying, "I remember you coming into the office when you were younger. You seemed really interested in the computers then."

Jeff grinned. "Yes, it was fun when I was little, but now banks of computers with people staring into them is definitely not my scene. I don't really understand why you computer geeks are so keen on them."

Colin laughed. "Oh yes. I am definitely a geek, but we can be quite useful when your computer goes wrong!"

"Well Ok, but just remember that computers take over our minds, whereas great drama stretches our minds. How did your Shakespeare trip go?"

Jeff was quite shocked to find out that Colin hardly knew anything about Shakespeare, and launched into a bit of a lecture on why he was so important and so modern. Colin asked the odd question to keep him going, and Wren was pleased to see how well they were getting on. Then, after a little more conversation, Jeff launched into something more personal. "So now you are not just my mum's boss, but her new man as well?"

Wren was about to say something, but Colin got in first. He had prepared himself for this, and she suddenly saw a rather different Colin emerge.

"So are you sure I'm not gay, Jeff? Maybe your mum has chosen me as a friend because she knows I'm not after her body."

So he knows why I am friendly with Julian, thought Wren.

Jeff wasn't thrown by this, "Of course, I know you're not gay. I remember the photo of your two kids on your desk. How old are they now?"

"They're both terrible teenagers. But you shouldn't make too many assumptions. Even today, some gay men get married and have children."

"Yea, yea. You're trying to divert me. Are you her boyfriend or not?"

"I don't really know. It's a bit of a mystery really. Would you like it if I was having sex with her?"

Wren gasped, but Colin continued. "Of course, I can assure you that if we were having sex, I would have asked for written proof first that your mother wouldn't give me any sexually transmitted disease."

Now Wren did join in, "And I would have asked the same information from him. You can't be too careful nowadays; you never know what people have done in their past."

She liked making that point because she had a feeling Jeff had been to bed with a number of girls, and she had sometimes worried what he might be getting into.

"And then there's the problem of making sure she doesn't get pregnant. She may be just over 40." Then to her, "Yes I checked the office records, Wren."

"But she isn't past childbearing yet. Would you like a baby brother or a baby sister?"

"You're very good," Jeff said, grinning. "I'm really impressed by the act you're putting on for me. And I think you are really great for my mum, so if or when you do get her into bed with or without contraceptives and a certificate of health, I will be happy. So mum," he said, turning to her, "You have my approval."

"Very kind of you," said Colin. "Now, tell me about this play we are going to see?'

Chapter 28: The Letter from Prison

Colin found Jeff's explanation of the play rather unsatisfactory. Jeff told him not to try and analyse it too much. "A play is not like a computer," he said. "There's no logic behind it, just lots of muddled and conflicting emotions. A bit like life. Just sit and let it happen in front of you and see what you feel."

Colin knew a lot about muddled and conflicting emotions, but this didn't really help him understand the play. "After all," he said to himself as the play progressed, "If I can't understand my own emotions, how am I expected to understand this?"

Jeff saw them briefly afterwards just to say goodbye, and they were soon in the car driving home. It was Wren's first chance to say what she thought of Colin's performance.

"Well, I don't know about the play, Colin, but you were superb with Jeff. I've never seen you like that before. I've always thought of you as rather withdrawn and formal. Where did that come from?"

"Yes, I even surprised myself! It's all from my past, of course. You see, I mixed with a pretty wild crowd to start with at uni. Looking back I am a bit bewildered at what I got up to. I don't think I ever really enjoyed any of it, but I wanted to be liked, and so I went along with it all….. And then Rita came along."

"But where did that bit about a Certificate of Health come from? It was a great touch."

"Funnily enough, it's based on what I actually did when Rita and I started going out. I began to realise that she wanted to have sex with me, and given some of the things I had been up to, I worried that I might have an STD or even AIDS, so I went and got tested."

"Did you tell her?"

"No. But I did ask her about contraception. I was determined not to just jump into bed with her without thinking it through. I'd had enough unsatisfactory casual sex by then, but with men, of course. By the time we were friends, all that had stopped, and I had deliberately cut myself off from those people. They tried to entice me back, of course, but I'd had enough. So I concentrated on my Course Work and went back to getting fit in the Gym and with the Swimming, and that's how I met Rita."

"So she was a swimmer too?"

And Colin told her the story of how he and Rita had met.

The following Monday, they both felt a bit awkward. Colin didn't want to appear too keen. He wasn't sure about sex. Despite his time with Rita, his sexual desires confused him, and he didn't want to impose them on anyone else, as he had been imposed on during his first year at uni, but he enjoyed her company and certainly wanted to go out with her again. Wren knew she fancied him, but was terrified he would back off if she pushed too hard, so she didn't know what to say. Also, neither of them wanted it all around the office. So it was all very business-like, with Colin working very hard in his office so as not to think about it, and Wren doing the same at her desk. That night when Colin was home and alone, he tried to work out what he should do. He was certainly attracted by her, but the idea of letting her too far into his life was more than a bit disturbing. He had failed with Rita, and he feared the same thing would happen again. The following morning, a letter dropped through his door before he set out for work, and that changed everything.

His heart missed a beat when he realised it was from Father Bill. In a way, he wasn't surprised, because the last time he and Walter had spoken about this, he had been keen for Walter to let Father Bill know where he was. But it was one thing to think about it and quite another to actually have a letter from him in his hand. He thought for a moment, and then realised that he did not have time to read it now, so he placed it carefully on the table and left for work at his usual time. Walking down the lane to the bus, half of him wished he had had time to read it, and his mind whirled around all the different things Father Bill might have written. He wondered if he would refer to the incident on the boat…he hoped that he hadn't. He tried to imagine what else he might say. Might he ask him to visit him in prison, and if he did, could he face that? How awful to see the place he had put him in because of his own confused mind. When he got to work, Colin found it difficult to concentrate, to start with, but gradually, as he got into a knotty problem for a customer with whom he was dealing, the worries disappeared for a bit, only to emerge every time he had time to think. He had his lunch at the desk, working away furiously to try to blot out his other thoughts, but every now and then, they came roaring back into his mind.

Wren could see something was wrong as she looked at him through the glass partition, and feared that he was agonising over their relationship. She wondered if she should go in and bring it up with him, but finally realising that she had a work matter to share with him, she went in.

Colin looked up, but before he could speak, she launched into the work matter, and a business-like relationship was achieved. She was about to leave when she plucked up the courage to speak. "Are you OK Colin? You look a little disturbed by something."

"Yes, I'm ok, thanks Wren. It's because I have received a letter from my past, and I am wondering what it says."

Wren was puzzled, "But haven't you read it?"

"No. It was time to come to work, so I left it on the table at home."

What a man! she thought, *So obsessed with being on time for work that he ignores a letter that is going to disturb him all day.*

But what she said was, "Why don't you go home a bit early if it's playing on your mind?"

Colin considered this for a moment or two and then said with an element of surprise in his voice, "I suppose I could.... Yes I will... Thanks... I'll just finish what I'm doing, and then I'll go." And he did, leaving Wren slightly miffed that he wasn't thinking about her at all.

He arrived home. There was the letter lying there on the table waiting for him. He sat down and looked at it for a minute, almost frightened to touch it, but saying to himself, "This is silly. Why would a letter from him upset you?" The problem was that it did upset him, because it brought into his mind all the guilt he now felt at putting this man into prison, as well as all the anguish he had felt when he first accused him. He knew that a letter from Father Bill would be kind and forgiving, but in a way, he didn't want him to be kind, he would have preferred him to be angry. It was his own fault, and he knew that now. He had told Walter that he would like to be in touch, but it was one thing to express that wish, it was quite another for it to actually happen. *Would Father Bill want a visit from me? No, he couldn't face that, but what if the tetter made that suggestion?* He shuddered at the very idea of seeing the place where he had put him and seeing him presumably in prison clothes. How could he ever tell him, how could he ever explain to him why he had made those false accusations?

He sighed, but then, looking up at his father's photo on the wall, Colin knew he was being told not to be so silly. He reached down, picked up the envelope and carefully opened it. He never tore open letters as some people did. He opened the letter and began to read.

Dear Colin,

Walter has told me how he met you and discovered your connection with me, and he tells me that you would like to be in touch. In the circumstances, I thought it might be easier if I started by writing first, as I imagine you might find it difficult to know what to say to me. Given that our letters will be read by the prison authorities, there is a limit to what we can say about the past; and anyway, the past is the past, and I am sad that we lost touch after you went off to university. Walter tells me that he explained to you, as best he could, my side of the story that got me put into prison, and why I pleaded guilty. Although nothing happened, what I imagined I might do was almost as wrong as actually doing it. It was my mistake, and I must pay for it.

Things are not too bad here. You will remember how when we were on the boat together, I would withdraw a few times a day to say my prayers from my office book. I am glad to say that I have been allowed to have these books with me, and saying the Hymns and Psalms and Prayers from them with the daily Bible Readings gives me a routine that helps a lot. Walter has also been able to supply me with various other books that are not available in the library here, which tends to have lots of novels. I have, however, enjoyed reading lots of those novels, some of which were awful, but some quite good, including some of the classics that I had never read before, like Jane Austen and Thomas Hardy. Mass is said here usually once a week, although not on a Sunday, so I can normally get to that too.

I was delighted to hear from Walter how successful you have been in building up your computer business in Sheldon. I am so glad that what you left us to study at university has led you to this success. Of course, I was sad to hear of your marriage breakdown, but he tells me that you are seeing your two children regularly. He says they are both teenagers now, so that must be difficult. You were not the first, nor will be the last, to find it difficult as a teenager to get on with your father, although Walter now tells me that the person we thought of as your father was actually your stepfather and that you have discovered and visited your real Irish family. I always thought you looked Irish, if you know what I mean.

I will quite understand if you do not reply to this letter as I expect you will find it hard to know what to say, but if you do remember that, the prison authorities have the right to read it. Perhaps you might tell me a bit about your children? But if you find even that difficult, I would appreciate a postcard, just to confirm that you have received this letter.

All my prayers,

Bill

PS. Yes, you will have to get used to thinking of me as Bill rather than Father Bill.

Colin sighed, as he often did. It was a lovely letter, and it was not nearly as difficult to read as he had imagined. He read it through again and then went to the computer to compose a reply. He sat for a long time, looking at the screen, wondering how to start. It was so hard to know what to say. Father Bill was right; he would never have been able to write to him first. Finally, he thought the best thing to do was simply to reply to what he said and then see where that led him. And so he began.

Dear Father Bill,

Sorry but I find it hard to think of you as Bill.

Thanks so much for your letter received today. I was so glad to hear that you have been helped in there by saying your prayers. I am afraid I haven't kept up my faith at all. I did go to Mass with Walter and Penny when I visited them in Oxford, and I went to an extraordinarily rapid Sunday Mass in Ireland when I visited my relations there. I found both difficult for different reasons bringing up mixed emotions from the past, as well as agonies over the slipshod altar servers! I am not sure what I believe in now, but I don't think I could ever be an out-and-out atheist as I just feel that there must be something underlying it all, even if I am not sure what that something is. I remember talking about this a bit with you and how you tried to explain to me that God is not some superhuman Dad sitting up in a cloud but more like a spiritual force. Am I remembering this right?

Colin sighed again. *How much should I say about my early life at uni?* He didn't want it to sound as if he was making his Confession, but he knew he had made some very wrong decisions… *perhaps best not to be too explicit..* so he wrote…

When I got to university, I am afraid I mixed with a very anti-religious crowd and went along with their views, and it is only more recently, not least talking to Walter, that I have begun to rediscover the good things about the Faith and not just the bad things. My wife Rita hasn't really got much of a religious background, so going out with her didn't make much difference to my religious views, although perhaps it stopped me being so anti and made me rather more indifferent. It wasn't helped by my anger against my mum for not telling me about my stepfather. You will be glad to hear that she still goes to Mass every week, and after a long gap, we are now friends again, which has been lovely for me.

My children are called Maria and Peter. Maria is 15 going on 25 and has been very tough on me, telling me off like mad for leaving them the way I did, and now regularly informing me how old-fashioned I am. We do have two things in common – computing – and, to my surprise, because she says I am a male chauvinist pig – steam trains. Peter is 13 and is much less critical of me as long as I go and watch him play football. I hated it to start with, but since he is a really good player, I am getting quite a lot of pleasure from being proud of him.

Should I say any more? He wanted to, but how should he put it, given it might be read by the prison officers. He wrote it a few times before he got it fairly ok.

I wish I could in some way help you to deal with the troubles you face being there in prison. Walter tells me there is nothing I can do that will make any difference. I am so sad about this, but if there is anything I can do for you now while you are in prison, and more especially later when you are finally released, please let me know?

Yours,

Colin

He read it through again a couple more times and then printed it out. Then, very quickly, he got out an envelope and a stamp, folded it neatly, put it in the envelope and hurried out to post it before he changed his mind. Once it was in the post box, he stood there, almost feeling faint with the emotion that welled up in him. It was too late now, but that didn't stop a part of him wishing he had never written it. He sighed, yet again, and turned for home.

Chapter 29: The Difficult Goodbye

John was gradually getting weaker. Helped by Wren and Julian, Colin had been able to push his anger away, and simply visit once a week, not least to give some support to his mum. Monica found his visits a great help. Colin didn't usually spend much time with his stepfather. He would pop in to say hello, and John would be pleased to see him, but it became more and more difficult to have a lengthy conversation, as the painkillers and the pain were making him more and more drowsy. John said to him every time, "Look after your mum, won't you," and he assured him he would; and John would try to give him more detailed instructions on what he should do, which Colin listened to patiently. But as the weeks went on, it was just "Good to see you. Look after your mum, won't you." This was a great help to Colin because he never knew what to say or how to make conversation with a man he had never liked, whereas he really wanted to spend time with his mum.

It had quickly become a custom that she cooked a meal for him, and then while he ate, she took something to John and tried to help him eat, although he could hardly take anything and had grown to be a skeleton of his former bulky self. Once she had done this, she would come back, and they would sit and talk for a while about all sorts of things. Then Colin would give her a hug and leave. She was so pleased to hear about his growing friendship with Julian and Wren. That first evening together had indeed become a regular event. It was good too to talk to his mum about Maria and Peter. Colin found this very helpful, as she knew them better than he did and could often suggest things he might talk to them about. Theirs was a classic case, in that, they found it easier to talk to their lovely grandmother than to either of their parents, and would tell her things that she could pass on to Colin, reminding him not to let them know she was sharing their secrets with him. Rita had been bringing them over one evening every week. Like Colin, they found it hard to talk to their grandfather, so they would say a quick hello and then go and talk to Monica. Whilst Rita stayed for a while with John, she knew what he would say every time she saw him. "Why can't you and Colin get back together again?" And each time she had to explain to him that she didn't think it was possible, he would say that he supposed he understood and would mutter about what an impossible boy Colin was, as if he was still a teenager.

Monica had been determined to look after John until the end, but she was very glad that soon the nurses were coming in every day, which took some pressure off her. She also had support from Father Jake, who brought them both Communion once a week. He had explained to Monica that she did not have to feel guilty about not coming to Mass, as her first task was to look after John. She and John looked forward to these times of prayer. They, too, were finding conversation more and more difficult, and so the set prayers and the Bible Reading that Father Jake said for them were a great comfort. At first, John had worried that he wasn't paying proper attention; but Father Jake told him not to worry. "This isn't like school, John. This is God coming to you in a special way, and all you have to do is relax and receive him."

John found the Our Father the best bit, as he knew it by heart, and Father Jake let him say it the way he had learnt it at school, even though it was a bit different from the Catholic version. "It's the same prayer," he said to Monica when she worried about this. "Remember that in the original Bible it's in Greek, so which English translation we use doesn't really matter." Towards the end, as John found it harder to swallow, Father Jake would only give him a tiny bit of what he called the "host" and John called the "bread," and Monica would help by giving him a sip of water after he had received it.

The arrival of Jessica from Australia was a big surprise for all of them. She and her mum had been talking, first on the phone and then on Skype, once Colin had taught Monica how to use it; and then one day,

Jessica simply announced, "I've just booked a flight and will be with you on Tuesday."

"But what about the children?!?" Monica protested.

"Come on Mum, you're forgetting that Lucy is 20, and Patrick's 18. They'll look after Jenny more than Steve would, and they'll look after him as well! Anyway, it was Lucy who told me to come, and when I hesitated, the other two and Steve all chimed in, telling me not to be silly, and that if I didn't come and see you and Dad, I would always regret it."

They hadn't told John she was coming, so when she arrived, he was amazed and pleased, although, in typical style, he told her she really didn't need to come and see him just because he was dying, whereupon she burst into tears. Then he got upset, too, saying sorry so many times that Monica had to shush him as well as trying to comfort her daughter. Out in the kitchen, Jessica wept again, "Why does he have to say such horrid things?" and Monica had to remind her that he'd always been like that, but he never used to say sorry did he, and now he did. She astonished Jessica when she told her about the letter of apology he had written to Colin, for she hadn't felt able to share it online. Jessica was intrigued and amazed. "So how did Colin take it? Did he accept it?" Monica explained that he had never talked about it but that he had continued to visit every week. "But he wasn't in touch with you for years, was he Mum? How did that change?" And she was told the whole story of Angela's intervention and how wonderful it had been to see him again.

She was soon able to see Colin herself because, knowing when she was arriving, he had arranged to come over that evening, and after the usual fairly brief visit to see John, they were able to have a good long talk about anything and everything. "You ought to bring Mum out to see us in Melbourne when this is all over, Col. She would never come by herself, but she would if you brought her, wouldn't she?" And he had to admit that she was right, and promised to look into it after John died. His blunt description of the impending death reduced Jessica to tears again, and Colin also had to say sorry. She kept saying, "No, no. It's not your fault Col. It's just facing up to it all that keeps reducing me to tears. And the jet lag doesn't help."

It was only a few days later that she phoned Colin at work. "Hi Col. I think you should come over now. They say he is dying, and Mum needs you." Colin didn't hesitate, quickly explaining to Wren what was happening. She insisted on driving him to his home so he could pick up his car and be there as quickly as possible. "You are so wonderful," he said as he jumped out of her car and into his. They had been out together a number of times since that time when they saw Jeff's play, but it was still no more than a good friendship. Yet when he said things like that, her heart would leap.

When Colin got there, he found that Father Jake was there too, waiting for him to arrive. He was a bit startled, but tried not to show it. The Last Rites were strangely moving for him. It gave them all something to do. John was hardly conscious, as he was anointed, but was clearly aware, as he moved his lips as they all said the Our Father that followed. Colin found the words at the end very moving, as Father Jake said quietly, *"In the name of God the Almighty Father who created you, in the name of Jesus Christ, Son of the living God, who suffered for you, in the name of the Holy Spirit, who was poured out upon you, go forth faithful Christian."* and then *"May he forgive your sins."* And then the repeated *"Free your servant Lord."*

Yes, thought Colin. Here was a man trapped in his own stereotyped view of how a man should behave. *Yes, free him Lord.* And he realised he was praying. But what finally reduced him to tears was the prayer to Our Lady. It was the prayer he and Father Bill had said every night when they were on the boat together: *"Hail holy Queen. Mother of mercy.... To thee do we send up our sighs mourning and weeping in this vale of tears/"* And he quietly retreated just outside the door because he couldn't control his weeping. Jessica came out and put an arm around him, which made him cry even more, as they watched their mother holding John's hand as he slipped away.

It was over. Monica brewed up tea and coffee for them all, and Jessica asked Father Jake if her dad really knew what was happening. "Oh yes" he said, "People can hear even when they cannot speak and seem to be unconscious."

"But how did he manage to die, Father, whilst you were saying the prayers?"

"People often do. Not everyone of course. But some seem to wait, almost as if they need to be given permission to die."

Hmph, thought Colin, *Typical of that man to do everything correctly.* And then he felt guilty about having thought it.

When Father Jake got up to go, Monica wanted him to stay longer, but he said that he felt the family needed to be alone together to talk through things, and Monica accepted this: "Thanks for everything, Father, and I'll be at Mass tomorrow morning to pray for him."

"Mum," said Jessica, "tomorrow isn't Sunday, unless my jet lag has got me more muddled than I thought."

Monica smiled. "I know I don't often go on a weekday, but Mass is said every day and I want to go and pray for him tomorrow. I expect I will go more on weekdays now John has gone, and I am free to do whatever I want." Jessica and Colin looked at one another. Colin had shared with Jessica Monica's admission to him that she had let John dominate her life, and both were intrigued by how quickly she was thinking of herself as at last free from her imprisonment.

Then Monica gave Colin the phone number of the funeral director that she and John had chosen together. "You mean he helped you choose them?" he said.

She smiled, "Yes, and he planned the funeral. The Hymns and the Readings are already chosen. Father Jake helped us too. You know what John was like. He had to have everything organised." Colin sighed; he had to stop himself from saying far more than he did, as he thought of "That man" trying to run everything and everybody. Instead, he said, "Oh yes." and rang the number she had given him.

Within an hour, a discreet white van was at the door, and John was taken away. They then helped Monica tidy away the many things that had accumulated around his bed, which for the last few weeks had been a special hospital-style bed provided for them in the sitting room.

Monica wanted Colin to stay for some lunch, but he said he had to get back to work. "You've got Jess with you now, and anyway, I'll have to take some time off tomorrow when we all go together to the Undertakers, sorry the Funeral Directors. So see you then." There were quick hugs all around, and he was gone.

Colin drove straight to the office. As he did so, he began to fume about all that he had just been through. He knew he was upset, but wasn't sure what it was that had upset him. It couldn't have been the death of a man he had hated for so long. Perhaps it was the fact that that man was being given all the trimmings of a Catholic death when he had been such a pain all his life? Or was it just guilt at his feeling of relief that it was now all over? Or was it his hang-ups about the faith because of Father Bill? The "Hail Holy Queen" had brought all those memories back. And with them his anguish at what he had done to Father Bill…? All these thoughts and more rolled round and round inside his mind. He came into the office with the anguish he was experiencing written all over his face. Wren didn't hesitate. She followed him into his office, saying, "Was it awful? Are you OK?"

Colin was relieved to have someone to share things with. Gradually, over the last weeks, he had told her more of the story of his relationship with his stepfather, but he hadn't told her all. He hadn't mentioned Father Bill or his Catholic hang-ups, and so he knew she couldn't understand everything that was now troubling him again. He mentioned his anger that John had received the Last Rites, but in her innocence, she said that she thought that sounded rather nice and was a bit surprised at the way he shook his head angrily and then apologised. "Sorry, Wren, you're not a Catholic are you, so you wouldn't understand."

"But I am a Catholic. Not a very good one of course, but I understand what the Last Rites are, and surely everyone must be given a chance to be forgiven by God, even at the last moment of their life?"

Colin was startled, and all he could say was, "It's more complicated than that. Maybe one day I'll tell you, but not now." She looked sad, even slightly tearful, by what seemed like a rejection. Colin apologised. "Sorry Wren. You have been such a comfort to me, and I am really very grateful for all your support and understanding." He paused, and then said, "But what you have done has given me an idea of someone I do need to talk to." And she had to be content with that. When she had gone, he phoned Walter.

Chapter 30: Talking Things Through

Walter was in his garden when the phone rang. Answering, he said, "Hi Colin. How are you?"

Penny was listening, and she heard Walter say, "What! Oh no. That must have been hard…... Yes no problem……. I am only doing a bit of gardening. That can wait, so all the time in the world….. What full Last Rites?" There was a long silence as Walter listened, and Penny longed to hear what Colin was saying. "Yes. I see. Look Colin, I think this needs to be talked through face to face. We'll come up tomorrow…………. No, it's no trouble. Penny's always happy to have an excuse to visit Angela, and I'm sure Angela will only be too delighted. Have you told her yet?............. Yes, you are right, she will be very kind, but not being a Catholic, she won't really understand. But you will tell her, won't you?....... Oh hang on. We will need to phone her straight away. We'll need to explain why we are suddenly coming to see her, so will it be ok if she hears it from us? …… Any idea when the funeral will be?.... Oh of course, you can't know yet………Hope that goes all right then…….. Right, so I'll come round and see you tomorrow night at about 8. Will that be OK?........... Take care. Loads of prayers. Bye."

Walter finished the call and sighed. "So he's died," said Penny.

"Yes, but Colin's all screwed up about him being given the Last Rites. It's silly really. If anyone needs the Last Rites, it's that awful stepfather, but of course Colin doesn't see it like that. For him, it's being given a privilege he doesn't deserve."

"Mm. And you were quite right; you couldn't tell him that on the phone. You'll need to talk it through with him. I'll phone Angela."

Walter was so glad to have someone who understood how hard it was going to be to talk this through with Colin. He wasn't at all sure what he was going to say, but as they talked more about it, he realised that Penny's advice was the surest. "Just listen to him. Let him talk." And so when he got round there the next evening, that was what he did.

When they arrived just in time for lunch, Angela told him that she'd been round the previous evening and that she didn't understand why her dear Colin was so upset. "He didn't even like him, did he?" she said, "So why is he so sad?"

Walter sighed, "It's probably precisely because he didn't like him that he is finding it so hard. His mum is sad, so he is sad; but he is glad he is dead, and then feels guilty for being glad…? Mixed emotions like that are much more difficult to deal with than simply being very sad, like you were when Tom died."

He wasn't sure she understood, but felt it best to be useful by going out in the garden to do some weeding. Penny would be much better at explaining things to her.

Colin was so grateful to see him. "You're the only one who knows about all my hang-ups with the Church, Walter. Seeing that priest praying over that man that I hated so much, and then getting us to join in the 'Hail Holy Queen', I just had to get out of the room. It reminded me how Father Bill and I used to say it together last thing at night on the boat…. It was too much…. Everyone thought I was crying because of the death, when I was actually crying for a totally different reason… My sister tried to comfort me by saying, 'But you didn't like him?' All I could say was, 'It's not that' and 'I can't explain,' which made her even more confused."

Walter didn't say much. He felt that he was there to let Colin pour out a lot more of his anguish, the anguish he couldn't explain to anyone else, and he was not wrong. Colin went right back to his days with Father Bill and began to tell Walter again and again how awful he felt about what he had done. He got out Father Bill's letter, "Look at this wonderful message I got from him recently."

Walter read it and smiled, "I can hear him saying this to you. Are you going to reply?"

"Yes, I replied straight away. I told him how sorry I was and that if there was anything I could do for him, he must let me know. But how can a letter ever express what I feel, Walter, especially when a lot of what I feel cannot be put into a letter the prison people will read. And I still do not feel forgiven, whatever he says."

Walter realised he had to respond to this, "Well, first of all, I wouldn't judge things by your feelings. I remember that he once said to me that I didn't have to feel God's presence in order for God to be with me. I remember his words, 'Feelings are fickle things. Best to just get on with life, and do what we think is right, and not worry too much about what we feel.'"

Colin nodded "Now I come to think of it, he said something similar to me. He tried to get me to see that my father, my stepfather, I mean, was trying to do the best for me, that I should ignore what I felt about the things he said because he probably didn't mean half of them in the way I was taking them. But I wasn't convinced.

"Mmm. Teenagers are not good at dealing with their feelings, and from what you've told me, that man was probably a lot worse than Father Bill realised. Father Bill always tried to see the best in everybody."

Colin nodded again. "Yes, such a lovely man, and that makes what I did to him even worse, and I can't see any way to put things right."

"Awful isn't it to realise how many things we did we can't put right. The damage has been done. We talked about this before, remember? And I explained that even if you confessed to perjury and went to prison instead of him, he would have to go through an appeal with all the publicity, and even when declared innocent, he could never be a priest again. You would have had to explain why you thought he had abused you, and many people would say that there's no smoke without fire, and the whole story would go round and round and just make things a hundred times worse."

"Yes, I know you're right, Walter. But it doesn't stop me agonising about it. And now that man who caused me so much pain, and maybe was partly responsible for what I did to Father Bill, gets to have a funeral as if he were a saint."

"That depends on the priest. Hopefully, this Father Jake you talk about will have the sense not to do that? After all, he had time to get to know him, didn't he?"

"I suppose so. He did persuade him to write a letter apologising to me. But that made me even more angry, and if he hadn't been dying, I would probably have told him so to his face. How can a letter make up for all that he put me through?"

"Sorry Colin. I haven't really got an answer. These things from the past well up, and there is so little we can do or say that will make any difference. I tell you what though. Now that you have been in touch with Father Bill, why not write to him again? Tell him that your stepfather has died, and how you are feeling about it. Putting it down on paper will be a kind of catharsis for you, and you will know that there is one man who has lots of time to pray for you, although, like me, he will not be able to heal your wounds. That's the problem really. The bad relationship you had with your stepfather will never really go away. So many people suffer from the way their parents treated them, and you at least have the comfort now of knowing he wasn't your real father."

Colin looked at that picture of his real father and sighed. "And my real dad would tell me to laugh a lot more and not let things get me down, or at least that's what Mum says about him, and I'm sure she's right."

"So there you are then. There's a bit of a solution. One, write to Father Bill, and two, talk to your real dad. Tell them both all about it."

"But I wonder what my dad would have thought about that man being given the Last Rites?"

"Well, he would probably laugh and say something about all of us needing to be forgiven and sent on our way. If I remember rightly, you told me that your mum said he was a bit of a rogue, not always a very good husband, but that he knew it and loved your mum as best he could, even if sometimes he let her down…?"

"Yes, that's true, and Mum clearly loved him to bits, even though she knew how irresponsible he could be."

Talking about his real father had helped to calm Colin down. Eventually, Walter was able to ask him about the funeral, and Colin was able to tell him that he had been to the funeral director's with his mum and his sister that morning, and the funeral was booked for 10 days time. "I didn't think much of the funeral director he's chosen. They seem a bit old-fashioned and bumbling to me. And then I have to face it all happening in the Church where I served at the Altar with Father Bill. So many memories, and they're all going to come flooding back."

Walter thought for a moment, and then an idea came to him, "Why don't we go over there beforehand to give you time to get used to it. We could even go to Mass if you could face it. Maybe a quiet weekday Mass where we could just slip in the back?"

"You know I would quite like that, but I don't know what time the Masses are."

Walter just pointed at Colin's Phone, and within minutes, they knew that Mass was every day at 10 am.

"Ok", said Colin. "I'm a bit nervous, but your idea of getting over going back before the funeral seems a really good one. Would Saturday be OK? I will check with my mum, as she might well be there too, and I wouldn't like to give her too much of a shock. Actually, I'd like you to meet her, and she will be over the moon at the idea of me being there. Since my stepfather died, she's been going to Mass almost every day."

Walter laughed. "Ah yes, a devout Catholic mum with her lapsed Catholic son at Mass with her. You will make her day. You couldn't give her a better present. Is it ok if Penny comes too?"

"Sure, and Angela?"

Walter laughed again, "She'll come to the funeral of course, but getting my wife's cousin into a Catholic Church twice would be quite an achievement." He paused and then said thoughtfully, "But you know, I think she might… for you."

Colin looked surprised, "Hang on. Are you all planning to come to the funeral too? Why would you do that? You didn't know him, so why would you want to come?"

Walter shook his head. "But Colin, we won't be there for him; we'll be there, Penny and Angela and me, for you." And before Colin could reply, he continued, "And by the way, I must warn you that Angela will weep like mad over you, and will hug you and soak you with her tears. Are you ready for that, or shall I find some way of imprisoning her in her house on the day? You think you know how emotional she is, well you haven't seen anything yet!"

Colin had to laugh. "But she is lovely, Walter. So genuine."

"Yes, well I suppose she is, especially for you. But for me, she is a bit too genuine! I have to admit that I find her quite hardgoing, especially when I am in the same house as her. That's how we met, you know. What was I doing going off to Sheldon early in the morning, except to escape from her ?"

"But…?"

"No I can't explain it any more than that, Colin. Doesn't your wife have any relations that used to drive you mad? A mother-in-law for example?"

"Ah, well yes, but…"

"No buts. That's the way it is."

Colin laughed too. "Of course, and remember, she's met my mum already. She was the strange woman on the doorstep handing Mum my mobile number!"

The thought of that moment made Walter chuckle, for Penny had described the whole scene to him. "Yes, and I think that for the Mass on Saturday, it is you who should ask her. But check first if your mum is going to be there, for I bet that once she knows that, nothing will keep her away!" There was more laughter. It was good for the soul.

Now that Colin was feeling better, Walter went back to talk about the Funeral, getting Colin to tell him what it would be like.

Colin frowned, "Well that's what annoys me, Walter. He's getting a full-blown Funeral Mass as if he'd been a Catholic all his life. He never used to come with Mum to Mass, except at Christmas of course, and for our First Communions. And I remember how often he moaned about her going off to Mass on Sundays. She often went on Saturday evening just to please him. Yet now he's being treated as if he had been a Catholic for years instead of only a few weeks. It just seems all wrong."

Walter wanted to give Colin a lecture on the Story of Jesus where those who work in the field only one hour get the same pay as those who had worked all day, but he decided it was better to approach things a different way.

"But won't it make your mum happy to see him get what she would think as a proper send-off?"

Colin sighed. "Yes of course it will, and that's why I just have to shut up and think of her instead, isn't it? Mind you, my poor mum might at least have had the chance to choose the hymns, but oh no, he made her write down exactly what he wanted. Even after his death, he is still bossing her around."

"Yes ok, so what are the Hymns?"

"Oh Abide with me, The Lord's my Shepherd and one other that I can't remember."

"Oh dear," said Walter, looking amused again. "Angela had those two at Tom's funeral. She will love it, but she will also be in tatters. I must warn Penny."

And they both laughed.

In the end, Walter felt that he had left behind a much happier man than the one he had started talking to earlier that evening, and he was right. Colin had a chat with his dad's photo once Walter had gone, and then went to bed and got the sleep that had escaped him the night before. He smiled as he drifted off, as he thought of Walter and Penny coping with an over-emotional Angela. The next morning, when he phoned her, after checking with his mum, he discovered that Walter was quite right, and of course, what clinched it for her was being told that

Monica had insisted to Colin that they all come round for a cup of tea afterwards.

Chapter 31: A New Name

Angela had never been to a Catholic Mass. Indeed, she had rarely been to any kind of Church and so was very nervous. As they drove over in Colin's car, she kept asking Penny what would happen and what she had to do; and she wasn't really satisfied with "It's easy, just sit and stand and kneel when we do." She wanted to know precisely what would happen and when etc etc. Penny nudged Walter to take over.

"I was just brought up a Catholic and joined in without thinking about it. Walter, you explain to her."

So Walter tried his best, but found that the more he tried to explain, the more muddled she got, until Colin finally said, "You don't need to understand Angela. Just watch and listen."

When they arrived, Colin became very tense. He quickly saw where his mum was sitting and hurried to sit beside her, pointing the others to the pew behind. He had hardly dared look at the Church, but now, sitting there, memories of the past came flooding back to him, and when the bell rang and the priest came in without a server, he felt terribly embarrassed. Part of him knew that he could easily go up and serve at that altar. He knew exactly what to do and felt for the priest managing alone, and yet the idea of going up there appalled him. Suddenly, he felt his mum taking hold of his trembling hand. She understood, and he came near to weeping. She let go his hand for the Gospel as she made the sign of the cross, but he found it very comforting as they sat, and then stood and then knelt in all the familiar places. Colin sat and looked at the familiar scene as Monica went up to receive Communion and actually felt a little less tense, until suddenly he thought of Father Bill, and he was on the verge of breaking down again. But this time, there was no Hymn to send him over the edge as in Oxford, and he held his emotions in check, determined not to upset his mother. He succeeded, but only just, and was glad to get outside in the fresh air and join the others.

Angela had kept very quiet during the Mass, but was full of questions afterwards as they drove to Monica's, with Monica squeezed in beside them in the back. Angela couldn't understand why there were about 30 people there when it wasn't a Sunday, and then she commented, "And most of them were foreign!"

Walter was quick to deal with this. "Actually, I expect most of them were British!"

"Oh Yes, Walter, but you know what I mean."

Colin was amused at Walter's response. He clearly wasn't going to let her get away with it! "You mean most of them were brown or black, don't you? But since the majority of people in the world are brown or black, it's not really surprising, is it, that an international Church like the Catholic Church would reflect that?"

This reduced her to silence, but by then, they had arrived at Monica's house, and Angela was soon chatting away with Monica and helping her make the tea. Colin was so pleased to see his mum enjoying herself. He sat there beaming with delight. He particularly liked the fact that these friends of his could come to his family home; now, there was no stepfather looming in the background.

It didn't take long for Angela to ask Monica to tell them about Colin's real father. Monica smiled. "Oh Paddy was a terror. It would take all day to tell you all about him."

"Well tell us a bit anyway," replied Angela as Colin nodded his agreement. "We've seen how like Colin he is from the photo. So handsome, both of them. Do tell us how you first met him."

Monica's face lit up. "It was after Sunday Mass one day. This handsome Irishman just walked up to me outside Church and said, 'Hello. I'm Paddy. Can I take you out one day?' I was a bit prim and proper with him, telling him that I didn't know him well enough, but he wouldn't take no for an answer, not him... it was, 'Well you won't get to know me unless we walk out together will you?' And so I said yes, but only for a walk. I told him he would have to come to my house first and meet my parents, and then we'd go for the walk. So he came, charmed the socks off them, and by the time we'd finished the walk, I was in love with him, and that was that. Then we got married quicker than we meant to, because I was expecting Jess, which didn't please my parents. He loved Jess to bits, but he was a typical old-fashioned Irishman, and so when his son was born he was over the moon about it. Of course, he went down to the pub to celebrate with his mates, and when I saw him next, he was more than a little tiddly – but I'd got used to that. Then we argued, but not because he'd had too much to drink, but because he insisted that his son must have a good Irish name."

"But I don't understand, Colin isn't an Irish name, is it?"

Monica looked at her son, clearly embarrassed that she had never told him this part of his story, and reached out a hand to him, "Oh dear, please forgive me. I'm so sorry I haven't told you this before Colin, but actually, your name at birth was not Colin but Colm. Colm Riorghan, of course."

Colin was astounded, but he couldn't be angry. He just looked at his mum, taking hold of her hand, and said very gently, "You mean that man didn't just make me take his surname but changed my Christian name as well?"

"Yes, I'm afraid he did. He said that people at school would make fun of you if you had a foreign name, so why not call you Colin which sounds almost the same, and so we did."

There was a stunned silence as the full implication of what she was saying dawned on them, but each in a different way. For Penny and Angela, it was just a feeling that it was a shame he had lost such a lovely name for a more common one, but for Walter, who knew more of Colin's story, as for Colin himself, it was a further revelation of the lengths to which that man had gone in forcing his wife and children to conform to his ways.

Still looking at her son, Monica said, "It was so difficult to resist him, Colin. You know what he was like, and remember, I was still in grief at the death of Paddy, and he was the only support I had with you and Jess, and there was hardly any money. Please, please forgive me."

Tears came into Colin's eyes. "It's all right, Mum. It's only a name, and it does sound more or less the same. In fact, over in Ireland, they called me Com, but I just thought they were using an Irish way of saying Colin."

Seeing him almost in tears, Angela found herself weeping too. "Will you want us to call you Colm in the future Colin? It's such a beautiful name."

Colin turned to her and held out his other hand. "I really don't know yet, Angela. It's all so sudden. I need to think. I'm glad it sounds almost the same, so that it doesn't matter too much which name I'm called by."

Colin had actually been thinking for some time of changing his surname back to Riorghan, but Walter had pointed out to him that then he would have a different surname from his children, and Colin had not wanted to do anything that might move him further away from them. But changing his name to Colm would be rather different. Peter and Maria would still call him 'Dad', and most other people would probably still call him Colin, but deep down, he would know he was Paddy's son Colm, and he knew that would feel good.

The next day was one of his Sunday trips to Coleshill to see them, and since the weather was chilly but dry, he quite enjoyed watching Peter play his game of football before they went home for lunch. They were quite surprised to find he had been to Mass the day before, and not wanting to tell them his real reason, he just said that his friends wanted to see the Church before the funeral the following Friday.

"So what's the funeral going to be like?" asked Maria. "We've never been to one."

"Well, just like any funeral, I suppose – prayers, bible readings, a talk from the priest and then the rest of the Mass."

"What do you mean, the rest of the Mass?" Colin had forgotten that his children hadn't been brought up as Catholics and so hadn't ever been to a Mass, and he felt a little guilty.

"Well, the priest takes some bread and wine, like Jesus did at the Last Supper, and blesses it, and then people go up and make their Communion."

Maria wasn't satisfied. "So what does Communion mean?"

"Oh well, they go up and receive the Sacrament." They looked blank. "Sorry I mean they receive a piece of the blessed bread.

"So how do we do that?"

"Oh no," said Colin. "we don't, because you aren't Catholics and…" he hesitated. "And I'm a bad Catholic."

Peter butted in then, "But Dad, you're not bad."

"Oh yes I am Peter. Think back. How I left you and your mum and didn't see you for years. That was bad wasn't it."

"Oh yes, I suppose so, but it's all ok now isn't it?"

Colin sighed "Well not really. I don't live with you anymore, and I only see you once a fortnight. It can never be completely right."

There was a long silence before Peter said, "Well I think you're a great dad. You come and watch me play football, and you took me to Cadbury World!"

Colin and Rita looked at one another and laughed. "Yes, well thanks for that Peter. That's at least one good thing I do, but I'm still not going to go up and make my communion, not least because I haven't done so, or even been to Mass since I was 18… except for yesterday of course, and in Ireland."

Then he had to tell them all about what had happened yesterday, and was able to say, "Oh, and by the way. I also discovered that my real name is Colm not Colin."

Rita reacted now. "What! Are you saying I married you under a false name?"

"Oh no. It was changed legally, but my name at birth was Colm, because my real dad wanted me to have an Irish name."

"Well," said Maria, "I think Colm is a great name, much better than Colin. I wonder what Maria is in Irish? So when are you going to take us to see our Irish relations?

"Well, your mum and I thought you might prefer to go somewhere with a pool and some sunshine in the Christmas holidays. How about that?"

Maria, however, persisted, "Why not both? We could go over to Ireland for a weekend like you did?"

But Peter said he preferred the idea of a Pool and some sunshine, and how about taking him to see a Game at the Villa, and Colin realised that he would have to do everything each of them suggested. They had now worked out the advantages of having a dad who felt guilty about neglecting them. This new dad was going to be busy.

Chapter 32: The Letters

Colin worried about his letter to Father Bill. He kept changing it as he tried to express his feelings about this Catholic funeral for his long-time non-Catholic stepfather, but he wasn't sure that he did a very good job of it. This was the final text:

Dear Father Bill,

Since I last wrote, my stepfather has passed away. Much to my astonishment, in his last few weeks, he was received into the Church, and so I then had to watch while he was given the Last Rites, and now I am going to have to be present at his full-blown Catholic funeral. I am so angry and mixed up about all this. I can see that the prayers asking God to forgive his sins were just right, given what he put me through, but I still feel very angry that he was allowed to suddenly become a Catholic after all those years when he showed no interest at all. Walter told me all about the story of Jesus – the one about the workers who only worked one hour and got the same pay as those who worked all day – but I still can't see that this is fair. I cannot see that my mum – a devout Catholic all her life – can be on the same footing with God as he is. It has just brought out all my anger against him. Anyway, Walter suggested I write about it all to you.

I realise that you probably won't tell me anything more than what Walter has said to me already, but I remember how often I poured out my anger about him to you when I was a teenager and just feel that since you know the background you will understand me better than anyone else about this.

Having gone over it twice, he sighed, and then, as he was about to print it out, he added:

By the way. I have just discovered that my original name was Colm, not Colin, so I assume I was baptised using that name. Did you know about this? Actually, although I was surprised when my mum told me this, I was actually rather pleased. Colin was the name that man gave me, and so I am really happy to now use the name my real father gave me. So I sign this letter.

Yours ever,

Colm

Father Bill wrote back almost immediately

Dear Colm,

How wonderful to discover you have a new name, almost a sign for you that now your stepfather has died, you can begin a new life and put all that old anger behind you. I don't think I ever looked you up in the Registers, so never noticed that you had been baptised Colm. I think I must have arrived as your priest just after you were confirmed and so had no reason to consult your entry in the Registers. I have such good memories of you serving with such efficiency in that Church, but always Colin never Colm.

I think that the reason you are agonising about your stepfather having a full Funeral Mass, is that you are thinking of the Mass as more like something that is put on for people as a kind of religious entertainment. In fact, the Mass is not that at all. It is all of us offering ourselves to God and asking to be drawn into his love in the hope that we can live out that love in our lives. If it were something the Church put on for people, then it would be quite wrong to do all that for your stepfather, but if you can think of it instead as all of you offering your prayers and thoughts to God, whatever they are – loving or angry – then perhaps it makes more sense. I often used to remind people at funerals that even good people are not perfect in the sight of God, that we all need God to have mercy on us, so it is wrong to pretend that the dead person is all good and perfect and never had any faults. We all fail in one way or another. St. Paul says, "We have all sinned and fallen short of the glory of God." Seen that way, your stepfather is just another sinner needing prayers.

Anyway, he is now in my prayers, but you much more so, and always have been. I do hope the funeral goes ok. Please let your mother know that I am praying for you all.

Prayers ever,

Bill

Chapter 33: The Funeral

When Colin shared with Walter the conversation he'd had with his children, Walter smiled.

"I think Father Bill would say that it sounds like you made your Confession, and they gave you Absolution. You're going to be busy aren't you."

Colin gave a slightly rueful smile. "Yup, and you know I'm quite surprised how well I am getting on with them. When I was with them, I spent too much time resenting the demands they made on me, thinking it took time from building up the business. Now I realise how wrong I was and how much more important it is to be a good dad for them."

"No chance you could get back to them properly?"

"No, I don't think so. Rita has made it pretty clear that she's not interested, but we have planned a joint holiday with some sunshine at one of the Red Sea places, with Peter sharing with me and Maria with her mum. But I think that's as far as it will ever go. I hurt her so much you know."

There was a slight pause, and then Colin added, "Oh and by the way, I have written to Father Bill and poured out my anger to him about the funeral, and you were quite right. Simply writing it made me feel better, and I had a great reply."

Colin also found great relief in sharing all this with Walter. Somehow, just telling someone else rather than wallowing in his guilt made everything different. He was beginning to realise that his mistake had been to keep all his dark thoughts to himself. He still had his dark moments, when all that had gone wrong in his life welled up in him, usually if he woke in the night and couldn't get back to sleep. But even alone like that, he could talk to his real dad, and then later, he could write to Father Bill or phone Walter. He found help too from the weekly evening meal with Wren and Julian simply because they talked about all sorts of ordinary things – work things, of course – but also things about their respective families and what they were up to. He was amazed when they told him when they met that week that they were both coming to the funeral, but did not need to ask why. Like Walter and the others, they were simply coming to support him. He was tempted to close the office altogether, but Wren said that there would still be requests for help coming in, and she preferred the office to have at least a couple of people there, even if some others might work from home.

Nonetheless, Colin found the night before the funeral really hard. He could feel the anger building up inside, even though he knew it was pointless. He worried about everything: about his mother and how he would cope if she became too emotional, about Maria and Peter that they would know how to behave, and about what people would think of him if he said or did the wrong thing. The funeral director had told them not to worry, that he would tell them exactly what to do and when, but it didn't really help. He tossed and turned and eventually did his usual trick of getting up at about 3 in the morning. This time, however, rather than sitting and feeling sorry for himself, he decided to do some work on the computer to keep his mind occupied. It worked, except that by the time he should have been getting ready to go, he felt exhausted. He wondered if he'd be able to stay awake even to shave, but he knew he must force himself if only for his mother's sake; after the shave and a quick shower, he was surprised that he was much more alert than he had expected, and was able to get over to the house and be the well-groomed son that he knew his mother would expect.

It was difficult to know what to talk about as they waited until it was time to drive over to the Church. Jessica was helpful because she chatted on about the phone call she'd had last night with the family in

Australia, and was able to tell them what each of her children was doing. They talked about who might be at the Church, as John had been an only child and there were no close relations. Monica knew that her own brother and sister were coming and a couple of people John had worked with on the Council but she wasn't sure there would be anyone else, so she was pleased to hear that two people from Colin's firm were coming and she wanted to know more about them. Colin had never told his mother about the weekly dinners in the house of this gay couple where the partner was away, and the other person present was divorced, so he just explained what they did at work and how helpful Wren was as his office manager.

Monica was still a bit surprised, but even more, she was intrigued, "I've never met anyone from your business before, so it will be nice to meet them. How kind of them to come when they don't know us."

"Well they know me very well", said Colin. "And having worked with me for almost 10 years, they will probably be able to tell you more about how things work than I can."

Monica wouldn't have that. "Oh no Colin. Don't put yourself down. You created that business and made it successful before you even employed them, didn't you?"

And he had to admit that she was right.

It was a cold day, so they waited just inside the Church, greeting people as they arrived. Colin was surprised but rather pleased to see quite a few of his work colleagues, not just Wren and Julian. Once the hearse arrived, Father Jake was there to lead in the coffin, and he and his mum and Jessica followed behind, feeling very conspicuous as they were ushered into seats right at the front. Colin was surprised at how calm he was. The Mass for a funeral was so similar to an ordinary Mass that he found it easy to let it flow over him. Father Jake didn't make the mistake of saying what a wonderful man John was, which

Colin would have found hard to take. Instead, he just said a little bit about the hope of life after death and then moved on.

It was soon time to leave the Church, get into the cars, and follow the hearse up to the large cemetery not too far away. It was up on a hill with great views out into the countryside, which might have been nice on a fine day, but with a biting wind, it was good that the burial didn't take long. Monica had been calm in church, but now she began to weep, as did Jessica, and Colin found himself too busy with an arm round each of them to think much of himself. He did feel, however, a grim satisfaction as Father Jake said the words "Dust to dust and ashes to ashes", and he said to himself, "At last, it is finished. He's gone." He was glad that Monica didn't want to linger. Father Jake handed her the sprinkler, and she and Jessica and Colin each sprinkled the coffin in the grave and then turned away. Monica had quickly recovered herself as she went round to greet the mourners and make sure they all knew where the reception was, as well as making a point of thanking the funeral director. In no time at all, they were back in the car and heading for the hotel where they had booked a buffet lunch.

Walter had been so pleased to see how well Colin was coping, especially as he and Penny had to keep comforting Angela, who couldn't stop weeping, especially during the Hymns, which she explained to them were Tom's Hymns, even though Walter and Penny knew this only too well. He knew too that Colin had organised the place for the reception himself. Colin had told him that he had been around to the hotel that his stepfather had chosen and just felt it wasn't right; and so he had simply told his mother that he'd found an alternative venue. He had watched her take in the news. He had seen her struggling for a moment, and had guessed that she was about to argue for the first hotel because it was John's choice; but then she'd looked up at him, taken a deep breath and said: "If you think it is a better choice, then that's what we'll go for." The fact that the hotel was his choice rather than his stepfather's was especially important for Colin. It marked a watershed into a new life where nothing that man had insisted on in the past mattered any more.

It was a small group of people standing around, eating and chatting in the usual manner when people who have never met before and will probably never meet again try to make conversation with one another. Wren and Julian were soon being interrogated by Monica about the office and what it was like. "It's just like any other office really. People sitting at computers with Colin in his office behind a glass screen. Why don't you pop in one day and see it?" Monica hesitated, and Wren knew why. "I'm sure Colin would like it, but just to reassure you, I'll go and ask him." She went over to Colin and found that he was surprised but rather pleased by the idea. "That man rarely let her go anywhere, so I'd never thought of suggesting it, but yes, and she'll love to see the picture of my dad on the wall!" As Wren turned away from him, she saw Rita not far away and decided to go and introduce herself. "Hello. I'm Wren, Colin's office manager. I wanted to say how glad I am that you and he are back in touch. It was so difficult when Colin left you and refused to talk to you. I'm so sorry. He insisted that we should say that he was unavailable. I tried to tell him he should at least talk to you on the phone, but he was so agitated about it that we were worried that we were going to lose him altogether."

Rita took her hand "Thanks so much Wren. I was so angry with him and with all of you at the time, that I think I was quite rude to you, so I think I should say sorry too. I am beginning to understand things a bit more now, even though I still think he was very wrong to cut off all contact with us like that."

Maria joined in. "Well, I still don't understand him, and I've told him so. It was really horrid. Most of my friends whose parents split up see both their mum and their dad like we do now, But when he just disappeared, it was as if he hated us."

Wren shook her head, "No, he never hated you. He had a photo of you and your brother on his desk. It's still there even though you are a lot older now. Can I take a photo of you two now so that he can have a more up-to-date picture?"

Maria and Peter liked that idea, and the photo was soon taken, and Maria then launched into another subject: "I've got to do a work placement next year. Could I do it with you?"

Wren looked at her in a slightly puzzled way. "Why don't you ask your Dad?"

"Oh I know he would say no. He'd say that we would find it embarrassing to have his daughter in his office or some rubbish like that, so I thought I'd ask you. After all, if he were suddenly to die, we would inherit his business, wouldn't we?"

Rita intervened, "Maria, that's a bit much… I'm so sorry, Wren. She tends to say the first thing that comes into her head."

"Don't worry Rita, I have a son who is just the same." Then to Maria, "Well, I'll have to check with your dad, but don't worry, I will be able to persuade him if he tries to say no. Take my email address and send me the details of when it will be, and I'll arrange it."

Maria was well satisfied with this, and as Wren and her mother continued to chat, she made a beeline for her grandmother, dragging Peter with her, and began to ask her to tell her more about the grandfather she never knew. Monica was rather pleased to have something to talk about apart from how sad people were for her, and she was soon telling them some of what she had told the others the previous Saturday. Her whole family then went home with her, and Colin watched his mum busy serving the dinner and revelling in having them all around her.

It was late when Colin got home to his empty house. He sighed. It had been quite a day, and he hadn't had much time to think. For a few moments, the old feelings of being empty and alone threatened him, but then, as he thought of all the friends and family he'd been with, he realised that his life had now changed. He was not alone. He slept right through till the following morning.

Printed in Great Britain
by Amazon

46463324R00126